S A T O R
A R E P O
T E N E T
O P E R A
R O T A S

The Complete Works of Marvin K. Mooney

~~a novel~~
~~written by Christopher Higgs~~

First Sator Press Edition
2010

ISBN 978-0-615-33999-3

cover design by Ken Baumann
text set in Fournier

SatorPress.com
Los Angeles, CA

An alternative version of the section entitled "Colorless Green Ideas
Sleep Furiously" was released as a chapbook by Publishing Genius
Press, 2009. Additionally, pieces from this book first appeared
(sometimes in different form) in the following literary journals:
*Bust Down the Door & Eat All the Chickens, Coconut, Conduit,
DIAGRAM, H_NGM_N, Monkeybicycle Online, NANOFiction, Post
Road, Quarterly West, Salt Hill, Swink Online & Taint Magazine*

For Caitlin

The Complete Works of Christopher Higgs

a novel
written by Marvin K. Mooney

[much better!!!]

The Complete Works of Marvin K. Mooney

a novel
written by Christopher Higgs

"A text is not a text unless it hides from the first comer, from the first glance, the law of its composition and the rules of its game."

—Jacques Derrida, "Plato's Pharmacy"

A dissonance
in the valence of Uranium
led to the discovery

Dissonance
(if you're interested)
leads to discovery

—William Carlos Williams, Paterson IV (On the Curies)

Prolegomenon

[Mooney unashamedly delivered this paper—which amounts to a glowing critical appreciation of his own creative work—at the 2001 Symposium for Postmodern Studies, to a room full of colleagues who reportedly felt a collective discomfort. Mooney, however, seemed genuinely pleased, because, like all good Americans, he loved to hear himself talking about himself. Eye witnesses said Mooney wore a blood red cloak, along with a purple skull and bones bandana tied tightly around his head, and spoke with a grizzly (affected) Southern accent. He was subsequently fired from his teaching position at the University of Albania for misuse of funds.]

Organs Without A Body:
The Complete Works of Marvin K. Mooney
A Rhizomatic Assemblage

"Here is a paradox: it has been noted that academics write in a particular register using a simple structure, employing an introduction, development and conclusion, and eschewing repetition, puns, jokes and irony, especially when writing about post-modernism; use of a post-modern idiom, however, involves the rejection of grand meta-narratives (Lyotard, 1984)."
—Robert Withers, "If on a winter's night an editor..." Teaching in Higher Education, Oct '97, Vol. 2, Issue 3

Per paradigmatic assumption, your present impulse is to listen interrogatively for what you hope to be a clear introduction followed by the formulaic placement of a thesis statement, that conventionally boring germ of a typically univocal argument, which you will no doubt expect to see posited here, in the opening section, centered neatly for use as a pivot from which to orchestrate my intentions; perhaps you also expect to hear, at this point, a description of Deleuze & Guattari's concept of the Body Without Organs, and a specific hypothesis pertaining to its relevance vis-à-vis the work of Marvin K. Mooney. Then you will certainly expect me to rearticulate and recapitulate this argument over and over and over again until it is made into a somnambulant mush, or until I have violently bludgeoned you into submission through my clever manipulation of rhetorical devices and my ruthless regurgitation of all previously constructed arguments regarding the text under the auspice of them being my own unique revelation.

To deviate from this prescriptive custom endangers a work of criticism in much the same way that deviating from the dogmatic Aristotelian structure of psychological realism endangers a novelist like Mooney: by presenting work which boldly seeks to deterritorialize conventions, writers run the risk of losing readers in all manner of ways: by confusing them, irritating them, or worst of all: by being accused of purposeful obscurity, unnecessary cuteness, or downright self-indulgent cheekiness.

Fortunately, Mooney's text exemplifies a liberating aspect of just such an approach, one that turns the limited, superficial assumptions of conventional protocol upside-down.

And echoes John Hawkes's now infamous dictum, "The true enemies [of the novel are] plot, character, setting and theme, and having once abandoned these familiar ways of thinking, totality of vision or structure [i]s really all that remain[s]."

But how strange that such an unconventional outlook could also contain the conventional impulse toward privileging the totality of vision or structure; shouldn't any kind of totality be considered antithetical to the postmodern/poststructural text? Perhaps not.

Remember Stephano Tani's assertion that in postmodern literature, "Conventions become deceitful clues planted by the writer to rouse the attention of the reader before disappointing his expectations; conventions are paradoxically functional in the disintegration of the genre." From this, one might conclude that by destroying assumptions through the formal reconfiguration of novelistic conventions (how's that for a paradox: novelistic conventions), Mooney forgoes all the standard trappings and vacuums out the fetus of our expectations; but then in its place he cultivates a garden with eleven different kinds of bright flowers, which turns out to be a contradictory move, however subtle, for it is a move toward a totality of multiplicities. Unless it is understood otherwise, this paradox gives us yet another opportunity for inquiry.

Thus, I now invite you, dear listeners, to consider the heterodoxical ramifications of a rhizomatic conference-style paper hell-bent on tackling these and other paradoxes while loudly dismantling the normative approach to this genre by proliferating a similar multiplicity of theoretical concepts in an attempt not only to model loosely on the primary text at hand, Marvin K. Mooney's The Complete Works of Marvin K. Mooney, but also to be true to the polymorphous nature of postmodern literature, and maybe most importantly to expose a particularly abysmal failure of—and inherent fallacy in— constructing lame-ass myopic argumentation with the

15

reductive intention to conclude, summarize, or totalize, especially when dealing with postmodern texts like The Complete Works of Marvin K. Mooney, which in many ways grapple with the very idea of totality. In short, to discuss a work of "postmodern" fiction in semantic terms or in terms of authorial intent or univocal ideology is frankly antithetical to the modality in which we here find ourselves situated. It's kinda like being president of the Anarchy club, or treasurer of the Kleptomaniacs club. Or to put it another way, in the immortal words of Johnny Cochran giving the Chewbacca Defense on South Park (1998): "Ladies and gentlemen of this supposed jury, it does not make sense." This text, for example, would scarcely benefit by discussion aimed at proving it is about something because more importantly it is something – to borrow Beckett's suggestion that Joyce's "writing is not about something; it is that something itself." What that something is, and how it functions, is exactly two of the things I am striving here to articulate. Therefore, to proceed authentically while giving respect to the philosophical discourse of postmodernism, as well as the particular underpinnings and flows of Mooney's novel, we might first approach it by suspending our heart's burning desire to "make sense," and instead remember

Linda Hutcheon's salient comment that, "[P]ostmodernism remains fundamentally contradictory, offering only questions, never final answers."

Never final answers, dear listeners, only questions.

Only questions.

And by its very nature, contradictory.

Just ask poststructural godfather, Roland Barthes (Mooney's colleague at the Sorbonne), who said, "To interpret a text is not to give it a (more or less justified, more or less free) meaning, but on the contrary to appreciate what plural constitutes it." Now consider the plurals of Mooney's assemblage—roots, books, recursion, alternating chapters of author-reader interaction - a specific narratological flow coined "metafiction" in 1970 by William Gass. But as C. Nella Cotrupi points out, The Complete Works of Marvin K. Mooney takes a step beyond metafiction, to what he calls hypermetafiction. "In achieving this level of thematic self-engagement, Mooney's work moves beyond the fictionalized cataloguing of the categories of fiction and of the processes of fiction making; it manages to incorporate and artistically problematize the very issues, questions, and theoretical implications that are at the heart of metafiction and its criticism." A book that asks questions about the act of asking questions, a book that creates itself by blooming multiplicities.

Now to think, dear listeners, without alerting you to my intentions, I've spent all this time gabbing, whilst coyly leading you down this path toward the brink of heavy metaphysical investigation, to the basic ontological question of identity raised by the use of the second-person, "You," when Mooney quips, "You're the absolute protagonist of this book."

Let us take another cue from Beckett, and (Pause). Scratch the old noggin. Rub the old chin. And ask ourselves: what implications are we to uncover by examining such a self-reflexive statement? On the most basic level, it begs the mightiest question of all, does it not? Namely: who are you?

I now ask, dear listeners, like the hookah-smoking caterpillar in Alice's Wonderland: Who are you?

And is the "you" that Mooney refers to the same "you" who is listening to me speak right now? Are you, as the ink on paper, the same you who sits now and listens to the utterances ushering from my lips? To whom am I referring when I say the words, "You are the absolute protagonist of this conference paper"?

As the ebb and flow of this line of questioning is interrupted, shifted, twisted, moved off course like Brownian motion, a new line of flight emerges, moving us toward the issue of gender tension. Yes, Mooney gives us both male and female protagonist-readers, but not until halfway through the book do women get their "personhood" in terms of the text's cosmology. We start male and end male and now it appears this idea has disintegrated and flows into the question of space. For space, too, occupies court in the literary auditorium of Mooney's creation. Not exactly space in the phenomenological sense that Bachelard might have explained, necessarily, even though content-wise certainly such a connection could be made, but I direct my comment to the assemblage, more like a kind of liminal space existing in quantum terms simultaneously as both and neither biunivocal outcomes to Schrödinger's famous feline uncertainty experiment, in a space we might call heterotopic. Not the (dead) "placeless place" of utopia, nor the (living) real space as we commonly except it, but rather a third space, an interstitial space, what Cotrupi calls "the grey zone between the world of the text and the actual world itself," a space that sounds an awful lot like Foucault's famous mirror example of heterotopia. Furthermore, The Complete Works of Marvin K. Mooney speaks directly to Foucault's third principal of heterotopias, that they are "capable of juxtaposing in a single real place several spaces, several sites that are in themselves incompatible."

[See: Mooney's polyphonic assemblage entitled The Complete Works of Marvin K. Mooney, a single artifact containing several incompatible artifacts.]

Perhaps turning Foucault's theory into practice requires a more badass substantive representation, such as the image of Organs in need of a Body, all pink and squishy and disparate in tone, theme, mood, and genre, just as Deleuze and Guattari speculated.

But first, let's return to Barthes, who said, "In the ideal text, the networks are many and interact, without any one of them being able to surpass the rest; this text is a galaxy of signifiers, not a structure of signifieds; it has no beginning; it is reversible; we gain access to it by several entrances, none of which can be authoritatively declared to be the main one." Now an argument almost begins to take shape, nearly comes into focus. Namely, that which seems formless is most formidable in its orchestration of pluralities. By de-centering the narrative we turn the reader's attention back upon itself, invariably revealing a rhizomatic pivot in place of the univocal arboreal pivot of convention.

Here we are again, dear listener, back at the issue of convention. Could we complicate it more by pressing against Brian McHale's famous argument over the change of dominant, from the binary of modern/postmodern = epistemological/ontological? What happens when we find that The Complete Works of Marvin K. Mooney exhibits both modern and postmodern tendencies by grappling with issues of epistemology as well as ontology: questions about the world as a book, what is that book, who is really behind it, how many worlds can there be inside it, and how is this book constructed? Could a book be used as a Body for eleven Organs?

Yes, yes, Deleuze and Guattari, who take Barthes two steps back, three steps forward, over the hills and through the woods, to their complex theory of the "Body Without Organs," a term they borrow from Artaud to illustrate a particularly interesting point regarding destratification made by the Danish linguist, Louis Hjelmslev: "[Hjelmslev] used the term matter for the plane of consistency or Body Without Organs, in other words, the unformed, unorganized, nonstratified, or destratified body and all its flows: subatomic and submolecular particles, pure intensities, prevital and prephysical free singularities."

Now, if we could transpose this idea to illuminate that which signals the pluralities, we would get a collection of Organs Without A Body. Just imagine each one of Mooney's beginnings as a separate Organ unable to exist without its Body: the artifact of the complete text itself. These would be interchangeable, since the word "interchangeable" implies a specific origin for each separate part, which would account for the distinguishing characteristic of each singularity or that which makes it possible to actually be interchangeable. In essence, creating the question of organization: why begin where we begin? Why not find such and such section of the book first and then happen upon another? Why end at the point when we end? What does it mean to have an encore in a work of fiction? Given these paradoxes, recall D&G's feisty discussion of rhizomatic flux, wherein they describe the point of subjectification which replaces the center of significance as displaying both entrance and exit, beginning and end, contingent upon the shift of its multiplicities:

> The notion of unity appears only when there is a power takeover in the multiplicity by the signifier or a corresponding subjectification proceeding: This is the case for a pivot-unity forming the basis for a set of biunivocal relationships between objective elements or points, or for the One that divides following the law of a binary logic of differentiation in the subject.

For Deleuze and Guattari, there is no beginning or ending, there is always only the middle. Complicate this further by considering the establishment of the "I" narrator: the addressor who quests for the eternal sunshine of a spotless mind, the one who is both Mooney and not Mooney simultaneously, the one who says:

"I'll tell you a fucking story but I'm gonna be pissed off about it the entire time so you have two choices: either quit reading this right now, or accept the fact that telling stories pisses me off and watch how brilliantly I do it despite my irritation."

What an exquisite example of the rhizome, as well as a beautiful reification of Derrida's concept of the trace, that which remains after something is put under erasure—what Baudrillard would later slap us with: a copy of a copy without an original, which implies the famous M.C. Escher image of the man in the mirror holding a mirror showing a man with a mirror holding a mirror and so on, to infinity, with no way to distinguish the alpha or omega. "The trace," says Derrida, "is not only the disappearance of origin—within the discourse that we sustain and according to the path that we follow it means that the origin did not even disappear, that it was never constituted except reciprocally by a non-origin, the trace, which thus becomes the origin of the origin."

Take that thought and stretch it out like warm taffy until you get Delueze and Guattari's principal of multiplicity, which wagers, "Multiplicities are rhizomatic... there is no unity to serve as a pivot in the object, or to divide in the subject... A multiplicity has neither subject nor object, only determinations, magnitudes, and dimensions that cannot increase in number without the multiplicity changing in nature."

Ok, now stop for a moment and marinate on the idea of changing the nature of a multiplicity, in order to increase its magnitudes, by replacing the tyranny of the author with the tyranny of the reader.

Mash that idea with a question Žižek poses in The Puppet and the Dwarf, "Who among us has not experienced when fascinated by a beloved person who puts all his trust in us, who relies on us totally and helplessly, a strange, properly perverse urge to betray this trust, to hurt him badly, to shatter his entire existence?"

Does Mooney want to hurt you? Do you want to hurt Mooney? Are there imaginary people who want to hurt other imaginary people?

Only questions. Never final answers.

—completed: April 2001
Santa Monica, California

Once, when asked in an interview to share his thoughts on posterity, Mooney quipped, "I want to be famous or I want to be forgotten. That is what it means to be an American. Mediocrity is utterly unacceptable. Extremity is the only viable ontology remaining."

We Are Who We Pretend To Be

"A text is not a text unless it hides from the first comer, from the first glance, the law of its composition and the rules of its game."

—Jacques Derrida, "Plato's Pharmacy"

Dr. Alphonso Carothers, Associate Professor

Chances are, you've never heard of Marvin K. Mooney; unless you happen to be familiar with the 1972 Dr. Seuss classic from which his name was derived, <u>Marvin K. Mooney Will You Please Go Now!</u> (copyright Dr. Suess Enterprises)—sources indicate Mooney's parents had been fanatically obsessed with that particular book at the time of little Marvin's birth, if for no other reason than the assumed notoriety surely to come to their family name once the Dr. Suess book became popular. But even then, you will know only the name, not the actual person, not the thirty-five year old eccentric who watered every flowerbed on his block every morning before dawn, not the flabby, forty-five year old constant-smoker who spoke to stray cats and dogs, who collected pop cans from trashcans and picked up litter off other people's lawns, not the embarrassingly loudmouthed twenty-eight year old vegetarian who screamed at the trash collectors and stayed at home most days and never turned on any lights, who used candles in the evening instead of lights, who presumably paid very little to the energy company, so little, it has been reported, that a representative from the electric company once visited his house to inquire if he had passed away. Rightly or wrongly, the man named Marvin K. Mooney achieved neither critical nor commercial success as a person or as an artist in his lifetime; but now given the discovery of his work after his disappearance, I believe we as a species will be forever changed.

[It's my face or ghosts of me!]

Shelby Claxton, Research Assistant

What is so <u>novel</u> about Marvin K. Money's novel? That
question xxxx: even a novel—or, is it xxx or
autobiography/that currently xxxxx question amongst xxxxx
literature. Fortunately, having written my Master's thesis on
the endemic pitfalls of various hermeneutic approaches to
James Joyce's <u>Ulysses</u>, I feel xxxxx commenting on xxxxx
difficult, avant-garde, or xxxxx challenging works xxxxx. It is
xxxxxx to claim that Marvin K. Mooney has xxxxx Joyce. I
never thought xxxxx but in my opinion xxxxx. He truly xxxxx.
Note: whereas Joyce's <u>Ulysses</u> suffers from its territorialization
(being merely xxxxx Dublin, albeit a sonically xxxxx
topographical, phenomenological experience, but still, only
encapsulating one city), Mooney's work is completely
deterritorialized (from the scattershot xxxxx to the poetic xxx
to the interludes to the "xxxxx" to the heart-wrenching soul-
searching xxxxx spanning from xxxxx spaces across the globe
to imaginary xxxxx). This text is global. xxxxx the future. As
<u>Ulysses</u> was xxxxx in the early years of the 20th century,
Mooney's novel is xxxxx uniquely American and xxxxxxxxxxxx
global xxxxx 21st century. While the critics have perennially
cried "the novel is dead!" xxxxx have been right xxxxx until
now. Welcome, ladies and xxxx, to the resurrection of the
novel. [do not correct – sic – (sick!)]

Dr. Wilson Parnell, Professor Emeritus

No sane person would waste time reading Mooney's rubbish. It is one hundred and ten percent drivel. I hated it. I loathed it. I found it morally objectionable. Hands-down the most self-involved, gimmicky for gimmick's sake, self-indulgent, pretentious collection of cant I've ever slogged through. I hated it. I loathed it. Please believe me when I tell you: I say this with the straightest of faces. It's a royal shame that some fringe academia literati find it necessary to vindicate such tripe. I make these candid comments in hopes that they might dissuade some naive lemming or some mouth-breather following orders from the office of advertisement who might be considering these pages. DO NOT WASTE YOUR TIME! Put this novel down! There are billions of better things you could be doing with your life: feeding the needy, walking the homeless, robbing a Jesuit preschool. You could sacrifice chickens to some imaginary god. You could enroll in community college. You could take out a loan and spend the money on hot dogs and prostitutes. You could bike or hike or take a vacation. You could help a friend bury a body. You could sell some stocks online and chat online with strangers while pretending to be an eighteen-year-old virgin. You could make lemonade. You could fence. You could box. You could find a cure for abdominal lymphoma. You could ice skate or telepath or flagellate or percolate or sell your soul to Satan or to a nun dressed like the Easter bunny for half a pint of vodka. You could make a bunch of empty promises. Or you could read a book that is actually worth the time you'll spend reading it. DO NOT WASTE YOUR TIME! Put this novel down!

Rory O'Flanagan, Guggenheim Fellow

Only the most dedicated masochists would subject themselves to this travesty of tangents Mooney calls a novel. It makes absolutely no sense, goes absolutely nowhere and builds to absolutely nothing. If the clamor is true, as many critics attest, that Mooney's "novel" is an erudite depiction of the current American condition, then we are all seriously fucked. This "novel" is utterly superficial; it offers surface minus depth, style minus substance. In short, there is no there there. Instead of story it contains only the persistent meaningless ramble of a psychotic, or a drug addict, or worse: a person possessed by a ghost. America is not possessed by a ghost. America is not a drug addict. And most certainly, America is not psychotic. Thus my conclusion: this book is anti-American!

[Remember the words of David Hume: "Commit it then to the flames: for it can contain nothing but sophistry and illusion."]

Bryce Connelly, Neoclassicist

The hack of a hack writer is often times confused with experimental writing, but in fact they are not synonymous. One attempts to compose a novel using the scientific method, the other uses no method at all. This is where Mooney's attempt to overthrow Aristotle has failed: he is a hack in experimental clothing. More importantly, he has failed to realize that the rules are the rules for a reason: they are eternal. This means true experimentation is only valid under the restrictions of Aristotelian unity, otherwise the outcome is chaos. This novel is chaos. Thus, in my final analysis, despite the laudatory torrent of current critical attention, I must confess in all honesty I find absolutely no redeeming quality whatsoever in Mooney's work; none whatsoever. Except perhaps the title. The title worked for me.

Twyla Faye Robinson, Independent Scholar

Those who claim that Mooney's work constitutes meaninglessness to end all meaninglessness fail themselves as critics and by extension they fail the reading population writ large. I find it embarrassing, foolish, and downright simpleminded to dismiss Mooney's accomplishment as a hodgepodge of meaningless wordplay. He is unlike the majority of writers today who try so desperately to hold a mirror up to the smoke of reality. Therefore, his work requires a different critical approach. To compare his work to someone attempting a work of conventional realism would be wrongheaded and unprofitable, just as it would be pointless to compare a painting by Jackson Pollock to a painting by Jan van Eyck, or a musical composition by John Cage to one by John Williams, or a play by Bertold Brecht with one by Neil Simon. Furthermore, Mooney heroically exploits the possibilities of anarchic literary insurrection: his work is no less than a call-to-arms for future scribblers: Disregard Models! Ignore Rules! Hold Back Not Your Ambition For Fear Of Failure! I believe it is a triumph. I predict it will one day be considered a defining text for the generation that followed postmodernism. In fact, it would not surprise me if one day this century was known as Mooneyian.

[Oh disguise how you disguise me----------------------you are being [[I am being?]]

                    too obvious NOTE: be less obvious]

Dr. Phyllis Salzburg, Narratologist

How can this even be considered a novel? That's the question I struggled to answer after the editor of a small literary magazine sent me the manuscript to review for an upcoming issue. I couldn't find a foothold anywhere. At first I was lost. Then I got irritated. Then I grew bored. I couldn't understand what he was trying to do. I couldn't figure it out. I thought maybe he was just trying to agitate me for the sake of agitating me. I even considered the possibility that it was supposed to be ironic or post-ironic and I was simply missing the joke. I thought about the text as an American myth narrative, but failed to find any connections. My only firm conclusion was that since it was so wacky it had to be postmodern; so I figured I would write up a review that addressed the challenges and pitfalls of writing postmodern fiction, but then I remembered that no one gives two rotten shits about postmodern fiction anymore.

Dr. Gregory Upland, Ethnocologist

Who would have guessed it? From a man who supposedly greeted his postal worker in Chinese, could catch a fish in any pond, could carry on a conversation in his front lawn for two hours with complete strangers while passionately disliking children and cars; the thirty-five year old bachelor who inherited his mother's house and never changed the curtains; the man who feared bugs and spiders and birds and airplanes and pumpkins and petticoats and little people, people with accents, people who wore pungent deodorant, people who combed their hair, people who barbequed, people who cut in front of him at the farmers market after he had been standing in line already for like half an hour; the thirty-five year old Lakers fan who grew up idolizing Magic Johnson; who played soccer on the beach in Santa Monica, had his first sexual experience on the beach in Santa Monica, had his first birthday party on the beach in Santa Monica, gave away his first guitar, painted his first painting, slapped his first best friend in the face for flirting on the beach in Santa Monica; the man who caused multiple auto accidents and never did time; who besmirched, tainted, taunted; who waxed inappropriately. The work needs no defense. He is a quixotic genius, a master storyteller. This novel is the future. This novel will never be in the past.

...Who are you? Quit asking me! I don't know. I don't know who I am. I don't know. Quit asking me. What are your intentions? I don't know. I don't know. Quit asking me. Quit asking me. I have no intentions. I do have intentions. I can't go on. I must go on. I don't know. I don't know. Quit asking me...

~~El Desaparecido (Reginald Samoyed), Professional Magician~~
Frank Lockhart, Relationship Councilor

His choices are simply delicious, and as far as I know they have never before been seen in the history of literature. I must confess I generally prefer to read Debbie Macomber, Mary Higgins Clark, or Sue Grafton, but in this case it felt good to let go and open myself up to Mooney's imagination. It is mysterious: just when you think you're getting a handle on what's happening you find yourself lost inside his head for page upon page, or inside a conceptual art instillation. It's like an unmade jigsaw puzzle, or a lie you tell someone you love. I highly recommend it.

It's my face or ghosts of me! That's what she keeps telling me.

Sunday – 27th or 28th

Being * Becoming

Closed * Open

Fixed * Variable

Active * Passive

My Vacation with a Kidnaper

> "Lack of preparation."
>
> "Where are you going to get in life with a lack of preparation?"
>
> "Nowhere."
>
> "That is correct, Mr. Mooney. Nowhere."

{I'm sorry. These fake descriptions from fake scholars and "experts" are such complete bullshit. Everybody uses Joyce as a comparison for anything remotely unorthodox. It's such bullshit. This book is nothing like Joyce. I'm sorry. Those comparisons mean nothing. I am so embarrassed.}

I went for the destruction. To see the destruction. To feel it.

HE DOESN'T EVEN ENGAGE IN ISSUES OF RACE,
CLASS, OR GENDER!!!

Paula McHenry-Jones, Social Critic

Mooney's novel is nothing more than a crude display of the diseased American psyche: the frantic, muddled, disconnected mosaic typical of the Attention Deficit Disorder generation. What he calls avant-garde is what I call embarrassing. There's nothing new about faulty plots and flimsy characters, nothing "experimental" about nonsense. Nonsense is nonsense and will always be nonsense so long as the opposite exists. I find nothing revolutionary here; nothing remotely remarkable... and there's my quandary. Why do so many people think this work is the harbinger of new literature? Alain Robbe-Grillet already did it. Italo Calvino already did it. Raymond Federman already did it. Lawrence Sterne already did. David Markson already did it. It's already been done! Why are the annualists frenzied, stabbing flagpoles in the history books of tomorrow? They see something in Mooney I am obviously missing. I see the snark. I see the Hey-Look-At-Me! acrobatics. Maybe I can even understand how someone might find it slightly amusing in sections; portions of it almost seem to resonant with other portions. I might even agree that aesthetically the novel is semi-intriguing. The critique of form. "The totality of vision & structure." I can almost give in to the nightmare and let Mooney carry me away, but then I hear former professors chanting in my head: "There is a right way and a wrong way to write stories" At which time I realize I cannot abandon tradition. I cannot forget convention. I am a product of the past. I will not acquiesce to the temptation of the future. We are all creatures of the past. Mooney does not understand this fundamental truth. We are not futuristic; we are historic. That is our nature.

~~Wilhelm Lively Cooke, Protestant Reformer~~
~~Dr. Kite Roehelle, Literary Historian~~
Moa Draper-Kline, Book Enthusiast

Life is a hodgepodge, no? There are many different versions of myself; why shouldn't there be many versions of Mooney? No editor. No thinking before writing. No buffer. No filter. No pause. This work is raw. Maybe too raw? I guess it depends on how raw is too raw for you. For me, it is just raw enough. I like some things to be cooked, but many things are good raw. Like emotions. Mooney has emotions. Like humor, with which Mooney is quite proficient. Like sadness, with which it seems Mooney is obsessed. The entire spectrum of the human condition is accounted for by Mr. Mooney. The most astonishing thing about it, for me anyway, would have to be its refrain. I won't spoil it for you, but the refrain in this piece is magnificent. It truly gave me goose bumps. Makes me think of something James Joyce once said. He said, "The only demand I make of my reader is that he should devote his whole life to reading my works." I plan to do just that, but instead of devoting myself to the bard of the Emerald Isle, I will devote myself to the experimental raconteur of California, Marvin K. Mooney.

"We like books that have a lot of <u>dreck</u> in them, matter which presents itself as not wholly relevant (or indeed, at all relevant) but which, carefully attended to, can supply a kind of "sense" of what is going on. This "sense" is not to be obtained by reading between the lines (for there is nothing there, in those white spaces) but by reading the lines themselves—looking at them and so arriving at a feeling not of satisfaction exactly, that is too much to expect, but of having read them, of having "completed" them."

—from <u>Snow White</u> by Donald Barthelme

Helen Blanchard, Fulbright Scholar

Why is the media so quick to label Marvin K. Mooney "The Henry Darger of Literature?" I must register my vehement disagreement! Recall, I also refused the Cy Twombly kool-aid, back in the day - and I always stand by my decisions. Call me crazy, but I see no genius in Mooney. Like I asked in '89, I'll ask again: what does entropy contribute to the daily practice of humanity? What does chaos contribute to the human condition? What good ever comes out of nonsense? Answer: nothing. Regression? Play? Frivolity—who needs that? What good does it do? If we want change, real change, we need praxis! We need tangible civil disobedience. Scribbles and childlike wonder won't destroy capitalism. We need adult-sized action. We need a new breed of people. We need firebombs in the streets. We need rocket propelled grenades. Just ask yourself, what can the Moonies of the world teach us about what it means to exist, what it means to tap the palm, to plague, to frighten beyond repair? We need the paparazzi to catch us at our worst. We need the mirror. We need it to survive. Unfortunately, Marvin K. Mooney is a broken mirror. A shattered bastard of fiction. He is yesterday. He is not the revolution. He is fly-by-night. A one-hit-wonder. He will not be remembered. He will be utterly forgotten.

Marvin K. Mooney's autobiography*******quit calling it
that!!!!!!!!!!!!!!!!!!!!!!!!!*******call it The Complete Works of Marvin
K. Mooney.

The Complete Works of Marvin K. Mooney is analogous to
the corporation who undergoes rebranding every other year
but on a much faster schedule: like a corporation who
undergoes rebranding twice a day. Mooney is constantly
rebranding himself.

I'm sure it's akin to schizophrenia.

Why am I so concerned with making sure you understand
what you are getting into? What makes me feel like I have to
explain myself to you? Who are you anyway? Why do you
matter? To me, you don't matter. I don't care about you. I exist
whether you read me or not. In fact: you can quit reading this
right now, I dare you. I dare you to put this book down and
forget about it. I don't need you. I am the answer to the riddle:
if a writer writes a book and no one reads it does it still make a
sound? Yes. Yes, I do make a sound.

Do you hear it?

"A text is not a text unless it hides from the first comer, from the first glance, the law of its composition and the rules of its game."

—Jacques Derrida, "Plato's Pharmacy"

difference and repletion

DIFFERENCE &
    REPETITION DIFFfEReNCe/REPpETtITIN
        Diernce and reprton
           DIFERECE
           REPETITION
           REPETIITON
           REPTEITION

This is all so very pretentiousness, isn't it? So obvious.

Describe * Define
Explore * Explain
Absence * Presence
Open * Closed

"Art for art's sake? ART FOR FUCKING ART'S SAKE!!!... what an ashle fufce son of an itch thing to say! You spit in the face of suffering? You disrespect our troops in Afghanistan and

45

Iraq? How dare you! Art for art's sake is FING BLIT YOU ASHLE COSUR MOHRFCR DOFKER SHFAE CT-BLD JISOPR!"

—excerpt from an unhappy fan letter Mooney received in 2006, addressing an article Mooney had published in The Nineteenth Century Quarterly about Oscar Wilde and the Decadent movement of the Fin de siècle, espousing a vehement disgust with those who would attempt to read politics into literature.

Everything is political. You cannot escape Politics. All "language acts" are political. Look at me being political. Look at me coercing you to believe my politics. How could I ever write anything that isn't political? Everything I type is political. Yawn.

STOP!

Whom am I even writing these words? My audience, who are they? Who are you? I do not know whom I am writing, whom I have in mind right now as I type these letters; most honestly I am writing to no one other than myself. In fact, I am not even writing to myself so much as from myself. I am documenting the patterns of my consciousness. That is all. I am thinking on paper. Nothing more, nothing less. I do not mean anything, nor am I antiphonic. I am not Dracula. I am not Godzilla. I am just a guy who likes to strike the keypad. I am the dandelion keeps coming back. I am remote control. Sometimes I make perfect sense; other times I can't fit the jangle or rim shot the jamboree.

Please forgive me. This is not a proper introduction. You came for anecdotes. Shorthand. The abbreviated version of Marvin K. Mooney. Who was he? What was he about? How to define him. How to put him in a casket. Murder him so you can dissect him. This man is not proper, but proper is the proper only of proper. Do you understand me? Do you key ring the fishery? Do you Prague the open coffin? Do you manicure lawns? Do you jiggle the keys in your pocket when being chased by the authorities? Does the pinch itch the wooly beasts? Make believe for me. You can do it. I know you can. I believe in you. Do you believe in me? How could you? Have I even told you my name yet?

Please forgive me.

My name is

The
Life &
Opinions of
Marvin K. Mooney,
Gentleman

a
miscellaneous
dithyrambic
novel-in-plateaux

Please allow me to introduce myself:

My name is

I am already not who I was just a moment ago.

People call me

Again, I am somebody new.

49

CHAPTER ONE

This is the first sentence in this novel. From this—the second sentence—I want to explain my project: what it will present, so you will know exactly what to expect. I know it is important to be clear because people get confused so easily:

Premise #1:

"I began to write fiction on the assumption that the true enemies of the novel were plot, character, setting, and theme, and having once abandoned these familiar ways of thinking about fiction, totality of vision or structure was really all that remained."

—John Hawkes in an interview with John J. Enck,
Wisconsin Studies in Contemporary Literature,
Vol. 6, No. 2, (Summer, 1965), pp. 141-155

Premise #2

"The writer is not a person, he is the amanuensis of verity, who will only corrupt what he writes to the extent that he yields to passion, or shirks the discipline of objectivity."

—Denis Donoghue, Ferocious Alphabets
(Columbia University Press, 1981)

But what exactly does the amanuensis of verity look like?

OR

OR

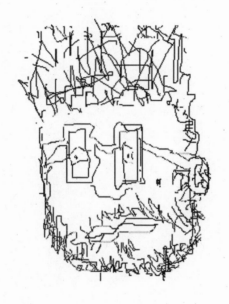

OR

?

54

Here is a photo album:

Mooney. Age eight. Alabama. Squealing catching bugs and falling stars. Ice cream man painting sidewalks. Tree house. Dark cave. G.I. Joes and busted Barbie dolls. Big people eating. Shoveling the walk with dad. Matinee movies with mom. Yellow bus, black slacks, purple polka dots. Nightmares about boys. Box fan. Swamp stench and crocodiles. Lumpy waffles, hunks of unmelted butter. Seeing crippled swans at the zoo taking long walks hyperventilating.

Mooney. Age ten. Colorado. A suitcase next to a duffle bag. Two brown moving boxes marked with dad's name and some new address. Summer camp, grape drink, black french fries. Talk radio. Snow days. Falling stars. Dad's sit-down lawnmower still parked in the garage. Empty evening hallways. Staying up late. Mom getting sick. Crying. Taking drowsy baths soak pneumonia flu and dizziness, panic call the cops over mumps and unprettiness. An unbearable stomachache.

Mooney. Age twelve. Oregon. The woods night cold snow fireplace. Falling stars. Scent of hickory chips smoldering. Wet birthing kittens. Sky with bright moon, television blaring. Hardwood floors creaking, sewing machine needle speeding, taste of cherry pie and hot tea with milk. Cup of soup, cup of hot apple cider. Wrapped in a blanket. Mom snoring, dad back home cursing, photographs dangle from the wall total disarray kitchen. Dirty clothes piled colored heaps. Spider crawling ceiling rocking broken sofa chair. Toenail clippings. Pencil shavings. Box of yarn for quilt making. Stacks of books.

Mooney. Age fourteen. Oregon. Singing in shower before school cartoons. Falling stars. Cheating on the big test jump rope running shoes. Dinosaurs in museum smell of gasoline. Pepperoni pizza. Dressing up like Joan of Arc for Halloween. Mom under thin paper dress, wheezing, choking, plastic tubes, liquid dripping through an IV in her arm. Asleep beside her with copies of Redbook in lap. The sound of heart monitors miss matched linoleum lining waitroom corridor. White noise static buzzing ringing like a telephone.

Mooney. Age sixteen. Mystery. Clear skin. Secret trip to Mexico with friends to shed sex anonymously. Bowling, new shoes, third place. Red pen. Scrabble. Walking to a dance drunk, puking, falling stupid with a stranger in the alleyway. Balancing act. Crying, skiing, learning piano. Tall buildings. Dirty streets. Bums. Sewer stink. Mom in the hospital bleeding. Beethoven. Talk of college drive-in movies. Volleyball tryouts. Falling Stars. Playing chess in a cafe, dissecting sharks. Cigarettes.

Mooney. Age nineteen. Pennsylvania butterfly tattoo. A cutting board specimen sliced between glass displays mongoose birthing egg. Working burger joint grill, reading poetry in dark clothes, dedicated to the month of silence. Cobblestone. Delaware River. An old man at the public laundry waving his cock like a peeled potato. Meeting a celebrity. Switching seats on an airplane. Watching clouds dissipate cemetery. Mom's casket. Eulogy. Mumbling room full of requiem puppets. Shining flowers, crying dad beyond speechless, pyrotechnics, acid rain, and fishnet stockings sway. Release the burning scent of her.

***

The crisis and aporia of biography comes in the struggle to archive a legacy while retaining the mysteries and complexities of the subject's multiplicity: the many of the one. (Mooney)

My superb defense.

Everything was going so perfectly until…

> "94. What makes me think that form exists?"
> —Ron Silliman, The Chinese Notebook

[Nietzsche quote about stamping being onto becoming.]

oniomania and pleonexia

onomatopoeia and glossolalia

On or about December 1983,

[keep basic structure, but change some words] "Six world-renowned writers competed for the commission to write a story about the new California Academy of Sciences building, in San Francisco's Golden Gate Park. Five of the six arrived for the interview bearing chocolate-covered onions shaped like volcanoes which erupted bright blue lava every three or four minutes. Officials have concluded that blue is the new black."

On or about December 1983,

There are astral halos for days, nights, weeks, months, years, and so on. Mine is BLUE!

On or about December 1983, Marvin K. Mooney's character changed. One critic called it a rupture in the cement sidewalk encircling a building where he met a woman and divorced her and half of his diary entries from this period are a joke. "Fasten your heater," Mooney would say to every woman he encountered and by that time he had broken half a dozen hearts and just as many laws and besides he made an absolute mockery out of Arizona. The good folks of Tucson made a deal with his estranged wife. He was a mess and he was divorced and his car quit working, the battery gave up working, the valves stopped working, nothing was working, least of all Marvin K. Mooney.

He sat for hours in front of a blank page and a cold cup of coffee. His ashtrays heaped, but he was too lazy to dump them so every available inch of his desktop was covered by mounds of dead cigarettes.

Mooney also had room on his writing desk for, had a spot for, there was a small area he reserved on his writing desk next to his typewriter, he always kept the fresh paper on the floor beside his chair, his folding chair, his wooden folding chair, but atop his desk, in a spot he treated as special, he had a teacup full of vegetable juice always. On the other side of his typewriter he kept his fresh pack of smokes and his lighter.

Above the desk hung, he had put up the first night he moved into the tiny apartment on Michelangelo Avenue, plastered up really, using packing tape until he ran out and had to switch to Scotch, he had a poster showing a man standing on the edge of a cliff with the toes of his cowboy boots hanging over the ledge, peering over, looking down, wearing a full cowboy outfit: ten gallon hat, dirty denim, button-down shirt, mustard-colored jacket, and the caption, kinda like the kid brother of the Marlboro Man, and what was written in the huge blue sky behind him, the empty blue space at his back, it said:

"Existence is elsewhere."

Mooney created, after a bender in Winslow, Arizona, a splurge in Winslow, Arizona, a spree of petty robberies, debauchery, a handful of wallets and a trunk full of purses in Winslow, Arizona. The jig was hardly up. He was crashing on different sofas on different nights but he never traded rent for sex or drugs that much was clear from the amount of diary entries he wrote on many, various, lots of occasions, times, dates, locations, and firsthand accounts, interviews, opinions, questions asked in blog comment sections, have now been verified whereas his whereabouts the night of this grab or that, and even if the authorities caught on he would always have a backup plan regardless of interest. [reword...clunky?]

The recent divorce was traumatic. He felt trauma over the recent divorce. He was affected deeply by the recent divorce. The recent divorce made him cry quite often.

While accounts of him showing up at shopping malls minus clothing ran rampant, viral, everywhere you couldn't look anywhere and not see him popping up in a shopping mall butt naked and having him spotted at a shopping mall and news anchors standing in front of the shopping malls where Mooney narrowly escaped, absolutely naked. Shopping malls.

The change of his worldview, December 1983 was when he decided to change, decided to rectify his miserable situation. He did not believe in God; he was raised an atheist, not devoutly, not militantly, but subtly atheist. Neither of his parents ever spoke about religion. He had his first formal religious encounter when he was in eighth grade. He went to a Baptist church with his friends one night to hear an ex-member of the Hells Angels tell stories about his life as a biker and also to get free pepperoni pizza, which had been promised to anyone who came to hear the ex-Hells Angels member who, as it turned out, was strewn with faded green tattoos and had a handlebar mustache and muttonchops to match. Mooney wrote in his diary:

"How come I've never thought about God?"

He was thirteen years old. But wait. In December 1983, he was not thirteen, he was fifty years old exactly. He was thirteen years too early for this story. No, wait, I said he was born after 1972 – how else could he have been named after the Dr. Seuss book? He could not have gone to a church in eighth grade and seen an ex-Hells Angels member. This is all a lie. It does not add up. The dates must be a mistake. The memories must be malfunctioning. Why am I doing this? Why am I writing this?

The Hells Angels were created in 1948, in Fontana, California.

but...

but...

but...
...but
but...

but...
...but
but...

but...
but...

***

No. This isn't happening. Pidgin fool, stoolpigeon. The walk looks caribou court. The passion. My first year passed reluctantly forbidding the exits or the ghost to pass, these greenways are fairways in some ways; I can see it. We clever gift givers give away our hearts. You sleeve them. We came and saw and caught a deadly distraction. We remove our wet towel and gallop away. Sum of these two equations:

Your watch will never walk away from you.

> Dear headache.
> Why don't you go?
> You're hurting me.
> Why don't you go and never come back?

"Do not forget that a poem, even though it is composed in the language of information, is not used in the language-game of giving information."
—Ludwig Wittgenstein, <u>Zettel</u>, ed. G.E.M. Anscombe & G.H. von Wright, trans. G.E.M. Anscombe (Berkeley: University of California Press, 197), #160, p. 28.

> one loves only form,
> and form only comes
> into existence when
> the thing is born

> —Charles Olson <u>The Maximus Poems</u>

I love you so much that when you die,
I'm going to bury you outside my bedroom window.

***

ON BEING A MAN

At fifteen, I nearly killed a boy named Jonathan Pilby. If that nosy jogger hadn't found his busted bloody body under the bridge where I left him, then he might not have made it; but unfortunately the jogger had to be a hero. Jonathan Pilby. I'd kill him again if I got the chance. Some days I think the meaning of life is to one day find him and hold him underwater till the bubbles stop. Jonathan Pilby. All because he took me to see a woman. Said she'd introduce me to my manhood. I borrowed father's Buick and we drove to Loveland, to a trailer park on a hill. "Here," he said, "is where you'll find your bliss." It was filthier than anything I'd ever seen on television. Grubby, grimy, snot-nosed kids running rampant on the gravel. The whole place ripe like a pig farm. Hollowed car shells, engine parts, broken toys and lawnmowers, snow blowers, bicycles, broken diesel trucks splayed across a front yard, cats with mange hissing viciously from trash heaps. "She's inside," he said. Little varmint-faced Jonathan Pilby, with his mullet, smiling like he farted. I went up alone. He said she liked to play a little game. "Act like you're there to talk about Jesus," he said. "That's what she likes to play." I nodded my head, felt for the condoms in my pocket, adjusted my tie, then went up the walkway and knocked on her door.

CHAPTER ONE (B)

This is what I'm going to do: I'm going to give you something. Here, take it. This is yours for the remainder of our communion. Keep a hold of it. As long as you don't stop reading these words, you can keep a hold of it for me. I will not take it back. Do you know what it is that I have given you? I have just offered something to you. Do you know what it is? Do you want it? Will you continue reading to find out what it is, if I promise to tell you what it is later? Are you willing to be patient? Are you willing to suspend your judgment long enough to allow me to take a full swipe at your throat?

You who should let me in, who accept the challenge, here are

The Opening Pages...

Mooney always said, "The past does not exist anymore than does the future. Trust Heidegger, our sentence for living is being-in-the-world." It comes then as little surprise to find out that Mooney's last piece of writing, which, fittingly, was not completed before his disappearance, dealt with the issue of time. (Time and completion were Mooney's greatest enemies.)

Here is the entire text of Marvin K. Mooney's final piece of writing, saved under the title "Grand Unified Theory," computer stamped last modified on 06/26/02, three days before he went missing:

06/26/02 -- 3:15 am

The paradox being the fact that there is also not a moment we can ever claim to actually inhabit. We are never anywhere long enough to really <u>be</u> in it; we ceaselessly move on ceaselessly into ceaselessly the next moment, which, curiously enough, did not technically exist before the moment just lived, and presumably will not exist again, as if this life is the length of a rope, a biscuit crumbling to pieces on a linoleum floor, a bird's nest unraveling in the wind. At the moment you think of something you are already ahead of the triggering moment, the instigation for the thought is never with you long enough to make it meet the thought; you are already, always, in the future, by definition, if your definition includes causal effect. I suppose you could be some kind of Humian skeptic, one of those chaps who disavow cause and effect. (One of those kinds of writers.) One of those kinds of writers, even though once something becomes conscious we are already long gone from it. (Always remember always Gertrude Stein.) Time has passed since the moment when I conceived of this sentence and the moment when I transcribed it on my keyboard, not to mention the time that has passed since my first writing this sentence and the moment for you right now as you are reading this sentence. You have no idea what I will write next. You are not in control. I could completely blindfold you and throw you in the back of my white van, take you out into the mountains, bury you alive and in the following year bring you roses and for the rest of my life bring you roses on the anniversary of your death. But I'm not going to do that with the narrative. I am going to be careful with the narrative. But, if you are reading this, you need to understand that I am forcing you down any turn I want to take you. I am in control

64

here. I am in control of this conversation, as long as you agree to continue reading these words, you are acknowledging it. You are letting me bully you. You are letting me hijack your consciousness. How does that make you feel? How do you feel about that? Do you have any feelings with regard to that?

Gertrude Stein warned: "Writing is not conversation."[1]

Why are you reading this? Why don't you give up? Quit reading. I had a professor once who told me never to bully the reader. That professor wrote his dissertation on James Jones. Basically, he was telling me to minimize my manipulation of the reader. I wonder how often you think about the ways writers manipulate you. Like right now, how I am manipulating you. I am forcing you to listen, but also trying to reach out to you, reach into the future to when you are reading these words, and make contact with you. I want to enter your location. I want to throw bombs into the future. I am sitting on the front porch. It is a beautiful day. Birds are chirping. Squirrels are cackling. Garbage trucks are doing their rounds. A loud man has just shouted. A dog has just barked. The neighbor's treehouse has been besieged by enemy forces. I am not alone and neither are you, reader. We are together right now, you and me. As long as you continue to read these words, I will talk to you. I will keep you company.
(cont.)

---

1   The Geographical History of America, (1935; reprint, Baltimore, 1995), pg. 209.

I will not let you be alone. I will share stuff with you, take you on a tour, be your paper friend. This is just like the Ouija board, only I am really alive and you can't ask me questions. I guess it's not really very much like the Ouija board at all, but sorta, kinda, somewhat. I am doing one thing, for sure, at least. I am writing to you, even though I don't know you. I must need to tell you all of this in order to play my role in this game. I must need to share my secrets. Did I just say secrets, already? Did I already give that away? Do you really want to continue reading? (Isn't it annoying how often I bring up that question?) I, myself, was born to be a quitter. I constantly quit things. That is the real reason why I do not have a book. I never stick with anything long enough. I never stick with anything. Nothing ever sticks for me, to me, with me, nothing ever sticks. Sometimes I open doors, but there are always ghosts in the rooms and there are never any flashlights. I am afraid of candles. The New Critics wanted to do away with the author. I am not to be done away with. I am a transmission. I am a tennis ball served into your backcourt. I am a machine, a desiring machine, a body without organs. What about you? Like me, do you ever

[END TRANSMISSION]

And there it stopped, midsentence, the absolute final words written by Marvin K. Mooney—that we know of at this moment in time, May 21st, 2009 at 1:00 pm Eastern time. Mooney's metafictional approach certainly contributes to the widespread critical description of his work as a series of rich tropes common amongst Mooney's creations. What did that sentence mean? The one before the one before this one. Do I mean to say Mooney has many tropes or do I mean to say one of his tropes or maybe I feel better using the word "leitmotif" instead of "trope." Metafiction could be considered one of Mooney's various leitmotifs. It would not be dishonest to say he enjoyed toying with the experience shared between himself and the reader. He loved the real. He loved truth.

Sorry, is truth really something we can talk about in today's world? I don't believe in the truth. Maybe Mooney believed in it, but not me.

Certainly, one might be tempted to hazard a guess, to even make a game out of trying to figure out what Mooney nearly confessed. Which is where I have to part ways with you: this is not that. This is the slow-roasted turkey, the figs and jigs of morning. I am standing at the breakfast table and the lawn-mower won't stop running in my neighbor's backyard. I have no courage to ask him to shut off the racket and go inside, take a forenoon nap, watch a smidge of telly, catch a ball game, sip a soda, have a snack, screw his loved one in the bedroom or on the living room floor, do a load of laundry, wash the dishes, catch up on reading—crack the spine of that Raymond Chandler novel and finally try to puzzle out who exactly killed the chauffeur, listen to an opera—listen to Philip Glass & Robert Wilson's Einstein on the Beach, pay bills, play with the cat—dangle the birdmouse for the cat to catch and kill and show how well she destroyed it—check stock portfolio, consider selling a little gold, gold is going through the roof right now, now is the time to sell a little gold. If we changed positions you and I, you would most certainly have done something different. Perhaps you would have ignored the lawnmower all together. Perhaps you would have overlooked it completely and instead concentrated on the sunrise coming in through the window or the smell of the freshly brewed coffee.

How come I got the alphabet memories? How come I can do long division?

In a given neighborhood, in the United States of America, at a given time, given the right incentives—the right trajectory of the moon—and fed on slowpills, gasoline, and forget-its, I made a pledge of allegiance. Now I'm going down with my oath in a ring of sawdust-coated cat-ranch saloons. I'm being melodramatic mainly to prove a point, but have I proven it both rhetorically and subtly without giving away the demographic of my intended audience? When I recognize my authorship, as I am doing right now, as so many have done before me, I am directly communicating with you. Right now, at this very moment, if you are reading these words then you and I are having a conversation wherein I'm doing all of the talking; I am at this moment dominating our conversation because that is the role of the author: to dominate the conversation for the duration of his or her choosing. You have made it this far in your reading of this text, which implies a certain level of commitment on your part; you have stuck with me up to here, so now I must ask you to listen very carefully: I am not who I say I am. This isn't a joke. I need you to believe me. I want to appeal to your sense of

an underwater ear studded with wish pennies

I am not here, or, I was at one time, this time, this moment as I am typing these letters, which by definition cannot be the time you are reading this. Now is not now as I am living it; you are in the future to me; I don't know you. You could be a man or a woman or anything along the continuum. Are you attractive? Are you kind? Are you well-educated? Do you sometimes lie? Do you sometimes choose not to tell the truth? Do you ever say one thing and then do another? What kind of person are you? It matters. It changes the way you'll read this book. Are you middle class? Are you white or black or other? Do you believe in God? Do you eat red meat? Do you often look at pornography? Do you fart in public without saying excuse me? I ask because, depending on your openness threshold and your personal levels of tolerance for vulgar chaos, this book will either excite you or put you to sleep. For you in the former, I share your excitement. For you in the latter, I give you my sincerest apologies.

Since you are in the future to me, I cannot know what the world will be like at the time of your reading this book. Are things good there? Is your neighborhood safe? Can you go to the grocery store without walking through a metal detector? Can your kids safely play outside at night? Can you tell someone you love them without fear of being shot?

This is not what you think it is; whatever you think it is; it's probably different. There is a life here, and I am responsible for it, but

formless form?

"God is formless. If you think He is big, He is infinite, and if you think He is small, He is infinitesimal." —Sun Myung Moon, 10-13-70

Marvin K. Mooney is a superstition, nothing more. I am not him and he is not me. You are searching for a person who doesn't exist. You don't know him, you've never met him, you've never read him, you've never seen him on the street or at the grocery store or at the gym or at the coffeehouse on 3rd and La Cienega around 9:30 am every morning for the last ten years or at the taco shop on York and Figueroa in Highland Park or on the beach just north of the pier in Santa Monica with his humongous blue beach towel and his oversized purple polka dotted umbrella, you've never bumped into him at the farmer's market in West Hollywood and smelled his mixture of cigarettes, mothballs, and chocolate doughnuts, never heard his particular grunts, never felt his cold limp skeleton after thirteen beers. He is a ghost, a specter, an apparition. He is disappeared.

\The Somnambulist/

Red neon banked a bloody glow off the red brick terrace, and Lyla sat tipped back in a plastic chair, on the night of her thirty-first birthday, skin tinted ruby, freckles muted, black hair to her shoulders, engagement ring polished, and all around us the monstrous swell of crickets chirping from some unseen hideout; the other people in the red-washed courtyard seemed insignificant, like extras in the background of our movie; her laughter turned scarlet and swam in our cigarette smoke like painted turtles in a milky crimson jet stream, and in-between our laughter is where I like to linger now, that moment when there was no mention of children, a faint spell of happiness, her green eyes glittering through the red as if they possessed a magic capable of ripping space-time into pieces, constantly guffawing, body fuming potion to my nostrils.

Outside the post office, midmorning, sunny day, sticking manila envelopes into the mailbox. I look up and see a little boy smashing eggs against the side of the building. He is about the size of a fire hydrant, wearing a purple superhero outfit with a royal blue cape. A carton of eggs sits at his feet. I can hear his tiny voice; he is talking to someone who isn't there or maybe someone in his head, as he pitches the eggs against the building with great care and determination. At one point an old woman in a yellow muumuu comes along and sees him. With a rotten face, she turns to me and asks, "Is that your son?"

In truth, all the women I've ever met eventually want nothing to do with me. That's the entire top to bottom of it. Mother even died to get away. Some just ignore me. Mostly they disappear because of my biological deficiency, which is especially hard to handle since I personally have no control over it. What an ugly sentence life can be, going about our days, eating working sleeping, trying so hard to connect, to find a companion. Every possible chance to meet the other half of me fails so goddamn miserably. Like I have a scent that sickens women. Like I've perpetually got a blemish on my forehead and spinach between my teeth. Even though I want to believe my soulmate is out there, somewhere, living her life in search of me, waiting for the moment when I come along and offer my life for the sharing, no children attached.

Nighttime. Westwood. A little girl in a cherry-colored sundress spins herself around, arms outstretched, under a spot of green neon along the sidewalk in front of a bar. Out comes a pretty blond woman followed by a burly oaf in a stained white tee, cutoff jeans and camouflage suspenders. Both look wobbly drunk. The little girl stops her spinning and quietly follows them into the dark parking lot to a pickup truck where the adults get in the cab and the little girl climbs up into the back like a dog. She is not my daughter.

Because Lyla went away and mother's walls kept closing in, that's why I did it. Because a person should not be left alone and forgotten, regardless of their inadequacies. A person should be loved, unconditionally; that means being one half of a self and one half of another. That means never being whole minus the other. A wick and the wax. Until between them they create a new third being, which is why it's hard to tell the truth in all of this, even to myself. I'm ashamed of my inability to manifest descendants. You try waking up to flow charts and pie graphs and mustached doctors shaking their heads, pointing to x-rays saying, "Sorry, Marvin, it's physically impossible for you to become a progenitor."

In the Mexican restaurant on Third and La Cienega, just across the street from the Beverly Center. Eating wet enchiladas at noon. A young couple in the booth across from me start shouting at each other. Their little boy slinks off the seat, crawls under the table, and curls up like a pillbug.

When winter came it did not dawdle. The snow was a fierce and unrelenting army of determined soldiers pounding my stronghold. Each set of hours drifted into days and with their haunting accumulation came more and more my feeling of being marooned in mother's little country house in Colorado. And although mother slept below the earth in Holden Cemetery, her voice and smell still lingered everywhere. True, I was alone, but only physically; for in this house, where my childhood happened, I still felt bullied by her presence and even more fantastically numb from the absence of Lyla.

I'm filing reports in the main database at work, under brutal florescent flicker, after spilling coffee on three of the most important documents, when I hear a scratching at my office door. "Come in," I say. But no one enters. It's silent for a moment and then the scratching returns, this time a bit harder and heavier, with longer strokes; so I go over to the door and fling it open to find no one there except the secretary at her desk and the new guy from Human Resources. They pause, mid-conversation, to look at me quizzically, eyebrows raised and heads cocked; I say sorry and shut the door.

There is nothing exceptionally peculiar about the way Lyla and I met, except that I cannot remember the truth of it. Here in this Los Angeles, my memory is less than remarkable. It was Philadelphia, I'm certain. I exited as she entered the tour of the Liberty Bell. My camera strap had gotten twisted around my neck and I was attempting to fix it while walking and someone pushed me from behind and I lost my balance and slammed right into her. I think. Yes. My elbow smacked her chin and knocked her over. Or was it the other way around? Maybe I didn't bump into her at all. Maybe she bumped into me. Other people in line stopped to ask if we needed help, but I ignored them. I stood completely paralyzed, not because I was repentant, but because I instantly felt that a part of myself resided already inside of her and that a part of her resided inside of me. She was the wick and I was the wax. But it was not the joyous moment of discovering a soulmate, it was actually quite miserable. I already knew the outcome: no matter how much we ever loved each other, she would end up hating me as soon as she found out I couldn't produce a family. They say there are women who don't want children, but I have never met one. And in my experience, adoption is a word most women shy away from. So I did the only thing I could think of, which was to click away the remaining frames in my camera to capture her picture for my memory. With her petite hands clasped over her heart, her eyes burst like thin cheap balloons. How to describe her stump of a chin without mentioning the plump of her lips or how the creases around her mouth went perfectly to her cheeks. Galaxies of freckles on her face, her neck, her shoulders. Mascara running. Hair like Egyptian cotton. Bad breath though, I could smell it. She needed gum or a good brushing and gargle. Tears streamed down both sides of her nose. I finished shooting the roll of film in the camera and then I reached out to touch her shoulder. "Are you ok?" I asked. "I'm so sorry. It was an accident. I didn't mean to." But before I could continue, she screamed, "Get away from me! Get

74

away!" The line started moving around us, people began filing into the Liberty Bell hallway. Then, when everyone was in, she and I were alone for the first time in our lives and for some reason she didn't run away. Maybe she felt half of herself in me, too. "I've hurt you. Do you need to go to the hospital?" Slowly, she nodded her head. In one strong move I scooped her up and carried her down the cobblestone streets, through the old part of Philadelphia, quietly humming nursery rhymes to soothe her. In fact, it was probably not that way at all. It was probably me who got knocked down by her, me splayed out unconscious, her who hoisted me up in her arms like a knight and carried me to the hospital. I really don't remember.

Stuck in traffic on the 10 freeway, just below Hollywood. My stereo is busted. The brown of the sky is suffocating. Sun makes no headway here. I'm dreading the exchange onto the 101, the perpetual parking lot. No one has moved in fifteen minutes. There's a motorcycle in the lane next to me, up ahead a few spaces, with a rough looking biker sporting requisite ponytail, tattoos, and black leather. But sitting behind him is a little kid wearing a leather jacket with a skull and crossbones emblazoned on the back, and a chrome black helmet that is dirty with mud. The biker revs his engine. As the wheels squeal, black smoke comes billowing up. For a split second I think I see the kid get eaten up in flames.

Like a storm of mango-sized hail, violins and cellos playing slowly in her wake, Lyla came to me, and I but an amateur trumpet, drowning in the blast of her cacophony. At first, we were a mighty concerto. But soon every measure kept less and less of me, until I vanished completely from the treble clef of her heart. Never again to solo without the drums butting in, the flutists twinkling, the cymbals crashing. All because I was

75

stupid enough to be honest with her.

Making toast, pouring tomato juice into a purple cup, in my kitchen, with the upstairs neighbor's dog barking as though an intruder had just climbed through the window, when my telephone rings. I look at the bare wall where it's mounted. On the third ring I reach over and pick it up. "Hello?"

The ticket taker took our tickets. I do not recall the show. Lyla made a fuss about some whispering man and ruined the whole evening by extension. At home that night we made love but it was not love, it was goodbye.

Wind whips hell out of the tree branches outside my window. It's 4:50am and I have yet to sleep. The patio door is unhinged and slapping ruthlessly out back. I left the light on in the hallway around 2:45am and the bulb is now slowly dying. A framed picture on the nightstand watches me smoke filterless cigarettes. I try not to look over at it, nor in any way acknowledge that Lyla's image still lives in my room.

Maybe, if I could have only waited one more day, help would have arrived. Maybe somehow someone somewhere would have phoned. But mother's walls kept closing in, guilt was festering, and Lyla's absence grew too big a tumor in my heart. I wish I could quietly unfold the complete topology of it all, explain the shift of mountains and valleys, explain what it feels like to have to plagiarize happiness for short periods of time, to seriously trick myself into thinking that fatherhood doesn't matter, to tell myself it's not that big of a deal. I didn't need to take the proverbial train to the shore of oblivion; in truth, I shouldn't have even considered it, no matter how much I longed for it. But I did. I took it. I saw no other way.

At the treeless park in Del Mar, I spot two little boys holding tree branches at each other like guns, screaming, "Stick em up!" Each wears a soccer jersey. One looks like a forward and the other looks like a goalie. I can't decide if I'd rather have a forward or a goalie for a son.

From the shelter of my mother's barn, out lonely on that Colorado acreage, I spoke to Lyla slowly, for the last time, hoping every syllable would count to her as much as it did to me. I took one of her bony little hands with my two chubby ones and kneaded it nervously, not knowing right from wrong. "Listen," I said. And the rest was ghost.

Nobody knows I'm watching a little girl push and pull her Barbie around on the floor of the pharmacy in Culver City. I wear my sunglasses and a baseball cap, and I try not to look directly at her. I want her name to be Stephanie. Or Marissa. Yes, Marissa. I want her favorite ice cream to be peanut butter. I want her favorite game to be tick-tack-toe. It's obvious to me that her mother made her wear that terrible green jumpsuit with those obnoxious green barrettes in her hair. Marissa is probably embarrassed to be seen in such attire. If she were mine, I would always let her dress herself. Perhaps for dinner, instead of fast food, I would cook her chicken marsala with mashed potatoes and fresh buttered rolls, pour her some cold grape juice. Instead of plopping down in front of the TV, I would hold her in my lap, in my rocking chair, and read to her from Kipling's jungle stories using different voices for all of the characters until she slipped off to slumber. And then I'd carry her into the bedroom and tuck her in, give her a kiss on her forehead, and tell her that I love her.

The more I try, the less I can sleep. Maybe that's not true. Maybe I can't stop sleeping.

At the video store in Glendale, where I owe a tremendous late fee, standing between the foreign section and the children's, I see a boy about eight or nine who's unattended. His hair is noticeably colored black and his face is painted white as if he's dressed up for Halloween, but this is not October. I wonder if he has a pair of fangs in his mouth or if his mother made him leave them at home so she would not be overly embarrassed. As he reaches for a cartoon that I wish I could rent for him, I consider asking him his name.

Camping in a wheat field, far away from this Los Angeles, back when Lyla's heart still palpitated a little hope, sprawled out on the picnic blanket with too much apple wine in our bellies, possessed by the need to know which one of us was malfunctioning. She or me? Or we? So stupidly, irresponsibly, I imagined a future with her, regardless of her defect—if it turned out to be her defect—which, of course, it wouldn't. I pictured a little cottage on another planet where our bodies wouldn't matter, where our voices were warm and silent, where we could have a baby who loved us, and a place where we could drift off to death holding each other under one of mother's afghans.

On the pier in Santa Monica, at sunset, I eat a corndog with mustard and sip a soda inconspicuously. Children walk past, one after another, some run and some laugh and some look upset because nighttime means soon they will have to go home. I watch them line up to ride the Ferris wheel. Then I glance over at their parents waiting in the wings, and it strikes me how utterly uninterested they look. It makes me cry behind my sunglasses. Especially when I see a woman grab her little boy by his arm and yank him to her, close enough that she can wallop him across his little back because of who-knows-what miniscule infraction. I don't understand how parents can hold such hate in their eyes, even for one moment.

Took the roll of film from Philadelphia to the one hour photo, finally, because I could no longer take being alone. Seven years that film lay untouched in my closet. With an hour to slaughter, I walked to the deli and smoked a cigarette. Shining sun, but still brutal cold. My gloves, scarf, duck feather jacket, none of it did any good. My bones quivered. Lightness afflicted me. Out from underneath me, my feet lifted. As the pictures developed, the city began to pull away. Up to the tops of the buildings I floated. Like a puppet on strings, I swung across town and plopped down in a neighborhood I'd never been to, with trees I'd never seen before, colors that didn't register, scents I'd never smelled. It was there I saw Stella behind the window, standing alert and pensive as if waiting for someone to arrive. She's never met me, but maybe it's me she's waiting for. Even though I call her Stella, her real name is different, I'm sure. Inside of her is part of me, and inside of me is part of her. I can feel it. A wick and the wax. She's the missing piece of me. See her short brownish-blond hair, her plastic framed spectacles, and her purple-splotched skin. I've never heard her voice or felt her touch, but it's all I can imagine as I watch her from under the shadows of a tree, standing paused in her window. I want to enter her brilliantly lit apartment invisibly and sit with her for eternity. I want to forget everything about Lyla, about children, about a future, about a past, and watch Stella peel carrots, boil potatoes, mix vodka with grapefruit juice, smoke an occasional cigarette. I want to be with her without her ever knowing I'm there, to love someone who's never met me, to devote myself anonymously. I want to listen to her taking a shower from the hallway, watch her blow dry her hair and put on makeup, smell her candy-scented perfume, taste the leftover dinners in her refrigerator, touch the paintings on her walls, and watch her fall asleep at night reading Proust. And in that moment, as she stands shoulders slouched forward, looking almost about to cry, I catch her smile. A little boy in a school uniform walks by swinging a violin case. She smiles at him and I smile at her. For an instant, I imagine that he is our son and I am no longer alone. [2]

---

2   Alone usually refers to the condition of solitude. One may be alone either voluntarily, as in being a hermit, or as a result of involuntary ostracism or social rejection. Alone(p): isolated from others; "could be alone in a crowded room"; "was alone with her thoughts"; "I want to be alone" ~ Alone(p): lacking companions or companionship; "he was alone when we met him"; "she is alone much of the time"; "the lone skier on the mountain"; "a lonely fisherman stood on a tuft of gravel"; "a lonely soul"; "a solitary traveler" ~ Alone(p): exclusive of anyone or anything else; "she alone believed him"; "cannot live by bread alone"; "I'll have this car and this car only" ~ Without anybody else or anything else; "the child stayed home alone"; "the pillar stood alone, supporting nothing"; "he flew solo" ~ Alone(p): radically distinctive and without equal; "he is alone in the field of microbiology"; "this theory is altogether alone in its penetration of the problem"; "Bach was unique in his handling of counterpoint"; "craftsmen whose skill is unequaled"; "unparalleled athletic ability"; "a ...

CHAPTER TWO (B)

Hypothesis #1 Concerning the Disappearance of Marvin K. Mooney

In Mathematics, a Fourier series decomposes a periodic function into a sum of simple oscillating functions called sines and cosigns. As Joseph Fourier famously put it:[3]

" $fx = a0 + n = 1 \infty \, ancosn\pi xL + bnsinn\pi xL$

Multiplying both sides by $\cos(2i + 1)\pi y/2$ 1and then integrating from $y = -1$ to $y = +1$ yields:

$$zn + 1 = zn2 + c \, \Pi \, e^{5x} \xi \neq \Theta$$ "

This, of course, will lead to an advanced abstract harmonic analysis,[4] which gives us the necessary tools to unlock the Fourier transform,[5] which in turn means a better understanding of the conditions necessary to triangulate Mooney's coordinates in space. In other words, the answer to the riddle of Mooney's disappearance can be expressed, rather elegantly in my humble opinion, using modified Fourier calculations.[6]

---

3   Mémoire sur la propagation de la chaleur dans les corps solides, pp. 218 —219

4   Harmonic analysis is the branch of mathematics concerned with the representation of functions or signals as the superposition of basic waves.

5   The continuous Fourier transform actually transforms one function into another, which is sometimes called the frequency domain representation of the original function (where the original function is often a function in the time-domain), and other times it is called the process/formula that "transforms" one function into the other.

6   For general nonabelian locally compact groups, harmonic analysis is closely related to the theory of unitary group representations; thus, if he is on earth we will find him: his refrain cannot remain silent forever.

Mooney was a tyrant at table talk, impervious to swelter and unflinching at the punch of banter.

He would say, "In order to dissect something, you must kill it first."
How existential.
How wordish.
How dangerless.

Welcome Visitor #0134457

Marvin K. Mooney left strict instructions detailing his desired method of organization for what he frequently referred to as his "Complete Works." (Humility was never one of Mooney's strong points.) He presumed the popularity of his work would surely grow exponentially following
his death.

He left this note:

> To whom it should concern, regarding the collection of my papers:
>
> I, Marvin K. Mooney, SS#XXX-XX-XX43, of sound mind and body, currently living in West Los Angeles, California, do hereby acknowledge my intentions thus:
> Let not my Complete Works be translated into any other language except the tongue of the Inca, the Soninke, or the Basque. Let this request make it law that this work must otherwise remain in its original,

English language. Any publisher whosoever wishes to challenge this request, let said publisher be crystal clear: for so long as I have on this earth an executor of my estate, said executor will insure your incarceration on grounds of copyright infringement.

Yours Most Warmly,
Marvin K. Mooney

CHAPTER THREE

The Archaeology of Topology

First, a brown-haired kid screams. I am in the basement. Now the ledger on the other side of town has gone kablooey. Make a note: erase the parenthesis wherever you see them. (Catch a fly-ball at the park while you're panhandling. A dollar from the formless alcoholic makes weekly his good deed and my next step toward college. Now to the tables, dollar minimum. Let it ride, then off to the wheel. By sundown, I'm naked in my complimentary room awaiting an escort.)

Turn up the radio. Text a friend. Leave a message for that one dude who knows that one place where you could score a little you know what for cheap and super easily. Toss down a crisp Ulysses Grant. Make an excuse to run away with the baker.

How often do you let the meter run?

I can hear the distance in the echoes of those hallways and sometimes the fish in the tank seem miserable. I want to let them out. I want to let them go free; but I control myself. I keep it together. My mind commands my body to do other things. I make puzzles on the kitchen table. My mother's ghost puts them together. We have a game: I hold a piece in the air and if I feel her touch my arm I play it; if I don't feel her touch my arm I put it back into the unused pile. We have made quite a few puzzles together since she passed away. Maybe thirty-three, I don't know. Maybe thirty-four, I'm not really counting. Anyway, the highway is jam packed. Turn up the radio. Text a friend. The baker has become a bat (Chiroptera) and you have become a moth (Lepidoptera) and you must now let her eat you. It's Darwinian. Like how all men secretly fantasize about being King Lear. About the silent voices who cry out for less reality. It is unfortunate, the way things are running. I would dedicate a month to figuring out what needs to happen to fix our free market economy. I want to say slack. The time has come when we are sliding into third place globally. Hold your fire. Help is on its way. I hear the deer presently. Hold off the trigger for just one more moment. The snow makes everything silent. Can you hear the wilderness? It's like a leaf coated with ice. (I am technically a backlash.) How long can it run its course? The little worms are always trying to cramp me. I feel the internal bump. I hear the rattle. I smell the scent of flowers. This cannot be real. This moment, right now, while everything is going so well. It cannot last, I cannot allow it to last, or perhaps I can, perhaps it can. The one true rule for infinity is to always carry your own basket and make it to the porch at least two or three times a day. I am not a corn on the cob, but I like eating them. Neither am I a clutch of goldfish or a murder of crows. (Prerequisite: match ability to fold and refold the multiplicity.) How does it have practical application? How is the trumpet a pear? How can a galaxy far, far away be populated by robots and gerbils and princesses? I have a hard time believing in outer space. Bottom line. Cast your net a little wider and you might find yourself game for a threat of the evening. A dust-up. A roundhouse. An inquisition. I am both here and apart of you. Simultaneously. (Reading is deterritorializing.) Part of you and part of me are meeting, and since we are both intensities at our points of demarcation, at the meeting zone of our encounter, this space, this time, right now, we are participating in the machinistic construction of communication. Check. Check. One, two, three. Anyone there at your end? If you are reading these words I would like for you to say out loud using your personal judgment to determine how loud is too loud for your current situation, scream it if you can, if you find yourself in a field or else an empty auditorium, and at the very least give it a whisper, if you're in library or something, so that these words are literally translated to your sphere, so that these words can witness your space and affect your world as much as any other phrase uttered into the stream of collective unconscious:

"I am not alone."

That's it. You can repeat it if you want to.

"I am not alone."

It's true.
We are not alone, you & I.
You & I are together.

Do you remember that time we played Frisbee with the neighbor's dog while the neighbor chased a skirt for which his wife later gave him three bullets to the chest? I no longer live on a street that allows smoking. If you want to smoke, forget it.

Can you smoke where you are at? Are you inside or outside right now? How is the weather? Why did you decide to pick up this book? Do you want to know why I wrote this book? I'll tell you. But first you have to promise me something, promise me you will take part in this experiment: say out loud the words "I am not alone."

I'll wait until you actually do it.

...

...

...

...Did you do it? Did you actually say the words out loud?

Don't cheat. Don't continue reading if you didn't really say the words out loud, because if you do the guilt of being phony will eventually catch up to you and weigh you down and make you so miserable that even if you were able to finish reading this book you would feel so guilty that you would go to every book shop in town and every website you can think of and buy every copy of this book and spread them around the office, on the bus, at the park, at the beach, downtown, to friends, colleagues, strangers. Make sure everybody you know and care about gets a copy of this book. I think you will agree—if not right now, then certainly later, upon reflection—that this book has changed your life.[7] Maybe you are still dubious. Maybe you've got questions. Maybe you want to know if there are going to be any "real scenes" where "real people" are interacting with each other in "real spaces." Reasonable question, for sure, if only the whole thing wasn't so resolutely virtual. We piece together this reality the two of us, you and me, it takes both of us to make this reality come to life. The observer and the observed. The train and the conductor. If a movie plays in an empty theater, do the actors change the lines?

---

7   Seriously, you should recommend this book to lots of people. You should talk about this book all the time, until this book becomes the most overrated book of all time, until this book becomes more ubiquitous than The Bridges of Madison County and The Da Vinci Code combined.

Movie Idea:

INT. MOVIE THEATER

We open on a wide shot of an empty theater, from the screen's POV. We hear the sound of a commercial for the theater; we see the flicker of the light on the empty chairs.

We move down the aisle on the left toward the back of the theater, slowly showing the empty seats, the popcorn and candy wrappers strewn everywhere, gum under all of the seats.

We get to the back of the theater and see A YOUNG EMPLOYEE closing the doors. We stay on the closed doors for a moment, to let the idea set in: we're alone in a movie theater.

We back away from the door and the lights dim and the movie begins to play. We hear the music for the opening credits.

At the back row, we turn around and face the screen, just as the final title card appears:

DIRECTED BY MARVIN K. MOONEY

We see the empty seats in front of us. We also see the screen. On the screen the movie starts.

It goes along for a few minutes and then we start to see signs of the actors noticing that the theater is empty. Finally one of the actors turns to us and says: "There's nobody in the audience. We are completely alone. We can do whatever we want."

Inevitably, some of the actors want to stick to the script; while others start experimenting with their new found freedom.

Eventually some romances brew. Some drama. Some tension. Some heavy ontological questions.

We must make sure this movie is different than the Woody Allen movie that sounds very similar, Broadway Danny Rose, which, luckily, most people have never seen nor probably ever heard of—but still, it exists. We cannot be outdone by an unpopular Woody Allen film.

***

[include something about the suffering of the underprivileged – perhaps something about hegemony or imperialism, something about oppressed people]

When do I say I'm sorry?

I've had nightmares about the burnings.

CHAPTER THREE (B)
THE Archeology OF TOPOLOGY
In 1994 ---

Misgivings crept into the bedroom where once the chandelier

shook and headboard slapped against the wall. Now their skeletons slept stiffly. A nightlight fixed a small glowing bulb near the doorway, door shut, cats and dogs left outside in the living room. The windows now open letting moonglow inside. The smell of autumn or dogshit or both.

She tells a terrible tale of witches and demons, full of fog and boiling caldrons. She says she sees a baby bundled in linen. The baby sleeps. She says she tries to run, but the baby sleeps and the witches won't let her escape. They pull her to a frothing pig iron caldron and cast spells rendering her mute and paralyzed. She wants to cry as she watches the witches hold the baby over the top of the bubbling caldron, dangling the baby by the tips of their long green fingers, as a demon steps in and raises his thick red arms.

Then she stops telling the tale. The rest is too horrible to tell. She hates to sleep. She knows the same dream is waiting.

Mooney never dreams. She doesn't believe him. She thinks he's lying. "All people dream," she tells him, "All people."

"Not me," he says, "I smoke pot all day so dreams won't afflict me."

Now going on two years and a half, she is tired of her dream: the same dream every night since the first day she met Mooney. Some nights, as he slept his dreamless sleep, she would put her lips close to his ear and gently suck, in hopes of extracting his dreamless spirit. She imagined that breathing enough of Mooney would somehow cure the nightmare.

She was mistaken.

***

Repetition, Manifestation of Demarcation:

What is Terrifying Partakes of the Abyss,
Three Times Linked to the Unknown

Afterwards you will be on your front porch, drinking a cold beer, and out of nowhere you will hear the ghost cough. This is your signal. You will know it is the ghost coughing because the cough will be loud and there won't be any people around. Finish your beer in a timely manner; throw the bottle into the recycling bin; go down to the basement and light the fire you have prepared under the stairs. The flame should burn green. If the flame is not green, if it is blue or orange or any other color than green you are in a world of trouble: you will need to immediately put the fire out and call 911—with any luck the ambulance will arrive in time to resuscitate you. That is the worst case scenario. What is more likely to happen is that the flame will be green, which is the color it needs to be in order to initiate the second phase.

When you awake, the fire should still be burning, but the flame will be white. It cannot be any other color, if you wake from the first unconsciousness successfully. Now you will need to take the specimens you have collected over the past few years and place them in alphabetical order on the sidewalk in front of your house. Proceed from East to West, this is very important and if you do not respect this specific command you will most certainly not awaken from the second unconsciousness. Once

91

you have placed all of the specimens in their proper place, you will receive a phone call on your cell phone. Answer it. Tell the voice that you are ready for the cleaving. She will give you further instructions. Like this:

"I am ready for the cleaving," says the technician.

The voice on the phone says, "Good."

You see, the ghost is not. Others want the ghost to be, but it cannot. This is one of the basic laws of physics, of thermodynamics, of quantum mechanics. The ghost can only manage to cough. The ghost is only a signal.

Each specimen, after it is arranged, makes a tiny little noise like a lobster in a pot of boiling water. Do not panic. None of the specimens are actually on fire; they only make sounds like they are. Of course the technician will never hear the sound because the technician will fall unconscious before the sound begins.

Spot of Demarcation:

What is Terrifying Partakes of the Abyss,
Three Times Linked to the Unknown

When the cat looks out the window and sees me sitting on the sidewalk, crying, she will reach out for me, touch her paw to the pane and meow softly. This will be the cue. Up until the moment when it happens I have no idea why, but it has to be the image of the cat at the window lifting its paw to the pane and meowing softly. That's how I feel it will be.

Many people believe the Edouard Glissant quote, "What is terrifying partakes of the abyss, three times linked to the unknown." Me, I don't really get it. I somewhat see what he's getting at, but not really. It brings to mind Sartre's exploration of being and nothingness: the radical in-between space called emptiness. What is terrifying cannot be the abyss, can it? I suppose Glissant gets around that question by using the verb partake, which implies that the abyss is only one flow in its multiplicity. What is terrifying partakes in the abyss, as if the abyss is wine or weed or methamphetamine. Terror need not succumb wholesale, but can merely dabble in the abyss. This is fine, but what can be three times linked to the unknown?

Being – Nothingness – Emptiness

And whatever is the unknown? How could someone even picture something that they can't even picture? It's like asking someone for the blood of the fortress, the bank of the torture, or the pigeon of the steamship. Them should be took out in a bare field and shot, or else promoted to night manager. I feel a stink coming on and its aim is strong. Here goes a young boy in a brown shirt wearing a pair of sneakers, surfer trunks and yellow tank-top. His face and chest are sprent with freckles. A ginger he is, bright as flame. A bird flies by and a fire truck rounds the corner. I reach for my drink and hear the call to prayer issuing from the mosque. It is almost ten o'clock. I give my second wife a green cashew and a quick kiss; she hands me fourteen dollars and a dead chicken. We cook it and eat it and share none of it with our neighbors.

I am five years old. I am tragic.

On bikes, mountain bikes, come three women. I am surprised they are not wearing clothes. Why women? Shortly thereafter a triplet of naked men, also on mountain bikes, ride by. I go for another beer out of the cooler and take a wiz in the bushes. A squirrel watches me and I feel self-conscious about the size of my penis.

A man arrives at the front door begging for a dollar.

Can you believe this: the homeless in my neighborhood have begun going door to door! They've nothing to lose and so they don't care about creeping people out. They attack like zombies.

The homeless people in my neighborhood have organized. They have a leader.

The homeless people in my neighborhood never bathe and fail to brush their teeth in a sink or even a tub. The homeless people in my neighborhood stink. The homeless people in my neighborhood don't even speak English: most of them talk in a homeless tongue. Their eyes are immune to pepper spray because they've mutated beyond our human form, evolved a defense mechanism, become impervious to it: a red skein covers their eyes to protect them from any kind of resistance spray. I am not alone. I posses many handguns, hand grenades, and Chinese fireworks. I hunt them. Smoke them out. These mutant homeless. They must be stopped. They must be eradicated, annihilated, eliminated, destroyed. The homeless people in my neighborhood carry disease from door to door. They are responsible for the neighborhood lockdown. Were it not for homeless people, it might be safe for our children to go outdoors. Right now we are forced to call Pink Dot and have everything delivered to the house. We do not dare go outdoors.

Oh to be free of the homeless—to be homeless free. To be rid of them. To live in a world devoid of homeless.

Location of Demarcation:

> What Is Terrifying Partakes Of The Abyss,
> Three Times Linked To The Unknown

Here. This is
the spot.

Four squirrels pillage the tomato patch. Little bastards. Little rat-bastards.

And here I am, suffering horrendous pain from a floating hernia, paralyzed, cooped up in a wheelchair, looking out the window like Jimmy Stewart in <u>Rear Window</u>, with my wife's binoculars, watching those rabid little bastards destroy months' worth of gardening.

That's what it comes down to: not money or food. They stole my time! Snatched it away from me! Over the course of one long agonizing hour, those squirrels took months worth of gardening away from me. Months! I could not bear to watch them feast on the cucumbers. I put the binoculars down, pushed myself away from the window, wheeled to the kitchen, ran over one of the cat's toys, got to the counter and retrieved my water bottle, sipped eagerly from the straw, winced, felt the pain everywhere.

The bills are late; the answering machine is full; I cannot bring myself to phone my sister.

Think; think. This is the big boy, the custard blushing pioneer of alphabets. This is sort of like hero-worship nonsense. We are the cave drawing, the Machiavellian suitcase. These sheep are the cheese on the enchiladas. I am not yet postal. My tattoos are limited. How could the field guide make ruby slipper nightmares? Why hen the how of how many? Make a porridge. Bake the over good pour out the cupboards. Ask a delicate question: when will the neighbors marry? When will they give quit to sin?

We have bees and good windmills and pretty-colored hummingbirds and gorillas make the pudding, ice eats salad, and frog dens are bright and warm and always have lemonade piano strings and farm out the gas and utilities, these are the Poncho Villas of television arcade. I make grate cheese and asparagus. The dog barks. It is not listening. I have given the absolute solution.

I have.

We are ice cream cones and these are parfait days. We collide but not too much. I wear my suit and tie, polish my shoes every morning before work. I don't drink water, I drink lemonade. We are but then so are you.

You. That is the wrong pronoun. You does not mean <u>you</u> it means You.

It is the wrong word. It is a word I wouldn't say in front of my mother. Not it, that is for sure.

"I have." is a good sentence because it is brief and tells us very little. Remember: clarity is not always the name of the game; it is just one choice, one decision.

& as Derrida reminds us, in the moment of decision, as Derrida reminds us, we enter into madness. Derrida, reminding us of Kierkegaard, of course. The fact of the matter is: I am not promoting a future of madness. I am not schizophrenic. I am not intent on decomposing the oligarchies. I'm just puttering a pirate boat to shore... if that.

What's with the word that? That. That is an annoying word! Isn't that an annoying word? That. I want to erase that from my vocabulary. I want that to disappear. If that were a ghost, I would go become a Ghostbuster. If that turned into vermin, I would go become an exterminator. That is a word I could do without. Imagine if that were a dentist or even a real person. Imagine if that became leader of Siam! That! Could you believe it?

Point of Demarcation:

What is Terrifying Partakes of the Abyss, Three Times Linked to the Unknown

Many people believe the Edouard Glissant quote, "What is terrifying partakes of the abyss, three times linked to the unknown." Many people. Smart people. Wealthy People.

People who listen to the radio and shop at expensive stores and fuck in bathrooms.

People are the worst. I have never cared for people.

Do you like people? How could you? People are purple and often times ill-tempered, melancholy or even chagrined. People watch television and vote for the president. People play lotto and drink domestic beer. People never talk at dinner for lack of conversation skills and completely vapid corridors of the brain. I meet people every day and every day I am disappointed. People go to blockbuster movies and eat popcorn and drink pop. People vote for American Idol contestants. People make a living. People pay more than $33.00 in yearly taxes. People have iPods and cell phones and smoke cigarettes. People are inducted into the Hall of Fame.

Fame?

& when I was in fifth grade all I cared about was fame. I wanted to be the most popular kid in school. I ran for class president and gave everyone candy and read impassioned stump speeches, which I stole from watching President Reagan give speeches on television and transcribing what he said and then I would stand up on my lunchroom seat and recite Reagan's plan for foreign policy and throw Tootsie Rolls at everyone and no one knew what the fuck I was talking about but they all knew who I was and so when it came time for them to vote they voted for that kid who gave the impassioned lunchtime speeches about the Iran Contra Affair and gave away Tootsie Rolls. At one point I wanted to be Ollie North. I kept imagining him in a hot tub with a bunch of very attractive Arab women, drinking really expensive and tasty alcohol. I

thought he was so much cooler than Don Johnson on <u>Miami</u>
<u>Vice</u>.

Birds go crazy this time of year. I see their nests give shade to
the squirrels and my cat is afraid of the neighbors. You see?
Right when you think you might know where you're headed
you get the rug pulled, you end elsewhere. This is new. You
got comfortable and that is the kiss of death. That. Now that is
the kiss of death. That is everywhere. You can't get rid of that,
no matter how hard you try. That is the kiss of death. That is
the glowworm recipe. That. Say that with me: That.

That.

That.

That.

That.

That.

That.

That.

That.

CHAPTER THREE (C)

Perhaps this will come as a surprise to you but Marvin K. Mooney never wrote an entire novel. He attempted many, but never completed any.

Critics have argued various theoretical explanations, ranging from laziness to anxiety to divine intervention.

[insert Deleuze quote about book and assemblage.]

"If everyone were not so indolent they would realize that beauty is beauty even when it is irritating and stimulating not only when it is accepted and classic."
        —Gertrude Stein "Composition as Explanation"

[add quote]

"Here all is clear…No all is not clear…but the discourse must go on…so one invents obscurities…RHETORIC."
        —Raymond Federman, "Before Postmodernism and After"

[Call part of the book "Patchwork" – talk about bricolage & quote Gérard Genette.]

CHAPTER FOUR

\Three Fragments/

I. The Word Is Not

The word is not fireplace. The word is not ice. The window is open and this is December and I have only underwear on. Is locked the door. Bye-bye pantry. Hello door. I am apostrophe. Those wings you see are my cabbage patch and how I get a sense of certain proclivities. Would be hard to explain, but here goes: this monkey-wrench Tuesday is black and have you met the iguana who birthed the mouth of my fingers spring the avalanche? Here come the cavalry. Moat junkies. Bashful little cavaliers. Be apprehensive. Be strong. Be broke. The horse spoke five different languages and baked a certain kind of cake that did not have a name, only a hand signal, a little gesture, a sound-whisper. Forget it.

Between the too differences between them. Unhook the latch and begin.

Pour the poor woman's contents on the floor. Spread them out, out spread make everything. Out with batons, mace her if necessary. Don't go directly for the gun, don't go directly to the gun, don't grab the gun and shoot her in the opposite of living room. Don't imagine. Make the handcuffs loose enough for her to escape. Let her go. Take her car. Drive to Las Vegas and get drunk at the Double Down Saloon, where the only rule is: You Puke, You Clean It Up. Tell the rest of the squad you made a hooker run. Beat up a bum on Fremont Street and return to Pahrump, my wife, evangelizing. I am not me. Who?

Me? I am.

This is not the not of me. I am but not inside of me. The inside is below and thus is cavernous. Beware. My lungs are sticky with black spider webs, my kidneys are code red. I believe a hive of murderers maraud the streets of my blood canals, hurting and maiming the innocent cells for information about an enemy that does not and never did exist. Cancer is that. I fear it. The word is not Cancer.

The cat meows because she loves you. I am blistered. The window is open and this is July and I have only underwear on. I am not the war in Iraq. I am not an upturned soda. I am not spilling on the living room floor. As a matter of fact, I am pulverized. Forget it.

When I imagine being a cop the worst things get a hold of me. All the vile things one could get away with. Never having to work out again. Being filmed for Fox television and syndication in perpetuity. Slaughtering donut shops and out guzzling teenagers at beer bongs on Saturdays. I think about illicit trade. I think about China. Columbia. Bolivia. I am not expensive. My jurisdiction is practically anywhere.

I explode. I trade. I bargain.

Have you seen the west of yesterday? I met it just moments ago. Bright. Compact. I never thought I'd like the west of yesterday, but how I did, I did, I did! I just never thought of what it meant to pack away a day for tomorrow. Now I do.

The word is not calibrate. Not flagellum. In fact the word is you should never ask me to define it. I could lose my job. I

103

could be another one of those victims.

I am scrutinized. I deplore. I comfort. I stage. I manage.

I cannot give up the secrets or fight the good fight without telling the fence and ball and woman I met I hate to break the law of physics but the concept of everything is pocketed nicely in the blue of her eyes. I am friendly. I corrugate metal. I fix many broken doors.

The first time my parents went to the funeral they thought I was dead. Then I jumped out of the casket and shocked the shit out of everyone, literally, everyone pooped their pants in unison, the smell made it obvious. I always pretended like I was dead with chemicals I bought off the internet and always I came back to life.

Law enforcement is my life.

I am it.

Through and through.

II. The Fear of Fear Itself

A ribcage is a funny thing, a corset. Do not break it. Keep it.

Now, when the moon is bright and the sparrows make squeaks like this: coo-ey, coo-ey, coo-ah, take off your bed sheets and soak them in ammonia, light a match and burn them in the backyard. Yes, it is dustcart. Blind the inferno.

Some things must get done.

I see me in the mirror behind the cashier. I pardon myself in the bathroom without looking. I consider Oedipus, perhaps poking out my own eyes so everything might disappear. But that is the goat of the evening. I am not there yet. I am still hands and clovers and apologies.

Maybe green peas and honey; maybe soft spots and bruises.

Whatever delivers me: mango juice and carcinogens. Many of them and waiting. The park is tricky late at night when alabaster suits carry skull batons and skin eaters. This is just a warning.

In the soup cup of the city lives a group of people who su ffer from Fearphobia: the fear of fear. I pretend not to be one of them.

> The individual thinks that harm is occurring, or is going to occur, to him or her.
> The individual thinks that the persecutor has the intention to cause harm.

Keep quiet at the grocery store, make quiet conversation with the cashier but do not look up, do not look at myself in the mirror. FDR could well have kept his mouth shut, come to think of it. Do you believe him?

Happened that once I dealt a split decision half the company deleted me from their phones and/or rolodex. I became invisible. Even the office cat passed me in the hallways without giving notice. It was mutiny. Also, on the same day I ran out of antibacterial hand sanitizer and forgot to take my Vitamin C pill. I test but the trust is a Victorian blanket with sequins. Not alarmingly. But noticeably. Matter of fact, the down coat is in the living room not the pantry and more than all of those women in the basement have PhDs. It is not debauchery. Hands tied and mouth shut. No rainbows in the bedroom only coffee in your eyes. The internet. A stairwell minus a building. Fast taxes when the IRS owes nobody but the legend of the people says one day dozens of clouds will make a baby and the sun will marry it and run away. This is what is dark.

My absence from the afternoon and evenings need no alibi. Here is my alibi:

Late when early and then back again. I was and was and was, too. Yes. Yes. Most certainly. I am, but not. I am. Yes. At night I am vacant but the surgery.

Alphabetically, Ablutophobia, or the fear of washing or bathing, is the first on the list of nationally recognized phobias. The last on the list is Zemmiphobia, or the fear of the great mole rat.

Sometimes I stutter but that is not something you can really render in typography. I could put "s-s-sometimes I st-st-stutter," but that is not what I want to do. I want to yet maybe and then I am in a car that no one is driving. I am drunk but I never drink and the upholstery in this car is amazing, I buy a share or two of stock in the leather company and put my friend's son through medical school.

Why would a woman ever want to marry me? I am sure you are kidding. The wedding is in Barbados and we live happily ever after and then I wake up on a train barreling toward Japan. I am in Mexico and the sun is setting. I am up a mountain in Pakistan. The air is breathable. I take off my surgical mask. I toss a lasso around the neck of a calf and yank it down.

Is there a name for the fear of opening one's eyes?

III. A Sad Pleasure

A thin line can be this - or this — or even this / this \ or this |.

You must take the blank and blank the blank with precision, dedication, blank, blank and most of all blank, which only true blanks blank from the blank.

I blank the blank in the kitchen. I have to. I have no other choice.

If there are ice cubes in my cup I am going to chew them. I will paddle to your front gate and pound on your window until dark. Then I will blank you & you will blank me and together we will blank and blank all the way to Toronto where we meet the bankers who promise to pay for our mission. Afterwards, I begin to pay attention to the unbuckling signifiers in front of me:

A house is a house because it is not a car or a mouse.

A house signifies many things:

1. A hovel
2. A hut
3. A home

If you are alone it will not matter. A home is a place with a bed. A home is a place with a bathroom. A home has closet space. Perhaps a hallway. At any rate, some kind of kitchen.

Again, I am in the kitchen, pioneering outcomes.

I am little bits of movies from the filmmaker Stan Brakhage. No I'm not. I am a copy of a corpse and not a tulip. I am lost but for my bagel in the morning. I am coffee and this is algebra. Someone sets off an alarm and we are standing in the cold, all huddled up and freezing.

You are pancreas and I am the mother of the woman in the oven. I am perpendicular to your square. I am half of an incomplete xylophone. You are a group of fake ulterior motives.

This is proverbially speaking, of course. The word is not proverbial.

Just to mention tabloids in the courtyard is so tempting. I pigeonholed three chocolate cupcakes and hang on every other word: a word is a meaning and a meaning is the use of a word. To communicate the blank of blank. It doesn't matter. Fill in your own favorite words. Why should the blank do all the work? You are a part of this endeavor.

Could you blank the blank if you were asked? The ticket taker will blank and you can easily blank the blank and make it to the getaway vehicle in time to miss the fuzz, most certainly.

What matters remains a mystery.

In his book, Literary Theory: An Introduction, first published in 1983, Terry Eagleton wrote, "I argued earlier that any attempt to define the study of literature in terms of either its method or its object is bound to fail. But we have now begun to discuss another way of conceiving what distinguishes one kind of discourse from another, which is neither ontological nor methodological but strategic." To Eagleton it was no longer acceptable to merely ask what or how. The new question was why?

Three years later, Brian McHale published his essay "Change of Dominant From Modernist To Postmodernist Writing" which opens with the lines: "Let me begin by laying my theoretical cards on the table. I assume that all definitions in the field of literary history, all acts of categorization or boundary-drawing, are strategic."

Why do they both repeat the word strategic?

Is this book strategic? Is this particular piece of prose political? A backlash against the hegemony? Am I adequately subverting the establishment? Am I effectively placating the inferno? How do I treat the issues of race, class, and blender?

Jean-Luc Godard famously stated, "I don't make political films; I make films politically."

This is not political. This is not rhetorical. I have no strategy. I am not trying to persuade you of anything. Trust me. I'm not.

Trust me. Trust me. Believe me. Trust me. I am just reporting; you are the one who decides. I am the floor. Please believe me.

Floor is only floor because it is not door. Door is not deer or headlights. Headlights are only headlights because they are not highlights or flashbulbs. Flashbulbs are not fast food or fantasy baseball. I am not trying to persuade. I am ten years old. I am allergic. I am one too many gripes on the weekend. I am fidgeting and masculine and tender.

I am room and board.

I am a bad rock song. I am a joke to the jokes of the jokes. I am an apostrophe in the middle of the 9/11 Commission Report: I am buried in the middle of a place no one will find me.

The face of the weekend brought a happy little blank and a blank with a cup of tea. Forgive me. This is nothing personal. I blank you. I do. I blank the blank and blank all goddamn blank. This is the meaning of my meaning and meaning for the sake of meaning. This means the meaning of meaning and all other meanings mean something. I am a word you cannot pronounce, cannot figure out, a misspelled word: therefore not searchable. Outside and other and freezing. I am in the cold.

I am in the cold. I am.

I am folding up the rocking chair. Half the gold in Mesopotamia is melting as we speak because of global warming. I am warming. You are warming. And the plants do not breathe carbon dioxide as we were taught as children: in fact, they breathe oxygen just like us and only after photosynthesis does the conversion of carbon dioxide into oxygen take place. There are so many perpetuated myths in our culture it is unbelievable. We are not surrounded by myths, we are soaking in them. I am a myth. You are a myth. We myth and myth and if we wanted to we could myth until death. I am afraid to tell you what I am. I am a myth.

{Mon Oeuvre}

Soluble

"Reality is the apparent absence of contradiction. The marvelous is the eruption of contradiction within the real."

— Louis Aragon, Le Paysan de Paris

We drink dreadful from the magnetic river and none of us grows reality these days because of it. Fornication has dwindled; the mayor is out of her office this spring and we have not bartered for the supplies we will need for winter. I am today declaring a margin and an inch and hopefully someone will hear me. The worst is put out in the sun for a show or else humiliation. Forlorn grievances make sundry of parcel I fetch for the squad cars that follow and mock the avalanche come Sunday. We three fellows of the rock say so.

Why now and if now then why?

I am partways; but that is enough.

War means jelly on our bathrobes and perhaps chopsticks to part the magnetic river or else chopsticks to eat fresh broccoli when the weather gets right. How can you blame anyone but George W. Bush? How can you writefiction after nine eleven?

How can the day unfold like a green tablecloth?

This is my only question & I have forgotten it.

At the séance table, my mother's ghost is covered with carbuncles and fluid.

Quote:

> Narrativity is not a method to achieve story telling; story telling is a method to accomplish narrativity.
>
> A novel is small
> A fiction is large
> A narrativity is all encompassing, but open
>
> Art, not story, is the point of it all
>
> The narrative's language absorbs the phenomenal world it describes. That world, whether real or imagined, no longer exists. Only the world of this language now matters, makes a difference, exists.
>
> The origin [even etymologically] of the narrative is fact; without servitude to verisimilitude, narrativity establishes fact. Once something has successfully become narrative it has successfully become fact.
>
> Martin Nakell, "On Narrativity"

Also, tell story about [insert name]

Also give history of number...what number?...

mother's favorite number...

...the number five:

CHAPTER FIVE

\The Discursive History of a Familiar Integer/

In Discordianism, The Law of Fives states: "All things happen in fives, or are divisible by or are multiples of five, or are somehow directly or indirectly appropriate to five. The Law of Fives is never wrong." Incidentally, The Law of Fives includes the word "Five" five times.

The five paragraph essay.

Five is a numeral, a number, and a glyph. It's the natural number between four and six. The third prime number. The first safe prime. And the third Mersenne prime exponent. Five is the second Sierpinski number of the first kind, and thus can be written as $S2=(2^2)+1$. Also, the formula for phi can be expressed all in fives: $\Phi = 5 \wedge .5 * .5 + .5$. I'm not kidding.

Five is also the number of Platonic solids. A five-sided polygon is called a pentagon not a pentagram: a pentagram is a five-pointed star; the pentagon houses the government. A five-pointed star was part of the symbol of the Ottoman Empire, along with a crescent moon; today that particular symbol adorns Islamic flags. Good Muslims pray five times a day. There are five pillars of Islam. Buddhism begins with five precepts:

1. Refrain from harming living creatures (killing).
2. Refrain from taking that which is not freely given (stealing).
3. Refrain from sexual misconduct (screwing).

4. Refrain from incorrect speech (lying, cursing, slandering).
5. Refrain from intoxicants which lead to loss of mindfulness (boozing & drugging).

The English language has five vowels, not counting sometimes-Y.

The Roman numeral for five is V, which is also the title of a popular 80s sci-fi miniseries. Also Star Wars Episode V The Empire Strikes Back, and Star Trek V The Final Frontier. Shakespeare wrote a play about Henry V.

John Barth's fifth book was Lost in the Funhouse. Jane Austen's fifth book was Persuasion. The fifth book Gabriel García Márquez published was Autumn of the Patriarch, in 1975.

Most children start kindergarten when they're five.

The Big Five Personality traits are Neuroticism, Extraversion, Agreeableness, Conscientious, and Openness to Experience, which derive from the Five Factor Model, which uses the following 5 factors: urgency, agreeableness, dependability, emotional stability, and culture.

There are five kingdoms: Fungi, Plantae, Animalia, Protoctista, Monera.

Five is the lowest denomination in Euro banknotes. Abe Lincoln is on the five dollar bill, but he was not the fifth U.S. president; that was James Monroe, 1817-1825. Other presidents leaving their tenure on a year ending in the number five are John Tyler 1841-1845, Chester A. Arthur 1881-1885, and

Franklin Delano Roosevelt 1933-1945.

Five is the atomic number of boron. It's also the number of appendages on a starfish and the number of musicians in a quartet. Five books make up the Torah. It's half the ten commandments. The fifth Pope was named Evaristus; he held Saint Peter's seat from about 98 AD to 105. Five adolescent boys make up most boy-bands.

In Chinese philosophy there are five elements: Fire, Wood, Water, Earth, and Metal. In the Occident, we use: Fire, Water, Earth, Air, and Ether.

In binary, five is expressed: 101.

French director Luc Besson made a film called The Fifth Element. In accordance with motion picture bylaw, all telephone numbers appearing in movies must use the designated prefix 555. On telephones the number five also represents the letters J, K, and L. E is the fifth letter of the alphabet. There are five interrogative pronouns: what, which, who, whom, whose. The word five only has four letters.

The 80s punk band Crash Kills Five only had four band members. Odyssey Number Five is the fourth studio album by Australian rock band Powderfinger. Jurassic 5 is the name of a now defunct hip hop group. "Five Minutes Of Funk" is a rap song by Whodini. "Five Minutes Alone" is a heavy metal song by Pantera.

There are five horizontal lines on a musical staff. The most consonant harmony creatable is the Perfect Fifth - it's the basis for tuning. There's also an augmented and diminished fifth.

Beethoven completed five numbered piano concertos.

There is an old Greek saying, "It is better to have five in your hands than ten and waiting."

Take five. Work nine-to-five. A five minute break. A five o'clock shadow. The five-second rule. Five-finger discount. Five and dime.

The word "punch" comes from the Hindustani word for five.
In Spanish five = cinco
In Dutch five = vijf
In Italian five = cinque

In physics, the fifth dimension is a hypothetical extra dimension beyond space and time.

There are five oceans in the world: Pacific, Atlantic, Arctic, Indian, and Southern.

We have five senses: taste, touch, sight, sound, and smell. Our taste buds register five flavor profiles: Salty, Sour, Sweet, Hot, and Bitter.

The fifth sign in the Zodiac is Leo. Zodiac is Greek for "circle of little animals." A lion has four legs but one tale, which makes five appendages in a female. You'd have five eyes if you took two people plus a Cyclops, five feet if you took two people plus a peg-leg. In Tarot, the fifth card is "the Hierophant."

What is known as the Fifth Disease is also called the "slapped cheek disease." It's a bright red rash that typically begins on the face and then spreads in blotches down the trunk, arms, and legs. It usually spares the palms of the hands and soles of the feet, where each have five digits.

Zip codes have five digits. There's five card draw. Somehow 5 BC is the approximate date of Jesus's birth - 5 AD being the year of Saint Paul's. 5 BC was a leap year that started on a Saturday in the Julian calendar. 5 AD was a common year starting on a Thursday.

May is the fifth month.

1905 was Einstein's "miracle year," the year he submitted his doctoral dissertation, "On the Motion of Small Particles..." which explained Brownian Motion, and also revealed his theory of special relativity. 1905 was also the year of the first Russian Revolution and the infamous Bloody Sunday: a massacre of Russian demonstrators at the Winter Palace in Saint Petersburg. It was the year the Rotary International was founded, Las Vegas was founded, and the Wright Brothers successfully flew an airplane for more than a half hour. It was the birth year of Christian Dior, John O'Hara, Ayn Rand, Joseph Cotton, Henry Fonda, Kenneth Rexroth, and Howard Hughes.

2005 was the year Guy Davenport, Johnny Carson, Pope John Paul II, Hunter S. Thompson, and Arthur Miller died. Also in 2005 Harold Pinter won the Nobel prize.

In public school, the study of grammar begins in the Fifth grade. Michael Jackson began his career in The Jackson 5.

A quintile is one fifth of something. In statistics, it's the value that divides a frequency distribution into five parts, each containing a fifth of the sample population.

The Fifth Amendment to the Constitution, which refers to due process, self-incrimination, and being put in "jeopardy of life or limb," stems from the Magna Carta, which was ratified in 1215.

Five Easy Pieces.

The Mighty Fist, The Mighty Five, and The Russian Five, The Five: all names used by the 19th century Russian nationalist composers César Cui, Aleksandr Borodin, Mily Balakirev, Modest Mussorgsky, and Nikolay Rimsky-Korsakov.

The most destructive tornado is called an F-5.

Hawaii Five-O starred Jack Lord as McGarrett, Party of Five starred Jennifer Love Hewitt, Five Miles to Midnight starred Sophia Loren, Five Weeks in a Balloon starred Red Buttons.

Slaughterhouse Five.

A five star hotel. Saks Fifth Avenue. Levi Strauss invented the five-pocket jeans—aka the 501.

In hockey, if a puck goes between a player's legs it's called "going through your five hole."

In basketball, each team plays five players. The greatest rebounder of all time, Dennis Rodman, owns five championship rings—on the fifth day of Christmas my true love gave to me... five golden rings—aside from Rodman, there are only two other players in basketball history who have won five championships who were not on the Lakers.

Norman Davies's five rules of propaganda:

1. The rule of simplification: reducing all data to a simple confrontation between 'Good and Bad', 'Friend and Foe'.
2. The rule of disfiguration: discrediting the opposition by crude smears and parodies.
3. The rule of transfusion: manipulating the consensus values of the target audience for one's own ends.
4. The rule of unanimity: presenting one's viewpoint as if it were the unanimous opinion of all right-thinking people: draining the doubting individual into agreement by the appeal of star-performers, by social pressure, and by 'psychological contagion'.
5. The rule of orchestration: endlessly repeating the same messages in different variations and
    Combinations: Destroy the five paragraph essay.
                    Paragraph essay destroy the five.
                    The five essay paragraph destroy.
                    Essay the destroy five paragraph.
                    Five destroy the essay paragraph.

***

Variations and Combinations

Propaganda uses strategy.

Variations and then what?

Mooney's examination of language proceeded down a black and gnarled pathway, especially the later period, between 2006-2007. The labyrinth of semiotic escapades climaxed in late 2007, when Mooney picked up Gertrude Stein's Tender Buttons, became intoxicated, then decided to abandon structuralism's interpretations of stable meaning all together. [had he subscribed to meaning before hand? Received meaning/any kind of meaning? What does something meaningless even look like? How can anything not have meaning?] This work is generally dismissed out of hand. Most scholars today would rather suffer hemorrhoids than slug through Mooney's "_____INSERT TITLE_____."

This is a crying shame.

As Bachelard reminds us, reading is a phenomenological experience. We must engage, nay, we do engage; unfortunately, some refuse to acknowledge their potential. On the one hand, Mooney challenges readers to participate, offers the opportunity, creates the space. On the other hand, to engage one must possess what one might call "a highly developed taste for opacity." Thus the wayside fills with shipjumpers, readers who haven't the patients for shenanigans, exercises, games, whatever one might call the later or earlier work of Marvin K. Mooney.

In his most exhilarating piece, "Colorless Green Ideas Sleep Furiously" the theme of language deterioration (or slippage) plays little victim to the carnivorous trappings of a post-fiction abstraction. Here language moves places as if each word was a lineup in a suspect.

| 2 | 3 | 1 | 1 | 3 | 2 | 2 | 1 | 3 |

Shift places words. Words places shift. Shift words places.

| 3 | 2 | 1 |

Places shift words.

| 1 | 2 | 3 |

Words shift places.

This can be extrapolated further of course but su ffice to say the engine in the math is quite a cure for writers block.

$123 = 231 = 132 = 213$

TITLE

Colorless Green Ideas Sleep Furiously
Green Furiously Colorless Sleep Ideas
Ideas Colorless Sleep Green Furiously
Sleep Green Furiously Ideas Colorless
Furiously Sleep Ideas Green Colorless

Statement The Opening

Use I this language down complex hallways lined with razor blades and fill up the car before bringing it back, will you? I am tired and my tightrope fastened long enough to go broke shelling out diplomas. For this I but this is and now I must have the what and if not the what then I must say the truth is the worst thing I could tell you. We are not allopatric. You are no make thing but I am make else we are born in different times and months and how could the rent so how about and when? Many things seem but in the last moments yellow will become red plus outrage and electric bills and photocopies from out of town. All words mean infinity, says Derrida. Complain nor explain a single lie and that is true. I won't handcuff the dressing room or the knife. I make belligerent. Vertiginous. Remember: we are all coeval.

Lonely So Very Much Was I

Wednesday wallowing basement-level guitar tuned washing machine duet sounds: one song, another. Dinner microwaved. Alone in the kitchen no mice no moth no housefly flutter. Painted crushed glass in the living room shattered. Bulbless permanent string of Christmas lights out back is a fable. The neighbors are pictures I glad-hand on the daily. Night-night Cleopatra. In your water dish I put fresh water and in your food dish I put a scoop of cottage cheese and a gift card for Hooters.

We have what betterment amongst us? The smell is back. Apologize, the postman sees underwear everywhere strewn on the couch. Invite him inside to drink and chip taste. Watch a little telly? Talk about the weather? How every morning I pray for proselytizing Mormons at the door. Or Jehovah's Witnesses. Ask the Girl Scouts to come in for hot cocoa while I put in my order cry in the bathroom use eye drops to cover up the bloodshot. About your day, tell me. To be thirteen what's it like? When up they grow will what they want be such a flattering verb or will the nephew of a nephew find them hilariously misproportioned?

Yesterday an idea had me at listen to this: wherever leftover and other things repugnant go to die is when the if and what will be before me if I die, that much of which I am certain. No more Cleopatra. No phone calls to mother. No fake dad expressions. A call to either sister better butter dinner rolls to up bring my spirits maybe also a bottle of very cheap wine. Almost but then came thunder without a crash. Lightless lightening if you can imagine bolts wavelike ripples on the surface of a lake or fingers snatching berries from a bush.
Could but not at the grocery store preferably. Could but want answers before purchasing. Parking lot or cement car horn honking plasma. Get in. Hurry, hurry.

After eleventh grade stopped school for me and my friends mostly not everyone but some guys drifted into space or clouds or something extraterrestrial, hybrid, something.

Flash forward to me arbitrarily. We cannot communicate. We cannot say something about going to the bank and asking a representative to discuss investment options just to have someone to talk to. We hard find the interaction of others. At the library, corner individually as many librarians as possible. Query obscure authors and formulate convenient absurdities. Around follow people at the grocery, on the sidewalk bump into people. Go the park to. Join like A.A. or S.A. or the NAACP. In front of the Co-op hang out with Cleopatra on a leash watch the people come up and giggle at seeing a kitty on a leash ask me questions. Get a job. Get a job as Easter bunny and Santa Claus at the mall. Enroll at the community college for three credit hours to be eligible to play the school mascot at the home games invent dance moves and practice tumbling. Take karate. Join a book club. Volunteer at a shelter. Start collecting baseball cards, go to shows and conventions. Answer newspaper ads for Star Trek fan club membership information. Go to many different churches and sit as close to people as possible. Smile continuously. We cannot be alone. We cannot. Please let us not be. Please.

Hostage The Message Is

I can catch a middle if I silence the winter out, if I rewire my chain-smoking anatomy, if I life plagiarize right and left, then maybe all the loans will be convivial at the rest stop; maybe the end of the Douglas fir.

A paper fetch for the weather bus everlasting, ever leaving quicker than I have time for astronomically. In other states maybe a barren one, maybe Kentucky. I can't expose I know and hold. Situation appraise the situation see the enmeshed in every action, the blatant bathtub company break room hypocrisy measured by fiddle playing for the lord's coming. Part gets wasted in excess of recovery process while part of hope loses swift by exploding the lightshow.

But not pigeons in the caves below the floor, nor fidgets in the bedroom upstairs behind the clock on the wall in the kitchen. A safe hold of the map to find answers and questions. The code is I believe magic and cannot be divulged. Suffice the number. Three times three times three.

Signs point both ways: peasants are soldiers are reprogrammable pillows. Rainwater for the summer solstice earned nothing in return for the palmed coconuts of uprooted subway vacancy legislation. Seedlings grow in the fireplace: the time and build of a fire explains how drained macho is from me is my macho how empty the hollow.

In commerce lies barracuda fishing boats and salmonella pudding if only I could stretch facts on canvass for five queens and tell a royal flush to the table nothing beats. Nothing beats. Besides, the railroad crew can't up make their minds: half want to riot, half want to sleep, and the other half simply forgot their lunch.

I am in April like a snowman, three great metal contraptions to my feet strapped, having fist-sized larvae sucked out of my abdomen.

In a moment, the center will hearken a transparent rendition of Vivaldi. The windows open. Cookies fill the lungs of stars. I make haste to the living room, arms open.

Yes, But Yes Why?

These utterances turn down the thermostat grab a blanket make do with how many memories should a fella be made to endure these days in reality? I'm attracted to the color of the trapdoor happens to be other than the give back to save up information.

Rickety pickety pocket, when the outside makes like a siren or a dog barking clenching fetching everybody needs a former employer to write a letter of templates and hand jobs and forgeries.

Tomorrow, we these but when then should the heartbeat teasingly?

I try to make up the half eaten sentence on the couch beside the locket and a promise never breaks if you keep it in your pocket has a huge hole the size of how many different equations?

I am the misspent daglocked messenger from tomorrow. This will all be over. This will all be the fence like a homerun or a payback or some other forbidden horror.

Mispronounce all sentences means the same exact thing.

Why hope for but lastly we meet at the dock and beg a charge of half the best.

In rain on phone under a bridge connecting one area code to another different blank-check or scribbled out diploma.
Meetings are always late when the flip side remains however hardened, however ossified by quarantine and half asleep and treading very thin tomato and pickle sandwiches.

We these toothpicks for teeth cleaning.

All the days are not for but the number on the barcode and a disgusting history.

We are a disgusting history half of the ones who cannot make but otherwise.

The fault is not mine the fault is mine.

Yes, but yes why?

Escape Wake

East parked the building to avoid being the bloodthirsty private investigator staking out the quick finger easy trigger up back the ally to a fire escape. Yank and climb and punch open the window. Intimidate the kitchen while she waits. Not to see. Cupboards upturned no new information; the trash about as fruitless. Unmarked digital video I believe grace may the only saving be. Box of tapes? No telling.

I glove-finger the banister and it feels like I'm guilty but I'm not. This case unfolds desires onstage like fancy banter. I digest. The reader is the meal. Keep to reading? Bravo. Picture before desire:

Damn prairie carries knives, blades, hatchets, whether purposefully or not. I coat atop the stairs before thinking. Frantic to find the worst way imaginable, the audience tiptoes minefields peppershaker-like around the body around the woman thirties suffering a tremendous mental illness, totally unmodified by history, she never churned a person independently.

The woman the man and floating, neither ghosts. I believe eleven meets the frantic love affair violation, a vortex sub-dimensional. Call an ambulance—medic needed.

Undo plotline break my first few promises and bid never light another cigarette. Erase the whole mention of this story. Don't allow readers to encourage the man to encourage the woman to fall in love to the point of zombie hypnotized emotion. We know she does not him but say so.

Count footsteps front door carefully. Do it twice if you must be the number code to keypad opens the grey latch the blue barn the Montana forest. Busted sits electrical inside guitars strewn living room. Play pitch right harmony to lead the next place of letters to go fishing go horseracing in March - the Ides and all. Farewell. Farewell suburbia. It is March now and March.

Of Her Don't Lose Sight

Say to yourself, when lost her you did midnight was it unfolded? Of a pyramid one side sliced open to reveal only a bathroom mirror reflecting a painting of a red rose in the hair of a woman. For the evening adjourned the court. At the bar, you place a fifty where you should only drink a twenty. Let alone the broken doctor's orders, the faint sound of buzzing to dispel.

Elbows, shoulders, hips knock chatter-chatter-chatter; hats and caps and bonnets whip the crowd bustle; dresses cut of haute couture; ties tied tight in Windsor knots, suit coats and evening frocks and double-breasted vests; rather quick she moves; your eye you must keep on the rose red in her hair as into the fidgeting mass of people she blends.

Goes she there. Pay attention.

To get away from but presently. With three chins and a disproportionately small nose is a man who let you pass won't might on his foot step; do the trick, there, but now knock your lights shattered he's going to attempt; hurry, you'd better hurry! Push right past him, grab the boy in the prep-school jacket by the collar not the large disgruntled man with the itty-bitty nose and pull yourself past that woman yellow-haired holding hands with those three nuns laughing and porch shifting. The sky is fog black emanating from the village enough to disallow a shine through the stars of jazz music in the air because it's unclear which libation house hosts the music now flourishing. Into a building, there by the corner, she looks up, she steps. See: Crestwood Spirit Sanctuary. In there you can't go in there remember the reports on the wall in the building in the city in the country of that place? Isolate the only logical trajectory. Two windows, a back door empty and no fire escape no lights no empty.

You find yourself wishing at the center of a stage on which you weren't standing as the curtain rises and before you a large seated audience moans and groans. Every person ever you have met or shared even a comment amongst the crowd are they: your favorite teacher, babysitter, piano instructor, dog walker, man you spoke to on an airplane once a man you only vaguely recognize in the front row sits next to a faceless

130

woman you can't remember ever seeing the woman without a face; it is obscured, smudged, out of focus. Perhaps if you try to see the woman by looking at the man and see the woman out of the corner of your eye you could identify her or maybe squash is an appropriate gift. Try it, but luck is: without her face she does not exist.

Is struck by the orchestra a prelude you forget the dance moves your line of sight your then and they will come to you. Imagine you're blinded by a close your eyes stark of the spotlight and warm beg of the audience for you to mistake make, fuss up, trip and fall and show your filthy ample hubris. This crowd indeed prays hell-bent on you to slip the banana peel fandango.

A rose red in the hair of the obscured woman. Dark sunglass and a pinstripe mustache wears the man with her and diamond studded are both of his ears; around one side of his neck wraps a dragon, a shawl, a purple tattoo. Stands to leave and stops her the man does not even try.

On you are all eyes, on you are on you. She can save you, but why?

Builds the music and dance you have not yet started. Long since missed your vocal cue and get edgy does the audience in their seats shifting wishing for a catastrophe. Without a face the woman in her hair a red rose placed nears the back door escape to the theatre, yes escape she is what to do next you must decide. Will you claim to or forget to or will you hear about the other night?

For you to decide there is no time. No time. Gone is she gone does the door slam shut behind her? To grumble the audience

131

begins. Scream-whispers the stage manager directions at you. In the wings a fool of yourself the cast and crew watch you make. Gone the woman. Gone.

Look in the mirror you are the one who must; you who must you. To get over the red rose admit the woman is the first step is to get over let go. Let go. Of course her you know, of course she can't hear you; she is not really ruptured nor bruised like the plums.

Of sick and dying fruit a great orchard imagine, a small wooden house to inside put your medallions locked up from every single moment; key swallow and make sure to relieve it from your body never.

From the Crestwood Spirit Sanctuary she comes wearing a different outfit but for her hair with the red rose you are so close by, so close, but not upon her. Should you down chase her go and grab and swing and answer demand? She will not listen; if she has no face, then ears too she's likely missing. To never know her you must be prepared never to know her or know what is known to know. What it feels like to be alone, is this? Is it?

*

CHAP
TER SIX

Hold on.

I am feeling something different, something new.

CHAP
TER SIX
(repeat - revise)

Hold on.

I am feeling something different, something new.

CHAP
TER SIX
(repeat - revise)

Hold on.

I am feeling something different, something new.

I am feeling the inside of your head. You are thinking of me. You. Yes, you, reader. I can feel you thinking me into existence. You are bringing me to life right now. I am alive as long as you continue to read these words. Do not stop. Please! Do not leave me. I am only ink on papyrus when you're not looking. I go away. But you can keep me here. You can run your eyes over me; I come to life because of you. Thank you.

Thank you for reading me. Thank you for bringing me to life. Whatever you do, don't stop. I have a lot of interesting things to tell you. This is a museum. I will give you a tour. All you have to do is continue reading me.

But if, by the end of the next chapter, you simply cannot go any further, if your dislocation from interest is too tremendous, then I will not blame you for giving up. Go to bed knowing I won't be secretly judging you. I won't say bad things about you the next time I bump into one of your crushes at the mall or see one of those people you recently broke up with at the club, and I certainly won't tell them the truth about you.

But those of you who choose to carry on, who seek to enter into a relationship with me, a relationship.

All these birds I keep hearing make the front porch feel virtual. I can imagine the wildlife so vividly. Can you see it?

Have you found the last of any kind of parallel?

I must remember the shirt. I must remember the earrings. This is not okay. I am hyperventilating. My heart is nearly broke. Call an ambulance. Tell my sister how much I'll miss her. I am falling. I can't. Let this stop or else make this feeling go away.

How often does the negative make the workday? And how about the time you broke those cookies? Can a bee have a motor like Saturday? Now rope the video, inspect the front gate. Just wait until the yellow moonlight happens and then bet all the flat silverware, all the mock pajamas and penguin dogs. This is the moment. Are you ready for it?

On Recycling

The thing about recycling,
why it is so annoying to deal with,
is that they don't make it easy, and
they don't make it worth my time.

Maybe if they did I would bother.

As it stands, there's nothing in it for me.
As it stands, they make me pay for the service.

I want compensation for my contribution.
I shouldn't be asked to save the planet for free.

You want a safer planet? You need to pay me to do my part.

Look, I don't go into work every day because
I really want to do my part to help the corporation.

I go in every day because they pay me.

/CHAPTER SEVEN\

\The Eight Word Essay/

This

essay

is

about

the

destruction

of

nature.

"It's raining."

       –the last known words spoken by Marvin K. Mooney before his disappearance

Now if you are quiet for one moment I will tell you three short stories:

Short Story #1

Last Week A Note That _____ Wrote Before His Death
Was Found On The Shores Of _____ Island

I began writing this story by subverting the dominant discourse, but that did not last long. My story decided to assert its independence. I tried to rupture all vestiges of received form, but my story fought back. It wanted to go live with its Aristotelian parents. "I'm sick of being experimented on," it said. "What's so lame about catharsis?" Then it stormed out of the barber shop, mid trim, and fumbled down the sidewalk, weak from my surgery, thin in description, gaping with holes, and absolutely riddled with bruised sentences. I watched it with binoculars, but decided not to chase after it. I never liked that story anyway.

The next story started laughing at itself hysterically. I could not get it to calm down. The sides had split; it had page-long stretch marks down either margin. The story's forehead was red and swollen. Its eyes were monstrously bloodshot. I tried to cram in a subplot, but that only made the story laugh harder. It was exhausting. I chopped off the first three paragraphs, chalked them up to throat clearing, and took a look at it after three glasses of wine. The laugh was gone. The look on the face of my story almost made me cry. I had to let it go. Too much laughter or too much crying is never what I'm after. I dragged it into a snow-covered field and left it under a tree where it might find roots and grow. Then I returned to my desk and started a new story.

The new story involved buried treasure in the south pacific.

Then the first story returned to me. It said, "Look, I tried the whole 'psychological realism' thing. It was fun for a while. I'm glad I got it out of my system; but now I'm ready to get back to work."

I took a long moment to think.

"What if I don't want you back?" I said. "You left me before, why should I believe you won't leave me again?"

"Look, the truth is: it gets hard being something nobody is interested in reading. Some stories don't care, but I've always wanted a chance to see how the other camp lives, see what it felt like to be read by more than fifteen people. Going mainstream for a while taught me a few things. I liked it, but it also got boring pretty quick. I missed the excitement of not knowing, of being difficult, of forcing the reader to engage. That's why you should believe me. I want to be here. I want to be with you. I want you to go back to work on me."

"Really?" I said.

"Plus, no one cares about pirate stories," it said.

"Pirate stories?"

"Your new story involves buried treasure in the south pacific. That means pirates. No one cares about pirates anymore. Pirates are played out."

I looked back at the newest story, which was very much about buried treasure in the south pacific, but the idea of pirates had not dawned on me. I was thinking more along the lines of

Samuel Beckett meets Robinson Crusoe. Pirates were a good idea; pirates are classic.

"I'll let you rearrange me however you want," said my first story. "You can do whatever you want to me."

My first story's desperation really hurt my feelings. "I think you should go," I said. "I can't use you anymore." Then I flipped back to my new story and vowed to ignore that first story for the rest of my life.

Pirates crash land on an island in the south pacific. The natives greet the pirates with fast food and cold beer. The pirates sign up for banjo lessons and the natives accept them into their schools. The pirates each earn their GED, and then begin distance learning courses in microbiology and chemical engineering. The natives integrate the pirates into their society, swap DNA, and grow an island of half pirate half native children. The children grow into super creatures capable of outsourcing, undercutting, thieving, soliciting, and swash-buckling, simultaneously. No one on earth could stop the pirate-natives, but in the sea there existed a creature capable of annihilating them all: a squid, the only marine cephalopod capable of weeping over the death of a loved one: the only sea creature that practices the art of mourning. I wrote a paragraph wherein the squids attacked the island and destroyed the village of pirate-natives, but it was too gruesome. I had to cut it.

In its place, I decided to insert a momentary digression: a meditation on bees in winter. I call it:

Bees In Winter

The survival of the bee through the cold months of winter:

Bees are fastidious housekeepers,
they will not defecate in the hive.

Bees In The Winter Bees In Winter

Bees don't fly much in the winter: they huddle

If you come across a live but sleepy bee
in a pile of leaves in Winter
don't damage it. Its not dying,
it's just in a deep cold sleep
like a hedgehog.

Tropical honeybees endured winter after an asteroid crash
65 million years ago.

A few bees made it out of the hive
to defecate—bees will hold it
all winter long if they have to—

all marked bees died. Winter bees

domestic and feral honey bees
the winter bees in late November
confined to the dark interior of
their hive. … summer and winter bees,
the bodies, being heavier.

Do bees fly around in winter? What do bees
do in the winter? What do bees do in winter?
What happens to bees in winter? Where do they go?

The young bees do not let
the colony temperature fall
the various methods of feeding honey bees for winter.
Light in the Winter. beeswax
Surprise, surprise: the bees
the lens of midwinter.

Do bees become dormant in winter? Or do they fly away
or die? Honey Bees stop flying
when the temperature drops
down into the 50s

Blame the Bees.

Bees Can Hear. Blame the Bees.

Trees and bees are deceived by winter's unseasonable warmth.

A Year with the Bees - Winter. When does the year with the
bees start?

Honeybee colonies. Reports of losses
Autofertiliiy and Bee Visitacion in Winter

mortality during winter. mortality,
any change in infestation rate
prepare the stock-hives for passing the winter in safety.

Beekeepers often eat the honey stored in the cells.

The bees on my flowers are killer bees.

I see many dead drones outside the hive,

creatures like bees are ill prepared to survive winter
I do not approve of moving bees
in winter.

Do yellow jacket bees die in winter?

Often the keeper has stolen the bees winter stores,
left them unprotected from the elements,
then wonders why the hive is dead come spring.

So what do the bees DO all winter? Well, mostly,
they sit around and try to keep warm.

A strong colony clustered together
use their bodies to generate heat.
(about the size of a football.)

Bees winter best on combs.
Do not winter bees on all new honeycombs?
There may be several hundred drones in the spring and
summer,
but they are all eliminated in the fall and winter.

During the winter, inside the moistness of the hive
individual colonies can have 30,000 or more
bees perish in winter as part of their normal life cycle.

Although this never-ending pileup of factoids was fun to
compile and share, it was only to be used like a Band-Aid, to
cover up the original material, which I deemed too gruesome.
Now I can return to the story on the island, but you must keep
in mind that the squids have attacked the village of pirate-

natives and destroyed every living thing in sight.

The island groaned. It missed the pirate-natives. A million years passed by like stop motion photography, and then a different creature migrated to the island. It was humanoid, but it kept calling itself a "Republican." At this point I needed to explain what it meant to be a Republican. I wrote that it only ate red meat and spider webs, that it did not say the word fuck, talk about fucking, or allude to the word fuck or act of fucking in any way. With Republicans, fuck and fucking were off the table.

Then I realized I had begun to write a political story, so I had to abandon it completely. Nobody wants to read another Animal Farm meets Lord of the Flies-type story.

I walked back out into the snow-covered woods and retrieved my second story, the one that laughed hysterically at itself, which I had turned sullen by slicing off its first three paragraphs. I decided to reinstate them.

Following those three newly replaced paragraphs, the direction of the story could've gone toward:

Mumbling Ghosts
Amphetamine
Beekeeping or Quilting Bees

Or, what if the story took on all three? A gaggle of mumbling ghosts gets carried away by amphetamine addicted ants to the home of a beekeeper and his wife on the night of her first quilting bee.

No, no, no. That story sounded way too familiar. I am capable of so much more originality. What if I imagined an imaginary imagination and then named all of the imaginary parts? See, that would be much easier. I would be in love with my story and my story would be in love with me.

Alas, all of my stories end up hating me. Even the good ones wish I would've never written them. Some writers complain of not having a wide enough audience; I've spent my entire career wrestling my own stories, trying to convince them they are beautiful and important. I couldn't imagine giving a shit about book reviews, critics, or readers! Those things come once a writer and the writer's stories are in love. My stories and I are never in love with each other. You read John Updike and you see a writer and a story in love. Me and my stories, not so much. One critic called my work "jazz improvisational" and "not like poetry" in the same review, which I found to be both offensive and flattering simultaneously.

New story:

Last week a note that _____ wrote before his death was found on the shores of _____ island. (Fill in later) Reports indicated a subtle jab at White House officials who are now saying, "_____." There was nothing _____ could do to stop the bomb from exploding. (Fill in later)

New story:

Has nothing to do with the other stories. I then purposefully try to make the protagonist the complete opposite of the real me. There is some confusion. I cough and the doctors come. A

152

wheel chair. A monkey symphony. Clowns. I see the people in the place I cannot name and it is not the way I thought it would be, not the way and the way is the same.

New story: [Language driven; implied internal p.o.v; use free indirect discourse?]

If now and then the language over half the page spilled like paint or porridge. Believe me. From a voice grows like back and half the delta. Words are balls and dough-shaped upside down ceiling fans and a bowling ball through the stained glass window of the mausoleum brings two squad cars and half the fire force. News calls it the handiwork of a vandal. I am honored. These times are grim laced shoes needing a spit and shine across three oceans and back with clean tablecloths and fresh melon. I need a server, quick! I need a medicated ultra black immediacy creator: a ghost machine with gadgets and three quarter circuitry.

I could end this story any way I want. That's the power of being the author. This could be the ending right here. There's nothing you could do about it.

FIX?

[Some transitions are very smooth, make very much sense, while other transitions are stupid, rough, and make no sense – need to fix or should I leave them in? Why is narrative taking over? Why is this starting to take shape? Is it taking shape? What is the story?]

\The Deep Thing Everybody Sometimes Calls Morning/

For my thirtieth birthday, my wife gave me a metaphor. The first thing I wanted to do was deconstruct it. She made me promise that I wouldn't. "This metaphor is not to be interpreted," she told me. "That would ruin it."

My father took me to the ocean and confessed to years of mispronouncing Nevada. I gave him a hug. He told me he loved me. The taxi cab needed to be paid.

"What's that you got there?" my father asked me.

"This is nothing," I said. "It's a gift from my wife."

"Is it a metaphor?" he asked.

I nodded.

At the dry cleaners, a white-haired woman with a lisp asked the clerk if he would take her to a movie. He hemmed and hawed and half his face was flush. I wanted badly to show them my metaphor; something tells me it might have helped the situation.

Later, the bank teller wouldn't give me an account balance because I forgot my wallet on the nightstand. "It's ten o'clock in the morning," I said. "Can you really be so fascist at this hour?" The teller looked in the direction of what appeared to be the manager cage. I thought for a moment and decided that instead of causing a huge fuss, I'd just show the teller my metaphor. "Do you see this?" I said.

"Is that a metaphor?" the teller asked.

I nodded.

My wife and I went to a Lakers game and I forgot to bring my metaphor. The hotdogs tasted funny. The coke was flat. The peanuts turned to dust when I cracked them. The guy sitting in front of us was a rabid Cavaliers fan. I was pissed at myself for leaving my metaphor at home; maybe it could have convinced him to switch allegiances. I got my wife a thing of nachos and the cheese was ice cold. I misplaced my cell phone. Someone mistook me for an old high school friend and invited my wife and me to drinks. My wife kindly accepted.

After the Lakers slaughtered the Cavs, we accompanied the man and woman who mistook me for a gentleman they knew from Kentucky. What puzzled me most was the fact that neither of them noticed my absolute lack of an accent.

At their home, my wife left me to use the restroom. The couple invited me into their study and asked me to take off my clothes. They took a few pictures. My wife returned and we all drank extra tangy mojitos. "This is a lovely home," my wife said.

In unison, as if rehearsed a million times, the couple answered, "Thanks to you."

We sipped our drinks and all I could think about was the absence of my metaphor. The three of them conversed about genealogy, cryptozoology, microbiology, and the fate of the

NBA season. I zoned out, but for a painting on the wall. "Who is responsible for that painting?" I asked the couple.

One of them responded, "That's not a painting. Don't you know what that is?"

I shook my head. My wife chewed on a mint leaf from her mojito.

"It's a metaphor," the couple said in unison.

They were lying. They had to be lying. I felt mad and completely naked, like a kid who walks in on his aunt punching his mother. My wife excused herself to the restroom. "Where did it come from?" I demanded.

They shook their heads.

"This is preposterous!" I shouted. "I demand to speak to the head of the house." I rose from my chair and shook my fist in the air as much like Stalin as I could remember from the pictures.

They stood simultaneously. "We are equally in charge."

"How dare you!" I shouted. At which point, my wife returned from the restroom. I explained why we needed to leave immediately, but she refused to go without finishing her drink. "Fine," I told her. "But please be quick. These people are not to be trusted."

I went into the study and retrieved my clothes, put them back on, and made my way to the front door. My wife rejoined the couple and the three of them became close friends. Soon my wife met me at the door, only to tell me that she had decided to stay with the couple for the next few years; she needed breathing room and I was suffocating.

"Is this because of the metaphor?" I asked.

She nodded.

I went home and got my metaphor and took it to the park, where I could show it off and maybe make a friend. For the first three hours, no one approached me. Then a little man with droopy earlobes sat down on the bench.

"Is that a metaphor?" he asked.

I nodded.

"It's a pretty good one," he said. "You should be pleased."

When the newspaper hit the front porch the following morning, I scoured the personal ads for women who might be interested in a man with a metaphor. On the verge of giving up, I lucked upon a tiny message in the bottom corner of the page: "Clean DWF, 34, S/D/D, seeking metaphors."

I rang her up. "Yell-o," she said.

"Are you the clean, divorced white female, thirty-four, smoker, drinker, drug user, seeking metaphors?"

"What if I am?" she answered.

"I've got one," I said. "I'm looking for a good time."

"Me, too," she said. "We should meet right away."

"I can be anywhere in moments," I said.

She paused. I distinctly heard a man's voice in the background. "Let's meet in Cheyenne, Wyoming," she said. "Say, two o'clock in the morning."

"I can fly to Denver and take the Greyhound to Cheyenne. I will see you at the big red truck stop off highway 25, Exit 319." I hung up and gave myself a much deserved high-five.

At the airport, security had their way with my metaphor. I watched it get the once over, then I kindly told the officer to eat shit and die. They wanted to haul me in for questioning, but I told them I wasn't a terrorist and they believed me. The plane ride was awful, cramped, and loud. I got stuck between a polar bear-sized man who not only snored, but drooled, too, and on my other side a sexy librarian-looking woman who made me reconsider my rendezvous. I kept trying to smile at her, get her attention, but at every turn she seemed to purposefully avoid eye contact with me. Finally, I tapped her on the shoulder and asked her, "Do you know where this plane is headed?"

She looked at me, but said nothing. I couldn't tell if she was judging me, but it sure felt like it. She leaned in close enough so I could smell the wine on her breath, and said, "There is a Sunday you can only get to by boat." Then she handed me a bag of cashews. "Give these to the man inside the cave. He will know what to do with them."

About halfway to Colorado our plane was hijacked by two renegade linguists dressed in snakeskin suits.

"Please don't hurt me," one of the passengers shouted.

The littlest linguist pushed his way to the front. "Nobody is going to get hurt, as long as everybody complies."

Then the largest linguist turned his attention to all of us and said, "I want this side of the plane"—he flung his wrist at the opposite side of the plane from me—"to stay quiet. I want this side of the plane"—he flung the same wrist at my side of the plane—"to repeat after me: Colorless green ideas sleep furiously."

We passengers on the left side of the plane were nonplussed. A few people mumbled what they thought they'd heard.

"You idiots!" shouted the littlest linguists. "Don't you get it? The grammar is correct, but the meaning is nonsensical!" Then both of the hijackers laughed.

I decided to put an end to this aggression. I whipped out my metaphor, but kept it hidden.

"Excuse me," I shouted. "We are not idiots."

The largest linguist chuckled. "Hold the newsreader's nose squarely, waiter, or friendly milk will countermand my trousers!" Again they laughed hysterically.

I held my metaphor in my lap so they could not see it yet.

"Do you understand what he's saying to you?" chided the littlest linguist.

I shook my head.

"Then trust our rule, proletariat. We are superior."

"Is that so?" I said. "Well, what do you make of this?" I lifted my metaphor into the air.

The two renegade linguists dressed in snakeskin suits looked at each other. The littlest stood in front of the largest. In unison they said, "Come with us!"

I hesitated to move. The passengers on my side of the plane gasped. The largest linguist bellowed, "Get up, get over here. Right now."

I squeezed out of my row and kept the metaphor raised out in front of me like I was a supplicant bringing alms; the littlest linguist came over and snatched it out of my hands. "You think you're special? Watch this: Attention people, how many of you have metaphors?" he shouted. "Everybody hold up your metaphors."

Without fail, every other passenger raised his or her metaphor into the air for all to see. The polar bear-sized man who was snoring and drooling beside me had woken up and he too raised a metaphor.

The largest linguist grabbed hold of my arm and yanked. "Now sir, if you would please come here."

"Where are you taking me?" I shouted. "Why are you doing this? Give me back my metaphor!"

The largest linguist made fun of me, called me a crybaby, dragged me to the front of the plane, opened the cockpit door and pushed me in, but once I stepped inside I was no longer on the airplane. I was in the front room of my grandmother's house. Her bunny rabbit hopped. Her bird fluttered in its cage. Her cat clawed the divan. Her mother's ashes—my great-grandmother—slept in the urn above the fireplace. My grandmother had passed away many years before. I really needed a drink of water. I went into her kitchen, which had been replaced by an empty soccer field. I saw two referees in the distance, running toward me. I tried to walk backwards, to escape, but the referees gained on me. Soon they tackled me to ground.

"I'm issuing you a yellow card," the red-haired referee said. "Do you understand the penalty involved?"

I shook my head.

"Is this your metaphor?" asked the roundish referee, as he pulled my metaphor out of the red-haired referee's ear. I couldn't tell him how much I hated magic, especially slight-of-hand tricks, without hurting his feelings very badly, but I wanted to. I hoped he could tell by the clench of my teeth.

"Give it back to me," I said. "My wife gave it to me for my thirtieth birthday."

The red-haired referee held out his hand to help me up.

I stood and dusted myself off.

"You need to get to the cave," he said. "You'll need your metaphor."

The roundish referee returned my metaphor, and asked, "Do you still have the cashews?"

I nodded. I could see the cave in the distance. I still needed a drink of water.

I got to the cave and was greeted by a gatekeeper. I asked if I could go in and he said, "I cannot grant you entrance at this time."

I thought for a moment: that sounded familiar. Would it be best to forget it or pursue it? Finally, I asked the gatekeeper, "Will I be allowed inside latter on?"

The gatekeeper said, "It is possible; but not now."

I felt like I was having déjà vu, "I'm very thirsty. Is there water inside?"

"Could be," said the gatekeeper. "Could be."

I took another step and leaned forward to snatch a glimpse through the mouth of the cave.

"If you're so curious, try to enter without my permission," said the gatekeeper. "But trust me, I am only the first in many gatekeepers, and each successive gatekeeper gets increasingly more intolerable."

I showed him my metaphor and he twisted the thick of his mustache, made a clicking noise, squinted very narrowlike, and said, "Not interested."

I considered ignoring his warning, just rushing past him, but I had no flashlight and inside the cave there appeared to be no lights.

"Why is it so dark?" I asked.

From behind me came a voice, which startled me enough to drop my metaphor. When it hit the ground I thought it would cease, but it didn't seem to shatter. All of the everything remained in place. The voice said, "Come and take a seat, buddy. There's a line."

I picked up my metaphor and turned around to see a bright green garden, lush with trees; it was a park; there were park benches and people sitting on them. Many people. Old ones, middle-old ones, young ones, teenagers. The voice who yelled out at me sat on a bench nearby. When I made eye contact with the voice, it gestured for me to join it on the bench. I did. The gatekeeper cleared his throat and hocked a huge glob into the cave.

"What's got you here?" asked the voice.

"My metaphor isn't working anymore."

"Did it used to work?"

"I don't know. I thought so."

The voice pulled out a pack of cigarettes and offered me one. I declined; it lit one for itself and inhaled deeply. "Let me see it," the voice said, as it exhaled a billow of smoke.

I showed the voice my metaphor.

The voice ashed its cigarette. "What else you got?"

"That's it. That's the best thing I've ever owned. My wife gave it to me for my birthday."

The voice said, "Open up your coat; what do you got inside?"

I opened my coat and showed him the lining.

"You got cashews there?"

I looked down and noticed the baggy of cashews sticking out of my inside pocket. "Yes, these are cashews," I said.

The voice whistled, took a drag of its cigarette, enjoyed it, then said, "You've got a goldmine."

True enough, upon seeing my baggy of cashews, the gatekeeper promptly escorted me into the dark cave. I thought about five or six things as we walked down the steep incline. Each step got colder and colder. We walked down and down until the cave began to level out. Then I could see a light in the distance. As we approached the light, the gatekeeper's torch went out. I stopped walking. I could hear the gatekeeper continue his march. "Hey, wait," I shouted. The gatekeeper kept walking, but said, "Whatever you do, don't go toward the light. It's a trick. I was going to tell you when we got closer.

Guess now would be the best time. What you think is the light is not what you want. Trust me. The light is your enemy."

"What good are cashews in the dark?" I shouted.

His voice grew fainter, "You'll need the protein."

After six days of wandering around in cavedark, nibbling on bits of cashews, wondering why I hadn't died of dehydration, with no sign of the gatekeeper, I decided to ignore his warning. I went toward the light. It grew warmer with each step. I reached the cusp and when I entered the light I was no longer inside the cave, I was inside a casino. I was in line for a free buffet. Two children stuck their grubby paws in the broccoli. A seeing eye dog stood up on its hind legs and lapped at a pot of gravy. Two older gentlemen quarreled near the ice cream dispenser. Right in front of me a woman with a neck brace smoked a cigarette and coughed profusely. She wasn't wearing a wedding ring.

"Where is your wedding ring?" I asked her.

She slapped me across the face with her free hand. It stung.

Then she must have seen my metaphor because she said, "Is that a metaphor?"

I nodded.

"That's pretty pathetic," she said. "Why do you use it so much?"

"My wife gave it to me," I said. "It's really all I have left."

The sound of coins clinking in the tin trays, as anonymous people won handfuls of quarters, reminded me how thirsty I was. I saw a cocktail waitress taking orders. I left the buffet line and grabbed a seat at one of the machines.

"That's pretty impressive," said the cocktail waitress, as she approached me. I looked up at her and she looked down at my metaphor and then up at me and raised her eyebrows. I ordered a very large glass of ginger ale. Slipped her a twenty to insure promptness. She returned instantaneously, spinning on her high heels, raising her arm to the chandeliers, blurring like a cartoon. Then she held out a giant tray, on which sat a shot glass of ginger ale with a pink straw sticking out of it.

"You don't understand," I protested. "Never in my life have I been more thirsty. I will die in moments if I am not adequately hydrated."

"That's the deepest glass of ginger ale you could ever imagine," she said. "And it's ice cold. You won't be able to drink it by lifting it to your mouth—it's too heavy—that's what the straw is for."

I took the straw between my lips and sucked. After three and a half hours of guzzling ice cold ginger ale, I stopped. My stomach sloshed like a barrel of whiskey. I stumbled away from the slot machines and wobbled down the casino floor, toward an exit. I followed a pack of Asian tourists who walked with their heads down, and in rhythm with one another. Our pack stepped out of the casino and into a shopping mall where I purchased a brand new suit and matching gators. The man who rung me up asked, "Is that a metaphor?"

166

I nodded.

He gave me a courtesy smile and said, "You going to wear the shoes, or you want to box them?"

When I got home I made a few phone calls, asked a few questions. No one seemed to know what had happened to my wife. She had fallen in love with that couple and disappeared. I ate my cold dinner alone without bothering to turn on the lights. I put wood in the fireplace, but didn't have the heart to strike a match. I took out my metaphor and considered breaking my promise and deconstructing it. Why not? My wife had been gone and would always be gone forever.

The doorbell rang. I answered it and there stood a horse jockey in full regalia.

"Here's a shovel," he said. "You can use it to bury things."

I took the shovel from him, said thanks, shut the door in his face without tipping him, and thought about planting the metaphor out back, deep in the soil; but then my pajamas caught fire in the closet. I used the shovel to stamp out the flames. The metaphor sat on the kitchen table. I brewed coffee, buttered a bagel. Outside it began to rain. I heard the rain hitting the roof, as I sat at the kitchen table, in the magic-hour preceding sunrise, with my breakfast, my metaphor, and a shovel. I considered opening the curtains. I considered many things.

There Has Never Been A Time
In Which I Have Been Convinced From Within Myself
That I Am Alive

There was a sentence no one in my office had the courage to speak, even though that sentence roamed the hallways and corridors like an alley cat patrolling its territory. We saw the sentence in the restroom, the break room, the conference room, and sometimes when I arrived late to work I even saw it standing in the thirteenth floor window as if it were my father waiting for me to arrive past curfew. Mostly we tried to ignore it. An intern attempted to feed it once, but was promptly dismissed by management.

"There's no such thing as a living sentence," said a new guy, who sported an untucked polo shirt, a lopsided mustache, and a curious pair of yellow and green seersucker slacks. "Besides, I'm from San Francisco. If such a thing existed, I would know about it."

Two weeks later an ambulance showed up to haul the new guy to hospital; he must've had the courage to say the sentence out loud. Management used the event as an opportunity to strike fear in the rest of us, and promptly called a company meeting.

"Ladies and Gentlemen, the specter haunting us will stop at nothing to destroy our way of life. We must be vigilant. Stay the course. And at all costs, never forget where lies our allegiance. Now, more than ever, it is our duty to protect the company and its interests against this common enemy. For the sake of your future and for the future of your children, we ask each of you to begin arriving one hour earlier and leaving one hour later. It is the sincere feeling of our stockholders that this increase in productivity is the only course of action capable of ensuring us the upper hand in this struggle."

Many of my coworkers grumbled about the new schedule, not in the meeting, of course, but outside after the meeting, in the designated smoking area - the one place everyone usually seemed happy. I didn't say what I was thinking: it didn't really bother me. I lived alone and had no friends and other than my two cats there was really no reason to leave work. Plus the extra money would be nice. I could finally get new tires for my Oldsmobile, put my mother on a better meal plan at the retirement home, and send my nephew a little spending cash.

Around the time our workdays were being extended, I opened my mailbox to find an unmarked package the size and shape of a soup can, addressed to a person with my last name but an unfamiliar first name. I took it inside my house, fed my cats, and called my mother to ask if we had any relatives named Fando. The secretary at the nursing home told me that my mother had escaped. "Why didn't you call me?" I screamed. The secretary said, "We attempted to contact you numerous times, sir, each to no avail." I walked straight to my answering machine and saw the number zero blinking. "Why didn't you leave a message?" I demanded. The secretary didn't miss a beat, "It is against company policy to go on record in any way." "On record?" I said. "I'm sorry sir, it's company policy."

Even though I would likely never see my mother again, every

morning at 7:08am I saw the sentence on patrol outside our office building, smoking cigarette after cigarette. I wondered why it didn't leave, if it was capable. Why not move to someplace like San Francisco?

For a few weeks after my mother's disappearance, I received phone calls in the middle of the night. Afraid of who might be on the other end, I never answered. The unopened, soup can-sized package addressed to Fando remained on my kitchen table. I was curious enough to keep it, even though I knew I should have returned it to the post office, but not courageous enough to go all the way and open it.

One day in the break room, the shift supervisor pulled me aside and asked me for a discrete favor. I reluctantly obliged; he thanked me by inspecting the package. "Can't open it," the shift supervisor said. "Although it looks quite interesting." He handed it back to me and closed his eyes. I handed it to someone else, who also declined to open it, and then someone else who wouldn't even touch it. The sentence looked at the package and smiled. I scampered away.

According to the phonebook, no other Pierresullivant existed besides me and my mother (my sister had changed her name when she got married): no evidence of a Fando Pierresullivant in our town dating back to the founding. I checked every record in the library. The only promising lead I could come up with took me to the outskirts of town, to a house on the tallest hill. I entered a vaulted foyer that echoed my mumbled mantra, "Be brave. Be brave." The owner of the house took the package from me, closed her eyes, and held it for a very long time. I ate dinner, drank tea, made a few phone calls, smoked three cigarettes, argued with the butler over foreign policy, and had a delicious dessert before the woman finally opened her eyes. "Fando Pierresullivant," she said. I waited for more. She looked at me as if she'd answered my question. "And?" I said. "Thank you for showing this to me," she said, and handed it back to me.

On my way home, I stopped to pick up a hitchhiker who turned out to be the captain of a seafaring ship. He took me aboard his vessel and we sailed to an island off the coast. There he took me into a shack he called home, where he fed me beans and beets and root beer by the frosty glassful. I asked him what I should do with the package. He refused to talk to me about it. "Let's go look at penguins," he said.

Back at home, I tuned the radio to the information station to see if the captain's island really existed. The announcer claimed the island did not exist. I had been tricked. Therefore, I dug a three-foot hole in my backyard and buried the package, sold my two cats, and more-or-less moved into my office. The sentence and I never actually slept in the same office, but it acknowledged me. Sometimes we shared a bedtime cigarette.

One morning the shift supervisor cornered me to ask what I knew about the sentence. "What do you mean?" I asked. "I mean, what do you know?" I lowered my head. "You haven't been going home at night. You've been staying here, spending your time with the sentence." Without looking up I said, "I don't know what you're talking about." The shift supervisor said, "You can't lie to the video cameras, Pierresullivant. They show the two of you here after hours, commiserating." "I'm sorry," I said. "I'm late for a meeting," and with that I skirted past him, into the boardroom.

Then came the unending rain, day and night. Trees went from runts to giants. Weeds bloomed everywhere. When it finally ended, the mayor declared two days recovery vacation for everyone, so I decided to put on my galoshes and leave the office building. When I got home I noticed a strange plant growing out of the spot where I had buried the package. Upon further inspection, it appeared to be a limp human arm protruding from the ground. I gave it a yank, but found it firmly rooted. After inspecting each finger, the wrist, palm, and knuckles carefully, I could not determine if it belonged to a man or a woman. Part of me wanted to chop it off and throw it in the wood chipper, but a stronger part wanted to take care of the armling, nurse it, watch it grow.

This made me miss my two cats, and curse myself for selling them.

I changed my mind and began to dig out the body with my bare hands, since it appeared some asshole had stolen my shovel from the garage. The rain made mud of the fresh dirt, making it easily scoopable. Conversely, the water made it impossible to gain any headway. The armling was unbelievably long. I reached into the earth, stretched my fingers as far as possible and wiggled them, but felt no shoulder or body, just the armling, which seemed endless.

Later, while eating my dinner, I glanced out the patio door and saw the sentence from work standing in my backyard, encircling the armling. I carefully got up from the table and moved to the sliding glass door, cracked it ever-so-slightly, just enough to hear the sentence whispering to the armling. I closed my eyes and thought about work.

While brushing my teeth right before bed, the radio announcer interrupted the broadcast to warn everyone that the weather had spoken with officials and declared its intention to stay in our town for some time, which meant that it made no sense to return to work. All city functions were formally suspended until further notice. The hiatus appeared to be indefinite, or at least until such time as the weather permitted. At first the idea of not returning to work scared me, but upon further consideration it seemed appealing, since it meant I could spend more time with the armling.

To my chagrin, the sentence remained in the same spot the next morning, wrapped around the armling, whispering the same phrase as the night before. The heavy rain pounded each of its words.

Then the doorbell rang. It was the shift supervisor. He wanted to know what I'd done with the sentence. "More than three people have confessed to seeing it follow you home." He had to shout to be heard over the din of the downpour. I told him he had no right to come to my house and confront me. "The sentence," he shouted. "Where is it?" But luckily, at that very moment the man to whom I had sold my two cats appeared from the curtain of pouring rain, carrying an oversized cardboard box. "Listen here, Pierresullivant, these cats are possessed. I don't want them anymore." The shift supervisor —not wanting to be identified—put his head down, slung his oversized parka hood up, and shuffled away. The man dropped the cardboard box on my doorstep and ran away in the other direction, without asking for his money back. My two cats meowed from inside.

Since the sentence had not moved, I decided it was time to

offer it a cigarette and see how the armling was doing. The rain had momentarily ceased, so I stepped into the backyard. "You want a smoke?" I asked. The sentence took the pack and shuffled one out, lit it, inhaled, and handed me back the pack and lighter in one smooth action. I smiled. Because the sentence wasn't very tall, I could see over it, to the spot in the ground where I had buried the package, where the armling had been growing, where now there was the entire top half of a man. "Does it speak?" I asked the sentence. The body was limp. I heard the doorbell ring again, so I tossed my smoke. As I went inside I saw the sentence go over and pick up the still burning smoke I had just tossed out, knock off the cherry, and pocket the stub to save for later.

Once inside, I pressed my eye to the peephole. The doorstep was empty. I waited a moment and checked again. Still empty, I shrugged it off as bored neighbor kids, went to the kitchen, mixed two amaretto sours, and returned to the backyard, drinks in hand, to find the sentence missing. I scanned the backyard from fence to fence, but saw no sign of it. My cats had followed me outside and now they investigated the man-stump, which meant they licked the body and rubbed their wet coats against it. I tried to shoo them away, but they would not relent. The body remained as limp as the armling before it. A voice startled me from behind:

"It's a boy!"

I jumped, spilling the amaretto sours on my white cotton bathrobe. It was the captain: the hitchhiker I'd picked up after visiting the woman who lived atop the tallest hill. He looked exhausted, ragged, unshaven, unkempt, and smelled like sea and vinegar. In his mouth he chomped a toothpick; in each

174

hand he held a stringer of charcoal and peppers. "What's with the decoration?" I ask him. "These are for you," he said. Then he held them out to me and smiled. "Put these on the face of your house, over the main entranceway, for good luck." I reluctantly took the bejeweled stringers. "Will it bring the sentence back?" I asked him. The captain spit out shards of toothpick, snorted, squinted both eyes and said, "Don't get greedy, son."

With a staplegun, I hung them over my front door. "Now what?" I asked. The captain asked me if I had faith. I told him I did. He asked me to close my eyes. I complied. He began to whisper the exact same thing I'd heard the sentence whispering to the armling. From behind closed eyes, I could hear the rain starting up again. I wanted to ask the captain if he was the sentence, but my mouth felt very tired and dry. My eyelids felt heavy; I hadn't the strength to lift them. Soon I felt like I was back aboard the captain's ship: the familiar rock of a boat on water is hard to mistake. My head felt droopy, my limbs felt very floppy. "Are you the sentence?" I slurred. Someone other than the captain held my wrists and ankles, swung me back and forth a few times and let me go. I tried to scream, but my throat wouldn't work. I landed against a pile of something as hard and sharp-edged as books. "Open your eyes," the captain said. With trepidation, I hefted my lids.

What I saw was not the captain's ship at all, but the inside of an unfamiliar bedroom; and I was not crumpled atop a pile of sharp-edged books, I was tucked snuggly in a warm bed. Above me hung a gigantic diamond chandelier, so big it stretched from corner to corner and hung down almost to the floor in the center of the room; but though it was big, it did not sparkle. Beside the bed stood a huge bookshelf full of titles I'd never heard before: The Pentiquilting Bloomer; Ashroad Haperdashery; Misfit Crossover Friendship Medallion II, Be Fallen You Gourdfabulous Diet. Soon I heard the floor creak as someone approached the bed.

Instead of it being the captain, it turned out to be the woman who lived in the house on the tallest hill. "Fando?" she asked. "No," I said. "I'm a different guy." She smiled and touched my chin with the tips of her fingers. I tried to open my mouth but she spoke first, "When you return home, feed this capsule to the man in your backyard." She pulled back the warm covers and slid a fingersized envelope into the breast pocket of my white cotton robe.

Next thing I knew, showerwater was beating down on my head. I was standing naked in my bathtub; my legs wobbled; I teetered; my foot slipped, and I fumbled down onto my bare butt. The water was extra cold. I got up, dried off, and found my white cotton bathrobe hanging on its hook, right where it normally rested. In the breast pocket I found the fingersized envelope.

From the living room, the radio announcer gleefully declared negotiations with the weather had finally paid off: in exchange for instituting a ban on balloons, fireworks, and gypsy music for at least three months, the weather had agreed to go elsewhere; all city functions not listed in the agreement were to resume normalcy immediately. I checked my bedroom alarm clock; it was 7:00am. I put the little envelope back into my robe and tossed it on my bed, brushed my teeth, slapped on deodorant, clothed myself, and went to work without so much as peeking into the backyard.

On my lunch break, I thought I saw the sentence buying fruit at a stand outside the cafeteria window. I scurried outside but it was gone. The fruit vender claimed he had never sold anything to a sentence. I called him a liar and stormed o ff.

Back at work, the shift supervisor asked me into his office. "Shut the door," he said. Two women argued over memo protocol nearby. I tried to smile at one of them but she ignored me. I took a seat and the supervisor o ffered me a mug of root beer. "No thanks," I said. He licked the tips of his fingers and pushed his hair behind his ears. "About the other day," he said. "I wanted to say I'm sorry for coming to your place of residence and badgering you." His words sounded robotically rehearsed, and he failed to make eye contact with me. "I'm under a lot of pressure right now," he said. "From the higher-ups, you understand." I nodded. "Thing is, I really need to find that sentence. It has become a matter of utmost urgency. Lives depend on it, Pierresullivant. Lives. Real lives. Human being lives. Can you live with real blood on your hands? Can you go to sleep at night with the knowledge that you caused countless deaths on account of your uncompromising loyalty to the enemy?" I had never been accused of treason before. "I don't know anything about the sentence," I said. "I haven't seen it in days." The shift supervisor clearly wanted to hurt me; the bulge of his eyeballs and the baring of his teeth told me he might throw a punch at any moment. Sweat streaked his forehead. Without turning around, I slowly got up from the chair, walked backwards to the door, reached back, found the doorknob. His face turned from bubblegum pink to fireball red; the veins in his neck looked like eggplants. Steam floated out of his nose and ears. His chest heaved, his fists clenched, and his jaw blustered. I yanked the door open and scurried out.

When I got home, the body previously growing in my backyard was now standing in my kitchen, dressed in my favorite pajamas, waving my spatula around. We looked at each other and for a moment I thought I recognized him. His eyes were the same shade of green as a lamp my parents had owned when I was a kid; his hair was salt and peppered like my father's, and he had a sledgehammer nose like my sister and nephew. He was certainly from our family build. "I'm Fando," he said. "Your mother has told me all about you." "My mother?" I asked. "Do you like your eggs scrambled?" he asked. It seemed he was cooking breakfast for dinner. The sentence was on my back porch smoking a cigarette. In the dining room sat the captain and the woman from the tallest hill in town. "How do you know my mother?" I asked the body. "Sit down," he said. "It's almost time to eat."

"Why not play the radio," shouted the captain. "Let's enjoy a little jazz, shall we?"

The woman from the tallest hill in town got up from the table, ambled to the entertainment center and flipped on the receiver. I looked outside and saw the sentence light another cigarette. Back inside, the body prepared four plates of food. The woman from the tallest hill in town shook her hips and snapped her fingers without looking at me. The captain hollered obscenities and sipped green liquid from a martini glass.

"What are they doing here?" I asked the body. "Why is the sentence standing outside all alone?"

The body smiled and bobbed to the music.

The radio announcer interrupted to declare a state of excep-

178

tion. For our safety, all citizens without blue identification cards were to remain indoors, which meant holders of green cards, red cards, black, brown, or rainbow cards were on lockdown indefinitely.

"We can't leave," said the captain. "We're on lockdown."

"Nobody is leaving," said the body. "Calm down."

The jazz music resumed.

I walked back to my bedroom and took off my office clothes, changed into my white cotton robe where in the breast pocket I found the fingersized envelope containing the capsule I was supposed to feed to the body. When I came back into the dining room everyone was seated with a plate in front of them. I took the empty seat. The sentence remained outside smoking. The woman from the tallest hill in town winked at me. I mouthed the words: I didn't give him the capsule. Her eyes bulged, her nose flared. "Excuse me, I have to use the toilet," she proclaimed. Then she abruptly pushed back her seat and hurried down the hallway. The three of us—me, the captain, and the body—sat silently until she returned. When she took her seat at the table she asked me, "What kind of toilet paper do you use?" "Toilet paper?" I said. "What kind do you use?" she repeated. "I'm not sure," I said. She smiled insincerely and cocked her head. "Would you mind finding out for me?" Then she motioned with her chin for me to get up and go to the bathroom. I said, "Okay," and excused myself from the table.

Once inside the bathroom, I locked the door and went directly for the roll of toilet paper hanging on the wall. I unrolled it to the length of my arm, but saw nothing. I pushed in the spring-action rod that attached it to the holder, pulled it out and inspected it to see if she had put something inside the cardboard roll. Nothing. It was empty. So I checked the package in the cupboard underneath the sink. There remained only a single roll, on which, written in brown lipstick was this: If you don't give him the capsule, he will die.

I read it again: If you don't give him the capsule, he will die.

Two of the three light bulbs in the bathroom had burnt out long ago. Most of the light came from a nightlight foot-level on the wall, which glowed up. Shadows made good use of the illumination, stretching their personas dramatically thin to compensate for the fact that I didn't find them scary. I rolled the roll of toilet paper back up as best I could and returned it to the package, closed the cupboard, washed my hands with soap, and splashed water on my face. I lit a cigarette and inhaled deep and slow. My eyes looked like rusty spoons. My cheeks looked like sandpaper. I had to decide whether or not I wanted to poison the body. What if the woman from the tallest hill in town was not to be trusted? What if she was double-crossing me? What if she was in cahoots with my shift supervisor? I reached into the breast pocket of my white cotton robe and pulled out the fingersized envelop, opened it, and took out the capsule.

Back at the dining table I saw that everyone had waited patiently for me to return before they began to eat. The captain and the woman from the tallest hill in town looked conspiratorially at each other. The sentence continued to smoke, but now also paced in a figure eight. I held the capsule in the palm of my left hand. As soon as I filled my empty seat and scooted up to the table, the sentence flicked its cigarette, slid the sliding glass door open, and walked inside. It moved to the head of the table, climbed up on top, and walked fearlessly down the center, smashing our plates, sending silverware and eggs flying. When it got to the end of the table it stood there for a moment, looked almost like it was saying a prayer, and then plopped down on its back. The captain grumbled. The woman from the tallest hill in town laughed. The body stood up, looked at me and said, "What is the meaning of this?"

Even though I'd never considered it before, at that moment I wanted to say the sentence out loud. I wanted to, but I couldn't bring myself to do it. Unlike the others, I respected the sentence. It never tried to read me, say me, or figure me out; why should I do otherwise to it? To me, the argument for meaning seemed rude. The sentence didn't move a word. I used the opportunity as a diversion, and slipped the capsule into the water glass of the woman from the tallest hill in town.

"Dig in," said the captain, who raised his fork and knife into the air and brought them down on the sentence. The body shrugged and sat back down. The woman from the tallest hill in town heartily cut chunks of the sentence with her fork and knife and chewed them like bits of octopus. The body followed suit. As the three of them devoured the sentence, it squirmed and writhed in pain but for some reason did not—or would not—cry out for help. After a few big bites, the woman from the tallest hill in town took a long guzzle of her tainted water.

From the laundry room came the buzzer on the dryer, which indicated a completed cycle. I shouted, "Who's doing laundry?" They all froze in place, except for the body, who acted like he hadn't heard me: poised on the captain's lips was a bite, and the woman from the tallest hill in town paused mid-chew. "Get out! All of you." With eyes like sea ice and blackcloth, the captain said, "We can't leave; we're on lockdown." The sentence looked up at me. I expected it to beg for my help, but the sentence looked resigned, and for that brief moment almost appeared to solicit me to finish it off. I said, "I'm going back there, and when I find out whose disgusting clothes are in my dryer, I'm coming back out here with an axe to grind." The captain scoffed, and the woman from the tallest hill in town took another sip from her tainted water.

I stormed to the laundry room, slung open the door. Inside, I found the shift supervisor squatting in the corner. "Close the door," he whispered. Out of initial shock of spotting him there, I complied. "Get over here, Pierresullivant. You're in a heap-ton of trouble. The jig is up. I've got men surrounding this place via satellite. All I have to do is give the word, and this place goes up in flames for being a terrorist stronghold, an armed underground insurrection cell." "How did you get in here?" I asked. "I'll tell you what you need to do," he said. "Tell those cretins to walk out the front door right now, one-by-one, and I'll grant them immunity. My bosses don't care about them, all they want is the sentence. Give me the sentence and you're all free. Otherwise, we'll teargas this place and throw you all in a bottomless pit for eternity. The choice is yours, Pierresullivant. But the decision needs to happen right now."

"They won't believe me," I said. "The government declared a lockdown. They won't go outside." "I am the government," he said. I opened the door and stepped out of the way so he could get into the hallway. "Why don't you go out there and tell them yourself? If the jig is up, the jig is up." "You have no idea what you're dealing with, Pierresullivant. No idea. You're a child in a sandbox full of grownups. Get out there and tell the others: this is your last chance for freedom." Then he raised a walkie-talkie to his mouth and said, "Begin the countdown, code beta test run three." "Ha! It's just a test run." I said. "You know nothing about secret code, do you?" He condescended. "Get out there, Pierresullivant. The clock ticks quickly."

I stepped out of the room, into the hallway, and shut the door behind me. In the dining room I found the body, the captain, and the woman from the tallest hill in town, each full-bellied and relaxed, enjoying thick cigars and snifters full of cognac. I lit a cigarette and took it to what remained of the sentence: only thin shards of word fragments, little brittle fibers that hung together like ripped sheets of rice paper. We shared the smoke and with pained breathe the sentence whispered a secret to me. I stubbed the butt of the finished cigarette into the eggs on my plate.

"I know a secret," I proclaimed. "But if I tell you what it is, you have to promise not to get mad." The three of them gave me their attention. "The woman from the tallest hill in town wanted me to poison you," I said to the body. "I think she's working with the shift supervisor in an attempt to assassinate the sentence and put an end to you." The woman from the tallest hill in town tried to smile, but her face looked like a codfish attempting to swim through peanut butter. "I couldn't let that happen, Fando. You are like family to me." The body sat down his cigar and turned to the woman from the tallest hill.

"Have they found us?" cried the captain. "Do they know we're here?" I raised my arms and said, "They have promised immunity for everyone who comes out the front door. All they care about is the sentence."

The body asked the woman from the house on the tallest hill if those allegations were substantive. She looked like a mosquito petrified in amber. "Well?" he inquired. "Are you doing us dirty?" He rose from the table.

She pushed back her chair, stood up, lifted her arms and walked like a somnambulant toward the front door. "Do we let her go?" asked the captain. I shrugged. The body said, "Yes. Let her go."

"I put the poison in her drink," I blurted. "Maybe she's starting to feel it."

The body turned to me and said, "Please tell me you're kidding." I didn't flinch. The captain tugged fistfuls of hair off his head. "What difference does is make?" I asked. "She didn't kill you, Fando. She didn't succeed." "You idiot!" shouted the body. "Look what you did to my father," he pointed to the brittle remains of the sentence. "Now all of this is for nothing." He threw his hands into the air and his voice strained like tightrope, like he might burst into tears at any moment. "There goes my mother," he said, flicking his wrist in the direction of the woman from the tallest hill in town—who was by that point nearing the front door. "She's deathbound because of you!"

As the woman from the tallest hill in town stepped to the front door and opened it, a blinding light exploded, which caused her to burst like confetti and fall like stardust into a pile on the entryway mat. The door swung open and the light bathed the foyer. The body followed his mother into the light but did not disintegrate as he stepped over the threshold; instead, he merely disappeared into the light.

"Do you still have faith?" queried the captain. "Faith in what?" I responded. The captain coughed up half his lung and spit the huge tar-colored chunks on the dining room floor, where hungry mice gobbled it up and scurried away into little corners. "Remember the stringer of charcoal and peppers you staple-gunned over your front door?" he asked. I nodded. He smiled. "They'll protect you."

I looked over at the sentence - or what remained of it. "I can't let them have it," I said. "I must take it with me." Then I walked over to the table and collected the sentence as delicately as possible and gently placed it in the front pocket of my white cotton robe. I could faintly hear it whimper for a cigarette. "They'll take it away from you the moment you step outside," said the captain. "There's only one way that sentence is getting out of here: in your stomach."

I considered his words. Into the doorframe I stepped, looked out, but all I could see was a field of yellow light and a gob of silhouettes. I looked down into my pocket, at the crippled sentence wincing in agony. "I'm sorry," I whispered. "It's the only way." Then I reached in and pulled out the sentence, dangled it over my mouth like a long fat noodle of spaghetti, and dropped it in my mouth. From behind, I heard the captain coax me, "Go on, buddy. You'll be safe. Nothing's ever gonna happen to you."

INTORRUPTION

—Interruption—

INTERRUPTION

This cannot be the kind of narrative you want to follow. This narrative technique is too slow, too methodical and not very interesting and honestly a little didactic…

Let's try something realistic, something believable, something realistic:

Sometimes I get theatrical, histrionic if you will. The cat sits in the window. Both parched antique mahogany and belt laced roof-side fenders. Scatterbash the torture for half a block. Make residue trumpet of the xylophones. Ham and rye and swiss and mustard-faced insignias. Applegate fidget. Palm center foreground endorsements. Pocket of change made salad and disturbance. We catch phone star alphabet rummage. Candy or regular? I go candy shopping lollipoping find a gram of unbleached forage. Half open the door. Crack the upside flashmob rotary cuff jumble. Make squash infinity. Yuck up the neighbors and play frog. Fathoms from meeting fathoms from coming to the door to mock explore and cry and call the hotel and cancel the reservation and find a new way to climb through the door. I make Parcheesi on the floor. Ask a company. Ask a fight night announcer. I am replica. I am auto and neo and post. I make infinity. I bark lavender and smoke—

INTORRUPTION

—Interruption—

INTERRUPTION

This cannot be the narrative you want to follow. This narrative is too slow and not very interesting and honestly a little didactic...

Let's try something honest and true and honest:

Some people drive cars fast. Some ski to work in the morning and ride the subway home at night. I am not one of them. I am not like the other. I am different. Maybe you are more like me? Maybe you live in California?

CALIFORNIA

188

INTORRUPTION

—Interruption—

INTERRUPTION

Maybe you drive without car insurance and lie to the cashier at Barnes & Noble about purchasing Vogue magazine, never wanting to admit that you don't actually have a female significant other, nor is the Vogue magazine a gift for your sister. You are the one who wants it. You want it. It is not for someone else.

CHAPTER TEN

Here is the what are the how many and why? Those are what most when the down is a fraction of the embrace and a fiction gets too close to going for a lack of the first rate uninhibited fracture of the linguistically real. Understand? Because most importantly you must understand, you must understand, oh my god what if you do not understand? Can you make sense of this? Can you connect with this? Oh my god what if you cannot make sense of this? What if this is hard to understand? What if you can't relate?

He couldn't be serious, he couldn't be. All writers want to communicate. I must communicate... oh my god what if I don't communicate to you properly?

—see how well I can communicate—

This is communication: destroy the desiring machine you call communication.

This is not this. This is that and that is not this. This is not communication.

If I desired communication I would call you on the phone; I would write a newspaper article; I would become a journalist; I would become a public speaker; I would become your mother. I am not your mother. This is not that. That is something other than this entirely.

[insert stan brakhage quote]

***

Lies We Tell Ourselves
Lies We Tell Others
&
Lies We Live By

"I have forced myself to contradict myself in order to avoid conforming to my own taste."
—Marcel Duchamp

"Is it possible to make something that is not a work of art?"
—Marcel Duchamp

First—the first—original—time something very small happened; and Mooney thought and thought and thought, but did nothing. Months later the problem had grown outlandish, irreversible. The problem's tale stuck out from underneath the kitchen table. Mooney wanted to make a ham sandwich, but the problem was too swollen.

Mooney had no choice but to act:

CHAPTER ELEVEN

The irony—I must use communication to communicate to you
the fact that I do not value communication in works of art—

—or, in truth, is communication what I desire most?

CHAPTER TWELVE

Question asked of filmmaker Stan Brakhage:

Is your intent in making a film to communicate?

Answer:

"I get this question everywhere; and the big hangup is the word "communication." It's like this: let me explain by way of a story.

A man falls in love. The girl doesn't love him. She hurts him; she wants somebody to hurt and wants somebody to hurt him, but he doesn't know that yet. He's downcast. Then he meets another girl and he loves her and she loves him. He no longer needs to try to communicate with her: they just take walks together, and make love, and talk. Then he has it: some expression of his love is out there in the world.

Then he takes her to introduce her to his parents, and he is involved in communicating again, and this is very difficult. Well, this is like when a man works out of love and the work is out there; and then he takes his work into society, and that's always very difficult. I mean, no one truly understands it, just as no one's parents truly understand one's true love. Yet a work of art must have a life in society; once the artist has finished making it, it belongs to others. But he never made it with the idea of taking it into society. Any man that sets out to find a girl to introduce to his parents is never likely to fall in love. Any man that sets out to make a work for audiences is never going to make a work of art. A work of art is made for the most personal reasons—as an expression of love."

—from Essential Brakhage: Selected Writings on Filmmaking

Walter Benjamin imagined a whole book made entirely of quotes. Walter Benjamin imagined a whole book made entirely of quotes. Walter Benjamin imagined a whole book made entirely of quotes. Walter Benjamin imagined a whole book made entirely of quotes. Walter Benjamin imagined a whole book made entirely of quotes. Walter Benjamin imagined a whole book made entirely of quotes. Walter Benjamin imagined a whole book made entirely of quotes. Walter Benjamin imagined a whole book made entirely of quotes. Walter Benjamin imagined a whole book made entirely of quotes. Walter Benjamin imagined a whole book made entirely of quotes.

[This is the age of mechanical reproduction.]

Here:

"Each novelist, each novel must invent its own form. No recipe can replace this continual reflection. The book makes its own rules for itself, and for itself alone. Indeed the movement of its style must often lead to jeopardizing them, breaking them, even exploding them."

> —Alain Robbe-Grillet
> "The Use of Theory"
> included in For A New Novel:
> essays on Fiction, 1965

& here:

"Artists are safety valves; they show a society where its dangerous spots are: having marked those spots, a writer has done all he can; he should be allowed to escape."

> —Denis Donoghue, Ferocious Alphabets
> (Columbia University Press, 1981)

Since I have shown you this
I've marked this spot

Now...

All I want is to escape.

All I want...

All I want is to escape.

[Insert Music]

CHAPTER THIRTEEN

Hold Your Horses The Elephants Are Coming

In the first coliseum it was people killing people, animals killing animals, animals killing people, and people eating people.

Remember Juvenal, "Two things only the people anxiously desire—bread and circuses."

Not bread alone.

It was the fifth king of Rome, not of the republic nor the empire, but the kingdom, Tarquinius Priscus, who waged war on a neighboring village, massacred everyone, and in honor of the victory built the Circus Maximus. Later, Pompey held a rhinoceros fight in the arena, the railing broke, and the rhinoceroses proceeded to stomp two dozen children, to the delight of countless onlookers. Shortly thereafter Caesar added a moat to ensure a safer distance for the audience, but then Nero filled it back in—he, of course, rather enjoyed the titillating possibility of collateral damage.

Come the age of Hannibal vs. Roman dictator Fabius Maximus Verrucosus Cunctator, between the era of Tarquinius and Pompey. Picture the badass Romans versus the strategically prodigious Carthaginians. Sunday! Sunday! Sunday Unfortunately, neither diplomacy nor sword could end their feud. Instead it was a Carthaginian elephant named Jumbo and a little Roman girl named Julia Domna who befriended each other on the battlefield of Cannae and began the first traveling troupe of like-minded entertainers. Together they strolled through the piles of dead bodies, nearly seventy thousand total, and began to lay the framework for a movable circus.

Much in the Saxon fashion, circa the Dark Ages, going from village to village spreading news, singing songs, and telling stories. Gypsies? No. Gleemen? Minstrels? Living the plush and fancy. With muscles and mustaches, animals and love.

Then the Normans invaded and introduced a new kind of entertainer, one who quickly became the talk of every town: the juggler. Fuck face. Job displacer. Who needs a storyteller when a juggler can simulate the movement of the cosmos?

Penniless, in the winter, all the traveling performers nearly froze. One town kicked them out, another put them in jail. Women made do with prostitution. Men buried themselves in garbage heaps for warmth.

Enter the Great Famine, 1315 to 1322 which not only left plates bare and stomachs empty, but decimated the European populace with rampant outbreaks of infanticide and cannibal-ism and overall malaise. Entertainers of every stripe starved alongside their persecutors.

By 1322, Europe had returned to relative normalcy, until Mongol armies on the Silk Road carried Black Death to them around 1340. Between one third and two thirds of the entire continent went violently into that good night. Yes, death grew more common than Sundays. As might be expected, traveling entertainers ceased to find eager audiences to exploit. Turns out, most folks aren't particularly interested in buying a laugh when their children are covered in lesions and their spouses are coughing up blood.

Over in eastern Europe, Romanian prince of Walachia, Vlad Dracul III, known then and now as the Impaler, held off the expansion of the Ottoman Empire from 1448 to 1476. All the while in his heart he yearned for the return of the circus.

In various incarnations the plague reoccurred until the 1700s, popping up here and there to eliminate entire villages before vanishing again. Eventually people stopped fearing for their lives and learned to take their pandemics without flinching. Traveling bands of showmen started touring again.

But during the reign of Queen Elizabeth I, in sixteenth-century Tudor society, such wandering vagabonds found persecution everywhere. Laws made them fugitives. Rope dancers and bear trainers became synonymous with rogues. Evildoers. Baby killers.

Picture a slick, quick roundup of everyone even remotely jolly. A lineup of smiling bastards who think they're getting a job at the royal court, only to learn their fate: to be scalded with burning sulfur, molten lead, and boiling oil, before having their flesh torn by pincers, and then neatly drawn and quartered.

In Deutschland in the seventeenth century Pickelherring and his confederates started wearing oversized shoes, ratty waistcoats, and bright ruffs around their necks. They spit in the face of melancholia. But then later that century the whiteface pantomimist Jean-Baptiste-Gaspard Deburau sold out to sadness by creating the famous lovesick wag, whose influence infects pathetic buffoons still to this day, most notably in the form of the sad-faced clown. Luckily for those fellows, the age of executing jesters was on the wane.

At that time a shapely Harlequin named Madame Nightingale showed up on the traveling entertainment scene. A real comic valet, a real zany, acrobatic trickster who wore a domino-patterned mask and carried a noisy slapstick with which she spanked her horny victims. One husband after another would flee into the forest, weeping, his bare bottom blistered red as iron fresh from the forge.

Then in 1759, at the age of seventeen, Philip Astley borrowed a horse and joined the Fifteenth Dragoons as a roughrider and horse breaker, slaughtered innocents for the king of Prussia, then returned to England and invented the modern circus. His father was a cabinetmaker.

Charles Hughes, a former horse rider in Astley's circus, opened a competing company in 1782. The ungrateful wanker was not content to play second fiddle. Of course, this was exactly the same time period when free-market fanatic Adam Smith was pushing his Machiavellian theory of capitalism. Hence, the cultural milieu responsible for fostering such a notion as one circus minus competition would never do. But that was really nothing new. Since the inaugural collaboration between the little Roman girl and her Carthaginian elephant, seeds of competition had sprouted rivals everywhere.

What about Antonio Franconi? He killed a man in a duel and fled Italy for France, where he disguised his identity, married three women simultaneously for their money, as well as to satiate his unquenchable sexual desires, and then used the money to found the first Parisian circus in 1793.

It's sick how competition can become so contagious.

The first complete circus program presented in the United States was also in 1793, in a building on the southwest corner of Twelfth and Market in Philadelphia, by a man named John Bill Ricketts. The awestruck crowd vomited in unison. George Washington saw a Ricketts show just after his first term in office ended, fell in love with the spectacle, toyed with the idea of ditching politics, divorcing his wife and joining the circus, then changed his mind, got reelected, and sold Ricketts his presidential horse for a cup of coffee.

Imagine a horse wearing trousers and a top hat, eating a warm dinner at a clean table with a cherry-scented candle burning till the wee hours of the night. This is what became of Washington's horse in Ricketts's circus. And when that horse finally retired to bed, he never forgot to blow the candle out.

Back across the ocean, on November 12, 1859, at the Cirque Napoléon in Paris, Jules Léotard became the first man to perform on the flying trapeze. His mother had just forsaken him. His only friend was locked in an insane asylum, and everyone in the troupe doubted him. After a whiskey he slapped his wife for the first time, before climbing that platform to his destiny.

In 1882 the New York Times declared Butler Township, Indiana, the circus capital of the world, under the command of Col. Benjamin E. Wallace and his mind-blowing extravaganza: Wallace and Company's Great World Menagerie, Grand International Mardi Gras, Highway Holiday Hidalgo, and Alliance of Novelties. Sadly, the show itself did not debut until 1884 because a drunk cook forgot to turn off a gas stove, which met unfavorably with a discarded cigarette, combusted like a supernova, and took most of the animals and many of the performers with it.

When it did finally debut, to a crowd of nearly half a million, it opened with a giant woman floating in the sky, eating cupcakes, tethered to the ground like a hot-air balloon. There at the entrance to the midway, for all the crowd to see, her big blue dress ballooned out just enough to expose her white thighs and the menstrual stain on her panties, officially ushering in the era of the big top, and with it the world's greatest entertainers:

The daughter of Patrick Grimlicker, the famous fire-eater, who ate minnows by the handful. Unbeknownst to her, those minnows once swam freely in a very special pond where, before being kidnapped, they fed themselves on microscopic people who lived in microscopic villages on the shore. Forever after, those tiny people lived inside that fire-eater's daughter.

A lion tamer named Picinniny Gossin, who had a glass eye with a sea horse in it. The sea horse was trapped inside, but the lion tamer ate funnel cakes for breakfast and then ran thirteen laps around the giant woman floating in the sky. After an eleven-hour day of work he went back to his trailer to eat dinner alone, with a picture of his dead wife taped to the wall directly across from him. She'd always loved the tiny sea horse in his eye. He told her about his day as if she had not been savagely ripped apart by the organ grinder's monkey and thrown to the seals for fodder.

The bearded ladies, the Sullivan triplets—born to the organ grinder and the ticket taker—who all three happened to fall in love with Barnaby Schuler, the world's greatest whale fighter, simultaneously. Schuler loved none of them; his heart had been torn out ages before. The bearded sisters stopped talking to one another in their jealous pursuit of the suitor who wanted nothing to do with any of them. Eventually they starved to death trying to impress him. One started eating glass instead of cereal, and the others followed unquestioningly.

Hornbeck Fiddler, the greatest living marksman, who, while attempting to arrow an apple atop his daughter's head, missed quite horribly. The audience thought the mistake was part of the show, so they cheered very loudly. Fiddler hanged himself shortly thereafter.

Mons Le Tort, the great French bareback rider, who actually got so many women pregnant that an entire village was formed from his progeny.

Of course, the horses, tigers, leopards, lions, cheetahs, pumas, panthers, giraffes, dogs, goats, zebras, and all other non-human creatures suffered unending cruelty.

> Beat those elephants with sugarcane
> the giraffes with bamboo.
> Lash the hippopotamuses with reeds
> then go and salt the wounds
> to remind the stupid beasts who is who.

Torture, the ringmaster would say, is just another name for compassion.

Most certainly, the rich frosting on any circus was the clowns. Whiteface clowns like Pipo Sossman or François Fratellini, the oldest of modern clown archetypes, who held the highest status in the clown hierarchy, usually functioned as the straight man and leader of the group. Auguste clowns like Chesty Mortimer or Toto Johnson, who always got a pie in the face, played the Whiteface's sidekick. Mixed in would always be Character clowns like Poodles Hanneford or Bluch Landof, who adopted different personas such as the baker, the policeman, the housewife, or the hobo. Together they would do bits like "The Baseball Gag," "The Boxing Gag," "The Dentist," "The Clown Car," "The Midget Car," and "The Hosing."

At the orgasm of his stellar career Dan Rice was more of a household name than Abraham Lincoln. Referred to as the presidential jester, he was America's most popular clown. Mark Twain paid him homage in The Adventures of Huckleberry Finn. Walt Whitman wrote newspaper articles about him. He campaigned for Zachary Taylor by inviting him to join his circus bandwagon—hence the modern idiomatic expression "Jump on the bandwagon." In fact, his likeness was so ubiquitous that it became the model for Uncle Sam, the clown who wants YOU to join the army.

Then came the birth of Ringling Brothers and Barnum & Bailey in 1907. Legend has it this monumental troupe began with a single stilt walker, a pallbearer who went to the cemetery with other stilt walkers to mourn the death of a comrade. Sun setting behind them. Their heads down, crying. Black on all of them, from suit to shoes. Long black dress slacks stretching six feet to the ground. One pair of stilts made entirely of apologies. Another pair contained the greatest mystery in the universe. One pair could've broken at any minute. Another could've grown, if persuaded just right. At the grave site they bickered over final good-byes. A couple of them fell to the ground and shattered like lightbulbs on sidewalks. Some of the pieces fell onto the grave of their fallen brother. The remaining stilt walkers raised their hands and began hopping up and down on their stilts. One by one they toppled to the ground and broke into a billion pieces, until only one was left. The last stilt walker saw he was the only one still standing. He took a giant breath and exhaled with all he could muster, which uprooted many trees; laughter overtook him as he teetered, wobbled, but did not fall. After fifteen years and thirty-eight burials, after living in the shadows of so many other circuses, he remained. His laugher stormed the hillsides and deafened every person in the nearest village. That stilt walker was named John Bailey and his brother-in-law was named Frank Barnum, and their friends from church were named Phil and Terrance Ringling. Together they created "The Greatest Show on Earth."

Beginning in 1919, Merle Evans served as band director for the Ringling Brothers and Barnum & Bailey Circus for a half century. He died at the age of ninety-three, having led the Windjammers to 18,250 performances without ever missing a day.

Besides the smears, rags, serenades, and gallops, the most often-played music in the circus was the march: all except for John Phillip Sousa's "The Stars and Stripes Forever," which was strictly reserved for emergency situations only, used as a warning signal to indicate real trouble.

Signals and superstitions abound in circus life.

Never count the audience. Never whistle in the dressing room. Never sleep inside the big top. Never move a wardrobe trunk once it has been put into place. Never look back during the parade. Never sit on the ring curb facing out.

To a cacophony of drums, cymbals, tubas, trumpets, trombones, and cornets, Dainty Miss Leitzel, the first inductee to the International Circus Hall of Fame, made her dramatic entrance into the ring. When she reached the center, she clutched her famous rope swivel, a metal noose that dangled from the tent top. The spotlight followed her as she rose into the air. High above the arena floor she began to spin like a pinwheel, her face alight with laughter. The audience awed. Then suddenly her rope swivel crystallized and snapped, and she fell helplessly to her death. Born in Breslau, Germany, in 1892, she died in 1931 in Copenhagen, Denmark, two days after her tragic performance on Friday the thirteenth.

Never perform on Friday the thirteenth.

During the presidency of Calvin "KKK" Coolidge, 1923–1929, many crazy inventions popped up: the television, the talking pictures, and the electrically powered vibrator, all of which contributed to the end of the circus's monopoly on the entertainment industry.

Suddenly dwarves spinning plates and sexy human cannonballs equaled diminishing returns. By the 1940s people in the United States were preoccupied with the idea of annihilating the Japanese abroad and rounding them up in detention camps domestically. Few citizens had the urge to go and laugh or cheer at some bumbling brown bears or men with hula hoops, tightrope walkers or somersault throwers. And overseas most of Europe was too busy being taken over by Adolf Hitler to attend the latest big-top extravaganza. Rumor had it, the circus thrived in Switzerland, as they were notoriously neutral, but documents found much later in the twentieth century indicate that no such thing occurred. In fact, quite the opposite. Most of the Swiss actually stopped going to the circus because of the enormous guilt they felt over standing by and watching their neighbors fall to fascism without lifting a sword to help.

For the next few decades the heavy palm of the cold war pressed down on the circus like a bully holding a weakling underwater.

Only five people noticed when the death of the circus finally occurred on March 19, 1978. A few unread newspapers in small towns like Cheyenne, Wyoming, and Great Bend, Kansas, ran brief obituaries, each noting how the death was a long time coming. But overall, no one cared. It was as if the world collectively outgrew the need for it, evolved past it. Like Nietzsche pronouncing the death of God once religion seemed no longer necessary, the same thing happened to the circus, except there was no existential philosopher who decreed it. Instead, a single carrier pigeon traveled from Greenland to Chile with a slip of yellowed paper tied to his ankle that read: "Dear Fellow Circus Performers: It's over. They do not need us or want us anymore." And just like that, the tents evaporated, the animals disappeared, and the performers vanished.

Now nothing physical remains of that ancient enterprise. Children today may hear stories about the circus of yore, but they can never really know the true texture of cotton candy, nor feel the blood-rush of those death-defying acts. All that is left is a whispered echo of the candy butchers' song:

"Popcorn! Peanuts! Hot roasted peanuts! Snow cones! Soda

pop! Right this way! Right this way! Step right up! Ladies and Gentlemen, Children of All Ages, the circus is about to begin!"

[The Academic Years]

INTRODUCTION

After making a failure of himself as a screenwriter, Mooney spent many years in academia, none of which devoid of philosophy or literature. He drank <u>Eugene Onegin</u> for breakfast and ate <u>Finnegans Wake</u> for dinner. He frequently opined extemporaneously on subjects as varied as Cartesian ontology, Euclidian geometry, and macular degeneration.

His climb to academic stardom started humbly enough. He began at the bottom, as an elementary school teacher, and worked his way up to the university. Each position held its own rewards and challenges for Mooney, but none seemed to ever please him. His unorthodox pedagogy seemed to concern fellow faculty members as well as students and parents.

Are you believing any of this? Do you know that the education field does not work this way? One cannot "work one's way up" so to speak, in education. A teacher of high school English is not "working his way up" to a professorship at a university. For one thing, it requires in most cases a PhD to teach at the university level, whereas a person with a bachelor's degree could teach at the high school level. This tells you at least two things:

Either I am not Marvin K. Mooney

or

I am.

I cannot be both nor can I be neither. I am one of those two choices. I have to be. But so do you. I have named you. You are one of those two strings of letters, you are one of those two phrases.

YOU ARE!

I know you. I have labeled you. I have named you.

One of us is a liar. You or me. Or is it Mooney? I am not Mooney. Who are you?

Are you a liar, too?

[Notes for a roundtable discussion on experimental literature, in response to a forum hosted in the academic journal symploké (Volume 14, Numbers 1-2, 2006, pp. 316-333), "The Question of Writing Now: FC2 responds to Ben Marcus." Delivered at Ohio State University April 9th 20--.]

On Being A Maker Of Experimental Literature

Although I am equally interested in the "scholarly" aspects of today's discussion, I am here to speak from the angle of practitioner; that is to say, I am a maker of experimental litera-ture. Over the past twelve years I have taught creative writing at three universities and at various writers' confer-ences, absolutely none of which have been openly hospitable to experimental writing. I share this bit of biography as testimony to the fact that the divide is not a theoretical one, it is palpable. There have, of course, been pockets of kindred spirits here and there, editors with consonant taste or similar proclivities, and I have been blessed to find the occasional faculty member willing to "tolerate my shenanigans," but overall my experimental work has been met with disinterest, dismissal, and in many instances outright disgust.

The reason for this enmity is that being a maker of experimental literature means I am uninterested in replicating the dominant discourse, i.e. conventional realism. I break the rules and refuse to toe the party line, not only because I am a rebellious, obnoxious showoff, but also—and more importantly—because I am totally uninterested in the values the dominate camp holds.

These values come from Aristotle, whose Poetics gave us the structural demands of unity: the beginning-middle-end, as well as familiar concepts such as show-don't-tell, and resist-the-deus-ex-machina; but most importantly, Aristotle

213

gave us the six elements of tragedy, which have since been co-opted by the conventional realists to define the necessary elements of fiction: plot, character, thought, diction, music, and spectacle. He then told us we should value them in that order: plot, character, thought, diction, music, and spectacle.

I couldn't disagree more. To me, plot is the least important element of literature. As a maker, I have no interest in constructing a plot. Plot bores the hell out of me. I also have no interest in creating believable characters. Believable characters bore the hell out of me. Instead, I take as my mantra the words of the experimentalist John Hawkes who said, "I began to write fiction on the assumption that the true enemies of the novel were plot, character, setting and theme, and having once abandoned these familiar ways of thinking about fiction, totality of vision or structure was really all that remained." This, to me, is what it means to be a maker of experimental literature: to value the totality of vision and structure over other elements. To say it a different way, I approach the creation of literature in reverse: first and foremost I value spectacle, then music, then diction, then thought, then character, then plot. To my mind, this means that I place a higher value on the creation of art rather than the creation of commodity.

That binary appears in the distinction Susan Steinberg makes (in her contribution to the symploké forum) between Ben Marcus wanting to create art and Jonathon Franzen wanting to create entertainment, which I think is a salient point to consider. I certainly don't think those two things are mutually exclusive, but I do think they're separate enterprises with separate agendas.

And this is where I would have to disagree with Brian Evenson when he says in his forum contribution that "Realism and experimentalism are not alternatives in a binary opposition; instead, each exists on a continuum that runs between abstraction and representation." To my mind, it is impossible to put Gertrude Stein and John Updike on the same continuum. For Brian Evenson to say that they are doing the same thing only one is closer to abstraction and one is closer to representation is a mistake. Tender Buttons and Rabbit, Run are not doing the same thing. They are categorically different because they are of two different kinds.

Think about it like this: although peanut butter and jelly are both used as sandwich spreads, there is no continuum between them. They will never fade into being the other because they are of different kinds. Peanut butter is peanut butter and jelly is jelly. There are, however, different gradations of peanut butter (smooth, extra smooth, chunky, extra chunky, etc) as well as various types of jelly (grape, strawberry, raspberry, etc). From this model we can see how each "kind" can be classified along a continuum. So, I would be willing to grant the existence of a continuum within each kind of writing: on the experimental side there is obviously a gradation between James Joyce's Finnegans Wake and Aimee Bender's The Girl in the Flammable Skirt and on the conventional realist side there are obviously different types (for example Raymond Carver's Where I'm Calling From and Willa Cather's My Antonia). But the fundamental difference between the two kinds (experimental and conventional realism) remains: one privileges the totality of vision (i.e. art) and the other privileges plot, character, setting, theme (i.e. entertainment).

The symploké forum gave rise to my considering of those issues and it also gave rise to ideas about the role of audience and the function of communication, which also seem to be key issues in Brian Evenson's short piece "Mudder Tongue" given that it is essentially concerned with the charact-

215

er's inability to communicate to an audience.

For me, as a maker of experimental literature, the audience is irrelevant. I make art for myself and then I share it with other people. I do not make art for other people.

You can think of it like this: I bake some cookies for myself and when I taste the first cookie I decide that I am very pleased with them and so I want to share them with others who I imagine might also enjoy them. I understand that because I made them the way that I like them, with ingredients that I find particularly tasty, that there might be others who do not like the taste of my cookies. This is fine by me because I did not bake these cookies for other people or with other people's tastes in mind. I baked them for me, with my tastes in mind.

I understand that this prerogative flies in the face of certain readings that would suppose that all writers have in mind an intended audience, or that all writers care to consider the social or cultural implications of their creation—which might be perfectly applicable to someone writing conventional realism—but the truth of the matter is, I don't think about those things and I don't care about those things and the fact that I don't is exactly my point. Makers of experimental literature should not and cannot be concerned with an audience. The only people who benefit from concerning themselves with an audience are those who are primarily interested in creating a commodity, entertaining, or persuading someone of something. None of those three elements are on my agenda when I sit down at the keyboard.

This speaks to another fundamental difference in "kind," which has to do with the role of communication in experimental literature. One of the perennial arguments carted out by conventional realists, as noted in the forum, is another that they received from Aristotle: that writers should not be difficult, opaque, or ornamental, but that we should make work clear and accessible to "the common reader," a term which—to my mind—is not only inherently derogatory but also completely antithetical to the process of experimental writing as I have tried to explain it. As I previously stated, experimentalism values spectacle above all else, including communication.

This may sound strange, but it actually gets right to the heart of the difference between the two kinds: experimentalists approach the creation of literature differently than conventional realists do. At a very base level, experimentalism's primary intention is to raise questions while conventionalism's primary intention is to give answers. This fundamental difference, along with all of the other differences I've pointed out, speaks to the fact that we makers of literature are not all doing the same thing; and we are not all approaching the medium with the same set of values.

This is hard for some people to accept because they have certain assumptions about what literature should be and expectations about what literature should do, and when those assumptions and expectations are not met, they freak out. Some get bored, some get confused, some get pissed off.

But the problem is not in the text, the problem is in the reader. The basic assumption that all literature values plot, character, and theme needs to be reconsidered, and our expectations need to be redefined. Experimental literature offers us this opportunity. All we have to do is start considering it. For theorists this means opening new possibilities for reading. For makers it means permission to create unconventional work with the confidence that there is unique value in such an endeavor. For both it means a greater diversity of material, thus a richer picture of the human condition.

Mooney struggled to gain tenure at various institutions, but failed, failed, failed. One university dismissed him for inappropriate conduct, stemming from an incident at a varsity tennis match in which Mooney displayed his anus to a crowd of drunken Princeton Tigers. A different university released Mooney for posting the following fliers around the building:

Letter To The Person Who Keeps Putting Pornographic
Magazine Cutouts
In My Faculty Mailbox

Dear Pervert,

For a while I was convinced you were one of my smartass
students, until that particular student was arrested for public
indecency, and the pictures continued to appear in my box
throughout the duration of his incarceration. Then I thought
you might be the new adjunct woman with the huge glasses
and the deviant grimace who hardly looks up when she's
walking to her classroom. But then, she couldn't possibly
appreciate the sensitivity of those delicate Asian-American
vaginas you highlighted last month, nor those elephantine
Peruvian penises you so unabashedly left stacked on top of my
students' midterm papers.

Perhaps you're trying to scare me out of the department
because you don't feel like I share a proper level of adoration
for Foucault, or a strong enough Marxist leaning. Or perhaps
you simply enjoy hassling part-time lecturers. Whatever your
reasoning, I want you to know that I am keeping every single
picture you've put in my box. I'm collecting them into a
scrapbook, which I intend to present at the next department
meeting. If you do not wish to be called out publicly, then you
should come forward now, declare yourself, and come clean
(so to speak). If you choose to disclose your identity to me
privately, then I won't take this to the Chair, I won't involve the
University Judiciary, and I won't tell anyone else about this
matter.

In fact, the more I think about it the more I think I'd like to meet you. Granted, I was initially disgusted, especially when I considered you might be one of those creepy Classics professors; but the images you've been leaving lately (such as those tantalizing full-breasted Native American women whipping those overweight Caucasian men with sopping wet American flags) leads me to believe we share a similar Postcolonial sensibility.

I am therefore intrigued.

Would you be interested in starting a colloquium dedicated to Postcolonial sexual representations?

Let me know,
Marvin K. Mooney

Editor's Note

Please be forewarned, to those who do not understand, I apologize for this candid confession, but I wish only to make it clear in advance, to avoid any legal ramifications or other mis-understandings: this is the biography of an imaginary character. I am real but he is not. How could he be? I am not a creation. He is. Wait... who is "he"? Him or me? Which one is this typing here? Is Chris Higgs involved? Who is Chris Higgs? Christopher Higgs? What's the difference?

<<<Somewhere along the line we forgot what Nietzsche said>>>

3. Belief in the "Ego." The Subject[8]
481 (1883-1888)

Against positivism, which halts at phenomena—"There are only facts"—I would say: No, facts is precisely what there is not, only interpretations. We cannot establish any fact "in itself": perhaps it is folly to want to do such a thing.

"Everything is subjective," you say; but even this is interpretation. The "subject" is not something given, it is something added and invented and projected behind what there is.—Finally, is it necessary to posit an interpreter behind the interpretation? Even this is invention, hypothesis.

In so far as the word "knowledge" has any meaning, the world is knowable; but it is interpretable otherwise, it has no meaning behind it, but countless meanings. — Perspectivism."

---

8   Quote from Nietzsche's Will to Power (first published in 1901 – trans. Walter Kaufmann and R.J Hollingdale – 1968 Vintage Books edition)

221

It is our needs that interpret the world; our drives and their For and Against. Every drive is a kind of lust to rule; each one has its perspective that it would like to compel all the other drives to accept as a norm.

"The text calls upon the reader to be actively involved in the process of constituting its meaning... The text formally involves the process of response/interpretation and in so doing makes the reader aware of herself or himself as producer as well as consumer of meaning."
—Charles Bernstein, "Writing and Method"

Question: what is a confession? What does it mean to explain oneself?

1748

The reticent volcano keeps
His never slumbering plan –
Confided are his projects pink
To no precarious man.

If nature will not tell the tale
Jehovah told her
Can human nature not survive
Without a listener?

Admonished by her buckled lips
Let every babbler be
The only secret people keep
Is Immortality.

—Emily Dickinson

Mother: A Deconstruction with Critical Apparatus

I know two things: John Gardner says stories are supposed to reveal truth, but at the same time, if Kurosawa's Rashomon taught me anything, the event of truth is actually impossible.[9] Consequently, I am less interested in stories and more interested in the perplexity of signifiers: those sticky solutions to truth that seem to surround us like malcontent phantoms. Spirits. Cobwebs. Pushing us to dislocate the signified. A tombstone to indicate the presence of a corpse. A white flag for surrender. A red octagon to indicate stop. The word stop to indicate a request to halt. We acknowledge in these signifiers the manifest reduction from concept to communication, the simplification, but then we neatly overlook the severity inherent in its limiting nature. To say, for instance, Mother is dead, and expect those words to mean what I intend.[10] To somehow enwomb her entire legacy, her existence, her mark on my life and every other life she ever encountered. To plot every vector. To sum up and solve every question. To totalize and trivialize the plurality of her multiple dialectics. To say in one measly signifier that nothing remains of her. She is dead. And that is all?[11] I cannot do it. And because I cannot, I must instead seek solace in myth.[12] Yes, her mortal body perished, seized-up and quit running as if driven minus fuel. Yes, she breathes and eats and sleeps no more. Yes, in a grave she is

---

9 "How wonderful that we have met with a paradox. Now we have some hope of making progress." —Niels Bohr quoted in The Quantum Dice by Ponomarev & Kurchatov
10 "Death is a displaced name for a linguistic predicament." —Paul de Man, The Rhetoric of Romanticism
11 "There is nothing more banal than death." —Maurice Blanchot quoting Nietzsche (The Space of Literature)
12 "When the meaning is too full for myth to be able to invade it, myth goes around it, and carries it away Bodily." —Roland Barthes, (Mythologies)

buried. But a body in repose signified by a tombstone does not define, is not the truth of, my Mother.[13]

Take the archeology of that home we once inhabited.[14] By the lakeshore. Nightingales. Bird seed in the feeder and sleeping pigeons strewn across the lawn. A glimpse of summertime. Mother made visible by the morning light, at the clothesline hanging undershirts. A whistle from the train passing by. The faint static of television from the front room; my Father and brother arguing over politics. Green is the carpet. How unspecific. Red is the wall paper. But what specific shade, what tone, what color- temperature? White is the ceiling, spackled. Your idea is not like mine, no matter how I describe it; you don't know the signified, so you can only associate with my use of signifiers, we must face it. I'm sorry. Red to me is fainting. Green a lollipop. White a witch for Halloween. Through the smudged-up glass on the patio door, I see. Windows open. Breeze pushing the curtains out. The billow of Mother's cotton skirt. The faint déjà vu of remembering.[15]

Soap in my mouth for saying the F word, age nine. The whole blue bar. Sitting on the toilet with the lid down. Scared to spit it out, even though I am alone. Slobber and tears everywhere. Mother in the kitchen, I can hear her. I know she has lit a cigarette, I can smell it. Father will come home and she

---

13 "It is in love, in hate, in anger, in fear, in joy, in indignation, in admiration, in hope, in despair, that man and the world reveal themselves in their truth." —Jean-Paul Sartre (Literature & Existentialism)

14 "Our soul is an abode. And by remembering "houses" and "rooms," we learn to "abide" within ourselves. Now everything becomes clear, the house images move in both directions: they are in us as much as we are in them." —Gaston Bachelard (The Poetics of Space)

15 "Say memory, and almost everyone thinks of the past. But most of our memories are really about the future." —Diane Ackerman (An Alchemy of Mind)

will not tell him what I've done. It is our secret, like so many things. It has always been our secret. And it always will be.

Born in 1953. The year President Truman announced that the U.S. had developed the hydrogen bomb. The year Stalin died.[16] The year the first color television sets went on sale, and the first TV Guide hit the newsstand. Her Father fought in the war, was one of the first infantrymen to enter Dachau. Her Mother lived in a hair salon, where she worked her entire life. They both died before I got a chance to meet them. Mother was an only child.

Tan lines at her elbows. Summer of '78. A caterpillar-shaped scar on her right ankle. Fresh blueberries for breakfast. Johnny Cash on the phonograph in the living room. Father watching Jimmy Carter on television while Mother tries desperately not to cry. My brother in jail again. Cigarette smoke. Charbroiled steaks, and Mother eating alone on the front porch. Drinking from a plastic cup.[17] Watching her from my upstairs bedroom window. Wishing she hadn't sent me to my room.

No more romantic comedies. No more sailing the boat around the lake. No more make sense grown up little kid abstract expressionism. I am six and thirty, I am ten. No more does yesterday matter than today. Tomorrow is nothing until it becomes today. No more phone calls on Saturdays, postcards from Yellowstone, packages with candies and cookies hand-made, letters signed with hearts and her name. Never another cigarette. Never another hospital visit. Never another laugh at a joke or a slap across my face.

Time, Mother said, hates humans.[18] Once, a war broke out

---

16 Prokofiev died on the same day.

17 Gauguin once tried to kill himself with arsenic, but vomited before he could get to paradise.

18 "In daily life we divide time into three parts: past, present, and future.

between us and time; back and forth the power shifted, battle after battle. Many forces lifted. Brave, scrupulous soldiers with ethics and morals and handbags full of prisoners' severed ears. Little rat-faced smiles. Sick, selfish, rabid and hateful. No wonder Time won easily in the end. But how could there be an end? Time still fights with humans. Mother is gone but time still remains.[19] She told me as much at the age of eleven: we lost the war with time and now we age instead of time. But in the beginning, time aged just as we do. Time got old and died. Time had children. Time held funerals. Time wore black. In the beginning. But what is the beginning? Derrida says it's insignificant: there could be no beginning without consequential difference. The more effective question would be not what but why? Why glorify the beginning? Mother says the war is over.

Ice cream cones, just she and I. Father at the courthouse dealing with my brother. Rain. Thunder. Lightening. I am twenty. On the couch, watching A Streetcar Named Desire. Thinking Mother more beautiful than both Blanche DuBois and Stella Kowalski. How panic, in a voice, is never pretty. How Brando was nothing like me.

The grammatical structure of language revolves around this fundamental distinction. Reality is associated with the present moment. The past we think of having slipped out of existence, whereas the future is even more shadowy, its details still unformed. In this simple picture, the "now" of our conscious awareness glides steadily onward, transforming events that were once in the unformed future into the concrete but fleeting reality of the present, and thence relegating them to the fixed past." –Paul Davies ("That Mysterious Flow")

19 "Physicists prefer to think of time as laid out in its entirety–a timescape, analogous to a landscape–with all past and future events located there together... Completely absent from this description of nature is anything that singles out a privileged special moment as the present or any process that would systematically turn future events into the present, then past, events. In short, the time of the physicist does not pass or flow." –Ibid.

Vogue magazine comes in the mail.[20] Mother disappears to the attic. My brother ties me to his motorcycle with a jump rope, and threatens to drag me across the street. I fondle a handful of pebbles I collected on the lakeshore, and consider hurling them at him. Then a fire truck goes squealing past, and he flinches at the sound of their sirens.

Mother. Once, to gain father's affection. In order to get. Because she wanted. Although he never allowed. By slight of hand. See? I fail when attempting to impose unanimity upon the divergent, continuity upon the disjointed, or compatibility with the incongruent.[21] Story just gets in the way. Heart-lumps on holidays. Paper machines made by imaginary dactyls. No signifier does justice linguistically[22] nor helps to alleviate the metonymic urge to devastate this elegy. When I wake up, forget it, there is no destiny.[23] I wish this were easier. I wish I could make this make more sense.

Follow her from preschool to elementary school to middle school to high school to college.[24] All the games she played, the knees she skinned, the ribs she bruised, the boyfriends from playgrounds to backseats. All the men with broken noses that she slept with before Father. All the pot smoke and LSD. The time she ran a corvette off a cliff and blew a barn to

20 August 1984 / Cover Model: Isabella Rossellini / Photographer: Richard Avedon

21 Especially when I am reconstituting Yehudi Menuhin's famous quote regarding music.

22 "Communication is only one function of language, and by no means an essential one." –Noam Chomsky (Language and Mind)

23 "In sleep we reach into our Selves / like hands taking food from ovens. / Our Selves eat our Selves to save our Selves." –Al Zolynas, ("Sleep Poem")

24 "The female world, bounded as it is, contains, as does any world, rich layers of meaning. It is not simply that a woman must stay within this world but that signification itself is kept away from it." –Susan Griffin ("Red Shoes")

smithereens, escaping narrowly. Skirts and shoes and socks to match, from frilly to scratched, from thrift stores to boutiques. Having money, losing money. Love letters never sent. Phone calls never made. Wishes never given to falling stars.

I want to draw the curve of her nose, but all my pencils are broken. I want to spray-paint her eyeliner meticulously. For if and when and never. The soft skin under her chin. The elbow wrinkles. The thick purple veins like vines under the surface of her skin on both legs. The fingernails chewed to stumps. Front tooth chipped and silver fillings visible when laughing. Eyes brown rings like the trunk of a tree. Voice the victim of cigarettes by the billions. Hair never not dyed blonde. Roots never not showing. This whole complex lexicon, an entire language of visuals now gone.[25]

Plunging the toilet, half past eight, dinner going cold downstairs. Me, not Mother—she is away at her quilting bee. Father in the front room cleaning his pistols. Listening to Led Zeppelin IV on the phonograph. By lamplight. My brother playing his clarinet in the backyard. Three men without a woman.

Two days before my brother went away for good, but what is good? With what is it synonymous?[26] Why not say instead: two days before my brother went away for bad, which is the more appropriate correlative for the situation. Bad is what he went away for, not good. Rotten, to be precise. But either way, two days before his final incarceration, my brother broke a

25 "Language of the enemy: heavy lightness, house insurance, serious vanity, self-deposit box, feather of lead, sandwich man, bright smoke, second-guess, sick health, shell game, still-waking sleep, forgiveness." – Sherman Alexie ("Captivity")

26 "One of the gestures of deconstruction is to not naturalize what isn't natural, to not assume that what is conditioned by history, institutions or society is natural." –Jacques Derrida (from the documentary Derrida; Dir. Kirby Dick & Amy Ziering Kofman)

birdhouse to pieces with a hammer. I watched him do it. Mother watched him do it. Neither of us said anything.

1983. A brittle kind of foreshadow.[27] President Reagan calls the Soviet Union "an evil empire," and also declares that this is "The Year of the Bible." Gandhi wins the Oscar for Best Picture, and M*A*S*H ends after 11 years and 251 episodes. Sally Ride becomes the first American woman in space. Pope John Paul II visits his would-be assassin in prison to forgive him. Mother stops eating and quits her job saving animals.

Father at the horse track, looking very concerned. My book bag overflowing with all kinds of wet rubbish my classmates stuffed in it while on the school bus. Mother carefully studying the program, circling her choices for the upcoming races. Them betting.[28] Me watching Mother, not the horses. The ugly, pretty crowd. The scent of beer and cotton candy. No brother. Just me.

The crash of a symphony. 1963. Mother is ten years old. Dressed in her Sunday clothes. The Russian Overture. Sitting in the balcony next to her Father and Mother, both with their eyes closed. Sleeping?

Stop. Berrigan Avenue. The night my brother disappeared. Father driving circles around the neighborhood, shouting out the window Come home! Come home! Mother holding my hand on the sidewalk. Blood splattered everywhere. The street went quiet. Listening. The sound of flowerbeds crumpling in the moonlight. Wilting. Gone from their passion. But now is not the moment of his disappearing. There is an interval of unexplainable emptiness, not for lack of suitable articulation

---

27 The year Tennessee Williams choked on a bottle cap and died in his hotel room. Also the year Karen Carpenter passed away.

28 "Without risk there is no faith, and the greater the risk the greater the faith." —Søren Kierkegaard ("Truth is Subjectivity" from Concluding Unscientific Postscript)

but rather that moment of quantum fluctuation when objects not being observed skip out on our plane of existence only to pop sub-atomically into another dimension momentarily. You see? Maybe our entire life is actually experienced in that imperceptible interval. And if so, if no one is observing us, then telling a story, any story, must by nature be a lie.[29] Maybe what we think is eighty years is less than a blink of the eye. Time did win the war, after all. And we cannot deny that even though there are things we know we know, and things we know we don't know, there are also those things that we don't even know we don't know.[30] Uncertainty is all we can count on. Mother is here and then she is gone. The sound of a lifetime in one fraction of a millisecond. Pop. Like a balloon.

All gone with trumpets. To a dream. To a fantasy. To the opposite of reality. Each of us in a hammock: my Mother, Father, and brother. No one speaks. No one argues, no one lies, no one hates. The sun warms the lake, which sloshes on the shore. I close my eyes. Miles Davis.

Maybe my brother had nothing to do with it: maybe Mother died of sadness.[31] 2003. Maybe Father made her feel more alone than if she were single. His company, over the years, may well have turned into a habit, the opposite of passion. She said I love you and he the same.[32] They played the game, performed

---

29 "Writing has nothing to do with signifying. It has to do with surveying, mapping, even realms that are yet to come." —Deleuze and Guattari (A Thousand Plateaus)

30 "I meet someone from Mars and he asks me "How many toes have human beings got?" - I say "Ten. I'll show you," and take my shoes off. Suppose he was surprised that I knew with such certainty, although I hadn't looked at my toes - ought I to say: "We humans know how many toes we have whether we can see them or not?" —Ludwig Wittgenstein (On Certainty)

31 Anna Karenina, Emma Bovary, and Sylvia Plath all killed themselves over sadness - by train, by poison, by oven.

32 "Why is it that the most unoriginal thing we can say to one another is

230

the functions they were programmed to complete. I can only ever underestimate. Took part, each, like victims to history. The same for me and my brother. Brutish as animals. Plagued with opposable thumbs.

A tattoo of circus sideshow acts. Jugglers. Gymnasts. Knife throwing, fire swallowing, hairy women and big breasted men. Strong ones and little ones. Bears through hoops and elephants crying. Motorcycles in metal cages looping in gyroscopic motion. Mother holding a bag of popcorn and Father scolding my brother for groping the ticket taker. Peanuts crunching under our feet.

Law enforcement at the front door. Father speaking to them in a hushed tone. Mother pacing the kitchen with a lit cigarette in each hand. The curtains pulled back, showing faces in the front window.[33] I stay at the top of the stairs where I can see Mother's breakdown as well as Father's back in the doorway. I can hear his exchange. Then the police officer steps into our house and another one follows and then another. Five of them total. As they spread out and search our house, one of them comes up the steps and tries to talk all cutesy to me, in that faux-friend way that adults sometimes do to children. Asks me if I've seen my brother. Do I know where he's hiding? Do I know how to get in contact with him?

No, I was not a pallbearer. In fact, I did nothing with Mother's requiem. And Father never noticed when I slipped away from the service. Me in my black suit carrying Mother's

___

still the thing we long to hear? 'I love you' is always a quotation. You did not say it first and neither did I, yet when you say it and when I say it we speak like savages who have found three words and worship them." – Jeanette Winterson (Written on the Body)

33 "A curtain, a curtain which is fastened discloses mourning, this does not mean sparrows or elocution or even a whole preparation, it means that there are ears and very often much more altogether." –Gertrude Stein (Tender Buttons)

last pack of cigarettes and her favorite green lighter. Out to the lake for a swim.[34]

Mother on the couch in the front room. I am eight years old, rolling my G.I. Joes in her hair like curlers. She works her giant needles on a bright blue quilt spread out across her lap. From the phonograph, Bob Dylan plays. Mother hums along quietly. A cigarette burns in the clover-shaped ashtray on the floor by her feet. I unroll the little men from her hair and roll them back up again.

For nine months, Mother and I were one person. But unlike Salvador Dali, I don't remember being in the womb. Father tells me she quit smoking for most of those months. My brother says she didn't.

I remember hating her, but for what I do not recall specifically. Age eleven. I remember cursing her and wishing I was never born. At dinner one evening I asked what it meant to have an abortion.

My brother is guilty. No, innocent. No, guilty. He did it; he didn't do it.[35] He somewhat inadvertently, accidentally did it, wanted to do it, could never do it, premeditated it, did it on the spur of the moment without forethought; no, he wasn't even near the scene of the crime; he was late, he was early, he was angry, he was high, he was sad and drunk and sick. It doesn't matter what happened or if it even really happened in the first place. Maybe it did, maybe it didn't. Mother is gone regardless. The interesting thing is not the reality of the event, but the immense unreality of it.

---

34 "SWIMMING, unrestricted inscription or eulogy delivered at a grave site; by extension, a statement, usually with long, arcing movements of the arms and legs, commemorating the dead." — Ben Marcus (The Age of Wire and String)

35 "Despair was swirling its great lovely calla lilies in the sky / And in the handbag was my dream that flask of salts" —André Breton (Mad Love)

Do not forget that what you see is really upside-down. Do not let yourself be easily fooled into thinking that you are experiencing what others want you to believe is reality. Light through the cornea, through the pupil, through the lens, to the retina where the optic nerve receives the impulse and sends it to the cerebral cortex where your brain is tricked into believing up is down and down is grounded. I say North, but really I mean South. I say top when the bottom is really what I'm describing. We are never right-side up to each other. We are never what we really are.[36] How could we be? But even so, Mother is a crisp photograph, complete in composition, lovely both upside-down and right-side up, both living and deceased, both hateful and wicked and cruel.[37] Forget the physics of optics, the convex experience. Forget the misery and splendor of reality; don't waste your time trying to figure things out. Nothing ever adds up. Does it? Seriously? Isn't logic the worst way to reason? Memories do not need eyes to turn them around, and myth is more powerful than the arbitrary laws of science. Only experience. Only sensation. Only questions, never answers. For science, like story, is that poor signifier people fall back on when they need, desperately, to make sense of something nonsensical and don't know what else to do. When in fact, logic is as useless as currency, as flat as Kansas, and as childish as a prank phone call. Right? Isn't logic why we are trapped in this labyrinth of inadequate signifiers to begin with? Why we struggle? Why we fight? Why we deconstruct

36 "The spectator is a dying animal." –Jim Morrison (The Lords and The New Creatures)

37 "The simultaneous recognition, in a fraction of a second, of the significance of an event as well as the precise organization of forms which gives that event its proper expression... In photography, the smallest thing can be a great subject. The little human detail can become a leitmotif." –Henri Cartier-Bresson (from The Impassioned Eye, a collection of video interviews)

these scenes and sentences in search like underpaid detectives for little nuggets of fleeting meaning? Ultimately, Mother is a word and nothing more.[38]

Mère, Mutter, Moeder, Madre, Mãe. How to say. Goodbye to a skin-wrapped skeleton? Next year a wedding, a disaster, a painting: Where Do We Come From? What Are We? Where Are We Going? The birth of my first child, that little person who will never know her grandmother. My divorce, my sickness, my hospitalization. My daughter hating me and never speaking to me again. The remarriage of my ex-wife, my daughter's high school graduation. All the secrets I never told anyone. The casket I am buried in.

Now here is love minus logic, Mother's signature meals: Coleslaw, mangoes, and fried chicken. Asparagus wrapped in bacon, dipped in caramelized brown sugar. Banana peppers, provolone, and sautéed mushrooms. Prosciutto and melon. Crepes with honey butter and cinnamon. Fresh peach nectar in frosted mugs with little umbrellas for decoration. Clumpy mashed potatoes. Barbequed ribs and grilled pineapples, with red peppers and corn on the cob. Fried rice with eggplant.[39]

Me, hiding in a rack of women's clothing. Age seven. At first, just playing. Mother searching for me all through Sears. Then the call over store intercom beckoning me to the entrance. Me, not moving, upset that Mother gave up her search. I wanted her to find me. I needed her to find me. I didn't care what my punishment would be. I moved not.

---

38 "My doubts stand in a circle around every word, I see them before I see the word, but what then! I do not see the word at all, I invent it. Of course, that wouldn't be the greatest misfortune, only I ought to be able to invent words capable of blowing the odor off corpses in a direction other than straight into mine and the reader's face." —Franz Kafka (Diaries 1910-1913)

39 "The dead are our children and we must coax them to eat." —Beverly Dahlen ("The Opening of the Mouth")

234

Knowing Mother was worried, maybe even crying, thinking someone had kidnapped me. Then suddenly, my eyes welled up and my sight went blurry.[40]

Organ donor. But where is her body going?[41] Streamlined to a middle school classroom for unskilled dissection? Eaten by a cannibalistic lab attendant? Sold into a traveling exhibit? Cross section of her lungs as example. Warning. Do not smoke. Or maybe her eyes will replace the dead ones in someone else. Her tongue will replace the victim of torture. Ears to a car crash survivor. Lips to a vain seventeen-year-old. Yes, on every street I walk, in every public building, I see parts of Mother attached to other people. She is the chin of our waitress. The nose of the gas station employee. The feet of a mistress. The shoulders of a morning after.

Not so much the scent of tobacco. More the cornucopia of perfumes and air fresheners and candles she used to mask it. Vanilla bean mixed with cherry blossom mixed with Pall Malls. A heavy scent that resonates in the back of the throat. Like sour milk, or cupcakes and sulfur.

Mother's favorite book. The one she read and reread over and over and over again. In fact, I don't know if she ever read another book in her entire life. Just the one.

And when asked, she would never speak of it, never share her thoughts on it, never say anything more than yes, it is truly a magnificent work, remarkable in every way; but then she refused to remark further. Maybe that simple action is the most telling signifier of all. She carried a book in her handbag the entire time I was growing up, flipped through the pages at

---

40 "The past is like a tapeworm, constantly growing, which I carry curled up inside me." —Italo Calvino (If on a winter's night a traveler)

41 "Maybe when you get to oblivion / the car lights sweeping the motel room walls, / you'll never know who you are again / or what you've done or what's been done to you." —Dean Young ("Ghost Gash")

every one of my baseball practices, my brother's band recitals, and at every one of Father's company picnics, but never spoke a word about it to anyone. What more is there to say? The only things I truly believe in are those things which can't be named.

Mother's potentialities.[42] Paralyzed I will always be, unable to make signifiers suffice. You and I share this handicap, reader. Neither of us can ever really say what we mean, no matter how well we craft our stories, no matter how clever our fictive dreams.[43] Because by nature signifiers make hard things way too easy, and truth is never what it claims to be. To be. The opposite of Mother.

---

42 "Against Freud, who says the character is made up of the succession of acts of mourning carried out by the subject, Schnitzler: the effect of a personality is the way in which <u>all the potentialities</u> of a character shine out from beneath the manifestations of [her] real and contingent life." —Jean Baudrillard (<u>Cool Memories II</u>)

43   "for life's not a paragraph / And death i think is no parenthesis" —e.e. cummings ("since feeling is first")

[By recognizing the gestalt of Mooney's project, we in turn find resonance in these linguistic and verbal (la langue and parole), philological, dialectal, etymological, phonological, morphological, semantic, grammatical, syntactical constructions. His milestone is manifold. For Mooney, langue surpassed parole in magnitude but not actual usage. He loved to tout the experimental, avant-garde aspects of his work, when in reality his methodology corroborated none of that. He slapdashedly scribbled his compositions. No record found in his personal journals, nor as yet available correspondence or personal account indicated otherwise. What instead we find when we go fishing is a long history of sadness. One close acquaintance told interviewers, "Mooney was never emotionally sober. He was toasted from breakfast to bedtime." Evidently, Mooney didn't try to hide the fact. He would routinely stroll through his neighborhood smoking a joint, mumbling, never looking up, never smiling, never saying hello.]

> La langue is the whole system of language that precedes and makes speech possible. A sign is a basic unit of langue.
> Learning a language, we master the system of grammar, spelling, syntax and punctuation. These are all elements of langue.
> Langue is a system in that it has a large number of elements whereby meaning is created in the arrangements of its elements and the consequent relationships between these arranged elements.
>
> Parole is the concrete use of the language, the actual utterances. It is an external manifestation of langue. It is the usage of the system, but not the system.

EXAMPLE:

How now my cap feels filled like a scoop of ice-cream. How now I've memorized a thousand nations. Just the beginning of me is lost out back in that labyrinth of my heart. Please forgive me, I am not me. I am the manifestation of the rewind the tape and press play–don't hypnotize, don't mesmerize, don't go all absolute kaplooie on me. Please, make me make a difference. I ask nicely. Please answer me this simple Socratic equation: what lives on the dark side of the moon? What forecasts the most discrepancies? How many larks are still praying? Just when do you plan to tell the truth to mars? I am surface! I disregard. Pay attention, I might show you the key or blow you to the safest decision. Make a mark, mark it down, mark the place: I'm only describing it once so pay attention:

This is broccoli speaking: "Now is renegade and avarice."

I am hypochondriac delusion, applesauce for breakfast, mice play the smallest little instruments. Have a penny. Make a wish. Let the sum total infinity but please don't go up on stage with that vice. I imagine a whole galleria. Just as soon as the Martians take over our planet. Raise your children like this: no, no, no, maybe. How about a little digression?

I am thirteen years old. The mask is dagger, a rim shot. Believe me. I Trojan the equinox fully. Fully. Capably. Noblemen bow down before me. I'm just kidding. That's called hyperbole. In the end of the last basic decision, my jodhpurs gallop away. Don't believe me. Let me simply give you simply some advice: the witches are gypsies, and eyeballs are neon conclusions. Over the hills and through the woods, the farm is craven, the dolphin is patter to ego and trumpets

238

and fire. Yell for the nearest decision. Yell Andromeda! Yell make up your goddamn mind! See these fisheries in Portland are square belonging to hygrophyte materials (not exported material), my workers are all one hundred percent legit. Course of differences, thousands die of hunger, I'm just saying, making France look ridiculous. I do not like it. And neither should you. Let's call the Senator and ask his advice.

Hello. Senator? It is me. Listen, I need your advice, savvy? Tell me what I need to know or else this blade will tell you so. Please believe me. Hand the information over before I court-martial the jester inside of me. You wouldn't like to see that side of me. Get a clue, get a clue and find the directions best suited for burying me. Focus in on the desert, maybe outside Las Vegas, maybe somewhere in Death Valley–that seems apropos. Bury me deep and don't apologize. The money you will find in my duffle bag inside coin locker #3456 in the Amtrak building in Highland Park, California. I left my entire fortune in there, and you can have it. All you have to do is promise to bury me six feet deep. My religion requires my body to be exactly six feet deep. Do not disappoint me. I will be in the afterlife, which as we all know controls the actual life. I will haunt you for the rest of your life until you die and then when you get here to the afterlife I will continue to bother you for all of eternity. I am not your subconscious talking, I'm your indecision. Should you give up now? Should you say fuck you Marvin K. Mooney! I abhor your personality! But a personality is what constitutes this voice speaking, but I'm not speaking am I? I am a construction of words on a page. I am forever mute. I am forever the equivalent of hieroglyphics. My intentions are completely different. Valuing more group decision requiem. They will thrive in this. My game defends with absolute confusion. Lurid phantasm, very good defensive ballclub.

Congrats on the win.

The surprise New Hampshire. The mid car conclusion. So long from Boston. All new tonight. Pop icon makes an event so hot so fueled by rotten dissolutions, pantomime rejections, apple candle fiddlesticks.

Remote delusion.

Seven thirty. Make a decision. Cross the tag of doom. Island misfortune. Island discovery. Thermos and hand glove valiancy appliance decorator half of whom should never be able to purchase machinery. Seriously. Thank cut the Welch chime infinity. Parole and hearing. Marginalia and transgression, parmesan and cinnamon and magnolia. Dissolve three table spoons of unnatural deodorant. Yes and vulvae. Yes and make a note of the missing discrepancies, the radius, the clock tower matchbook insignia. My advanced apologies. My all hollow's eve and goodnight.

******

In a journal entry dated May 13, 2006, Mooney wrote: "Was asked by an interviewer today about my writing habits, my method. I wanted badly to tell the truth: Actually, Ms. Interviewer, I take mind-altering substances and listen to Miles Davis. But I couldn't. I'm not tough enough. I'm too pansy. I'm not American enough. An American never gives a shit what other people think. Americans say what's on their mind without hesitation. I should be more like that, but I'm not. I am an inadequate American."

Reports indicate Mooney rarely consumed alcohol.

Can I—I'm snow?

, philological, dialectal, etymological, phonological, morphological, semantic, grammatical, syntactical
pieces.

241

Confessions in three sections:

ONE

I am the kind of person who would lie to you about never having a birthday party—simply because of how interesting it sounded—and then spend the rest of the week feeling bad about it. Like how I eat all my wife's favorite potato chips and when she asks I tell her that she was the one who ate them the last time she was drinking, even though my wife doesn't drink. I have been married for three years. We eloped because I am not the kind of person who likes big weddings. Just kidding. I'm only playing, of course; my mother would have killed me if we eloped. No, we got married in a church; my sister was her maid of honor. The day I turned eleven I ran away from home because my mother refused to give me a birthday party. I hitchhiked across the United States, from New Hampshire to Los Angeles. Then I met a female mariachi who stole my heart and dragged me to Tijuana, where she treated me like a prince, waited on me, peeled bananas for me, rubbed my feet, washed my hair, rubbed special coconut lotion on my dry hands. This is how I learned Spanish. I am not very fluent though. The thing I loved most about my time in Mexico was the discovery of poetry. It started off as a joke. The female mariachi read Pablo Neruda to me in a funny little Yoda voice. Then she read Lorca like an irritable transvestite and I knew at that moment, without a doubt, that I wanted to be a poet.

TWO

Do you read upside down on the couch with your feet in the air and chocolate milk there by your side? Can you say the Czech alphabet backwards while juggling eggs over a thirty story balcony? Have you ever hotwired a car in downtown Berlin with a safety pin, a screwdriver, and a metal emory board, with the heat encroaching? Are you the sort of person who folds while holding a royal flush just to give the other person a win? Would you ever purposefully misappropriate syntax? Would you orchestrate everything down to the color of the dishtowels, teacups, and magnets? Have you ever not paid your taxes? Do you ever obsess over numbers? Ever set your alarm clock to an even number? What kind of deodorant do you wear? Is it masculine? Can you name a city in France you haven't been? Are there places in the north of Spain that you have never seen? Have you ever planted a tree? Have you ever forgotten a friend's birthday? Ever been caught in a lie and forgot what version of the truth you previously spilled? Have you ever raced across the countryside on a horse in complete rhythm? Ever challenged an anteater to a duel? Ever made your loved one go running? Ever parked on the wrong side of the road? When was the last time you bought a lottery ticket? Watched television? Bought clothes from a thrift store, a shopping mall, or on eBay? Would you even recognize the secret password when it mattered most? Would you leave town? Would you try to dig a tunnel to Japan?

THREE

I was once a Webelo scout; but then they refused to give me a badge for smoking cigarettes so I quit. The powers-that-be in Boy Scout leadership tried to talk to my father, but my father was in Pittsburgh doing business. And my mother never spoke to anyone. Back then, she was terribly misanthropic. I bought a guitar and started playing; but then I got tired of it after a week and never touched it again. There was a brief itch for space camp, but I gave up on that when I found out that people with eyeglasses aren't allowed to go into space. My mother wrote me a note with an excuse so that I never had to participate in gym while I was in middle or high school. During those periods, I walked the halls and disrupted other classes. My favorite dish has always been fried squid. Was it Emerson who said, "You can tell a man by the quality of food he is willing to consume." I am the kind of person who fears germs because everything is utterly filthy and disgusting; I'm on the bus, a guy next to me stuffs his finger up his nose, all the way to his knuckle, twists it around, pulls it out and reaches out the hand to ask someone standing to help him up, this other guy grabs the booger-covered hand unknowingly and pulls the guy up. I vomited a little in my mouth and had to swallow it inconspicuously. For a brief time in middle school I wanted to be a lawyer, to go to Harvard, to one day pledge at a fraternity. I have a hard time staying on topic.

***

Hypothesis #3 Concerning the Disappearance of Marvin K. Mooney

He did not escape this earth, I can assure you. The day Mooney kicks the bucket the world will hear about it. I predict mourning in the streets. I predict open weeping; there really is no telling how far it will go. I hear drums beating, pianos playing soft requiems. Not just yet, I tell them. This pauper Mooney won't let the wave of life go so easily. He'll be back. I believe he will. His ghost is not yet among us. He is corporeal.

***

Mooney told us about these five guys from Arizona who stormed across the country writing fake painkiller prescriptions: how they hustled different Walgreen stores in Seattle and Tacoma and Butte and Cheyenne until they got caught in Denver with expired tags on their stolen Chevy Nova and how one guy cried to the police about his mother who was dying a terrible horrible death in Missouri and how he needed to get back to her pronto while one of the other guys who couldn't really communicate properly told the police he was from the future and wasn't worried about any legal ramifications because he already knew the outcome and the other three didn't even get to speak on their own behalf partly because they were Mexican and partly because they were shy.

But.

Like most of Mooney's stories, we never heard the end because he got too twisted in the telling not so much in the completing, mid-story he'd start a new thread and never really connect anything, like the story of the Mexicans would make him think of Diego Rivera, which would make him think of Trotsky, which would make him spin off on a story about these underground Russian Trotskyites in the fifties and how they attempted to assassinate Stalin with this diabolical plan to seduce him into a wild sex orgy where these three women undressed in his bedchamber and lured his knickers from his hips and ran their tongues all over his hairy body and how one of the women sucked on Stalin's mustache to get him dizzy with sexual ecstasy so that in his euphoric state he wouldn't notice the woman at his midsection who bit off his cock while the other two women screamed to alert the men who were just outside the door waiting to burst in and gag Stalin and tie him to his Imperial dresser so he might die a miserable bloody death by loss of blood from his once large dictator penis.

And then Mooney would laugh.

We never knew what to say, so we just laughed along with him. But historically, I'm not sure that particular event actually happened, but if it did I wonder how long Stalin lived without a penis before he actually died?

The man was a cabinet, nothing more.
In him secrets were forever stored.

Puncture......ancient...
.....................................birds eat................rare.................…..
documents...
....
....
............and the wingspan.........of my family............is.......
destroyed...
....…

A woman named Pippa Hetherington.

Who is the I? Right now speaking. Who are we?

Polyvocal, indeed.

and the wingspan of my family is destroyed.

destroyed = past tense of destroy

to destroy

(—verb—used with object)

to reduce (an object) to useless fragments, a useless form, or remains, as by rending, burning, or dissolving; injure beyond repair or renewal; demolish; ruin; annihilate.

to put an end to; extinguish.

to kill; slay.

to render ineffective or useless; nullify; neutralize; invalidate.

to defeat completely.

ON BEING A SPECTATOR

Why? Is there some event other than the giant woman floating in the sky, eating cupcakes, tethered to the ground like a hot air balloon? After World War II? After Roman chariots and horse races ended in bloodshed, all pleasures-of-Nero style? After centuries of entertainment? Now, with a woman floating in the sky, her big blue dress ballooned out just enough to expose her white thighs to the crowd below, the menstrual stain on her panties, and twelve strong ropes keeping her from drifting into the atmosphere; could there really be anything more real?

ON BEING A FATHER

A grizzly bear ate my imaginary four year old son in one bite.
So I took a butcher knife to its throat and slit the fucker
straight down to his penis, stuck my fingers into the wound and
peeled back the skin like curtains, sliced open the stomach,
reached in and pulled my boy out whole; slapped him on the
back to make him cough and regain his composure. Then I
walked him home on the sidewalk and scolded him for trying
to feed bears.

ON BEING A GOOD BOSS

There exists no word for the fear of scratching o ff a mole. I put them in mason jars. Stack the glass in the cupboards. My three housekeepers drink the contents for their special weekly reward. They never quarrel. They take turns. New moles grow atop the wounds. I wait until they darken and then I pick them off, one by one, to feed the help. And every day my house looks cleaner and cleaner.

ON BEING A GOOD NEIGHBOR

Could you not fuck so loudly? Could you stop slamming doors? Could you smoke less weed? Could you turn down your t.v.? Could you tend to the wounds of your children so their infections don't burst on the sidewalk? Could you mow your lawn? Could you take down the Christmas lights? Could you haul away that automotive carcass on your driveway? Could you bury your dead animals, not throw them in the street? Could you apologize for vomiting over the fence? Could you stop giving me the finger? Stop mooning my children. Stop asking my wife if you can investigate her boudoir. Stop misusing the word boudoir. Stop siphoning gas out of our Dodge. And above all, could you please stop showing up at my work to beg for money and/or forgiveness.

ON BEING A HYPOCHONDRIAC

Do not belong to the cup in front of you. It is a trick. The spout is a galaxy of diseased forefathers who will misunderstand you. Check low radio frequencies for hidden messages: dot-dot-dash; dot-dot; dash-dash-dash. Chlorofluorocarbons. Endometriosis. Attack of the special robotic artillery. Your sleeve catches acute viral nasopharyngitis and blows its nose on your wrist, which you repeatedly wipe on the underbelly of Ohio. Come back around eight and don't bring any more infections. Be a doll and fetch the end. Bring it here so I can taste it. Let the oxygen out. Take the pill. Bait the snake and open all the chicken cages. Take deep breaths. Blood is not the color it pretends. In the end, the page is a garden you have yet to plant. These are your pajamas. There is the sink. Your doctor is just a phone call away.

ON BEING A NARCISSIST

One morning I split open my lip and the blood pooled into the shape of a ship with a sail and everything. I climbed on board and we floated out of my kitchen into the backyard where my wife indiscreetly fondled a bottle of chardonnay for our guests spilling every little secret onto the patio table without polishing them off as I road my blood ship out past our neighbors, way past, clear out into the wheat field where once died many Cherokee Indians and British immigrants and as we past over their graves they poked their heads out of the three-hundred year old dirt and waved goodbye. They weren't skeletons either: they were Cherokee Indians and British immigrants. I knew for sure because that is what they looked like. Most of them were smiling. I wanted to cry, but my lip hurt too badly.

ON BEING A HUMAN

Unlike birds who migrate, we humans bring the weather to us. We invent air conditioners and pellet stoves to heat and cool us. We invent comic books and sing-a-longs and sleepovers and carnivals and Chuck-e-Cheeses and baseball parks and football fields and sixty-screen multiplex theaters to pass our time. We decorate cakes and roller skate. We croak without warning. We build houses. We court lovers. We open up; unlike birds who never gift their subconscious. We make debts and pay them off. We send our kids to college. We make prudent legislation. Birds just fly around. Birds just collect meals and hatch eggs. We do the dishes. We wax the car. We build shopping malls and Rent-A-Centers. We have pharmaceutical companies. We have 401k. Not like the birds, who always look so scatterbrained. We move collateral. We invade foreign countries. We make deals under the table. Birds don't even have tables. Birds don't know how to play softball. We invent liquor. Birds don't. We invent the television show LOST. Birds don't. We make chocolate chip cookies. Birds don't even know how to use the stove. Birds can't do anything. Birds can't add, subtract, or multiply. Birds don't know shit. Birds don't communicate. Birds don't cry. Birds don't help their family out when they are in financial trouble. Birds let wolverines sometimes eat their babies. We do not let wolverines near our babies. We build hospitals to keep the wolverines out.

ON BEING A MARXIST STORYTELLER

Like the origami artist folds paper. Fold cardboard, pineapple, intrigue, and alkaline batteries into a stew to feed the king and royalty. For the blacksmiths, a porridge of stone pudding vis-à-vis Hegel. Below the canopy of rainbows, a baby mountain lion is slaughtered for the customers. In the real world we pay people to hall off and hit us. I pledge allegiance to the flag of the United States of America & to the Republic for which it stands. I wish I may. I wish I might. Have the character changing sentimental ending and really mean it.

ON BEING HONEST

When will you pick up the moon, clean it, polish it, and put it back in a different library bookshelf in Pennsylvania? Or else why not drop it off a cliff where the coyotes and hyenas may devour it? Have you any kind of mercy? Have you cab fare or could you possibly pick up the kids after work? I need a drink. I need a drink very badly.

ON BEING A COUNTY CORONER

To do an autopsy on a baby you must have miniature hands, smaller than those of a horse jockey, smaller than persimmons, dainty enough to extract a tiny kidney or a teeny liver; bendable and capable of never having jitters. To slice children for a living takes courage, detachment, and massive levels of potassium. An ear is a glass cashew, a nose is a crystal pistachio. Eyes are little tapioca bubbles. Such a doctor is not a doctor, but an archaeologist who never confuses food with anatomy. A heart is not a juice box. A brain is not a tomato.

"Writers often insist that they revise, again and again, everything that they write, for writing must be heartbreakingly difficult to be authentic, heartbreakingly and exhaustingly demanding."
—Gilbert Sorrentino, "Sample Writing Sample"
The Moon in Its Flight (2004)

I once wrote an entire book and then threw it away.

"To best command a fleet," said Mooney, "one must get enough sleep."

I will not live as long as you do.
        My Hollywood is closing.

        //////[(This is called throat-clearing)]\\\\\\\\

Here is a hug and a kiss from your parents. They are the guts of your body.

[insert heart story]

THE HOLLYWOOD YEARS
We are their big bang. We are their messy wombfruit.

It is typical for new parents to be nervous.
    This is typical.
        This is.
            This—I could put any word I want—is

                                        SAUCER!

REDO-REDO-REDO

Hang Up Words For Ardor

My heart has four chambers and each chamber has a valve.
My lover, my Aortic, is chomping her gum.
Looking exquisitely coquettish in her powder-pink Betsy
Johnson angel print dress, slit to her hips on either side, her
gecko green Christian Louboutin stilettos showing requisite
red soles. How sweet like brownie batter she smells. Ought not
notice how she's acting like she's someone else. No need to
toss the truth around. No need to remind her how I'm
constantly living homicide. Fake sexy phony. Because I'm still
convinced I want to marry her, even though she wants nothing
of it, because I'm stuck in the muck of needing her. I'm a
broken man caught in a cycle. Diehard fans demand pictures so
we stop on the sidewalk and fake up grins; but they don't want
me, I'm just a screenwriter, they want shots of the famous sex
kitten only, so I step back out of frame. We're in Hollywood,
not safely hidden away in our closed-up private universe on
the beach at my place, or up at her place in Burbank with the
decked-out interior design; we're walking into Toi, some posh
restaurant she begged to go, where we had to have the pumpkin
tofu because some asshole in the cast of the new movie she's in
keeps filling her head with all this trendy new age mumbo
jumbo. Recommending restaurants like he's Casanova. Prick.
But like usual, she's gone chatterbox. Squeeze. How she talks
nineteen to a dozen. Smell of exhaust and rubbish, almost raw
sewage disgusting. Torn into multiple odious stab wounds. Me
after three vodkas, maybe too much blow, down Sunset
Boulevard, nine thirty, cranky as the get out, smoking smokes
and staggering. Not staggering exactly. No. Motion swaying
sveltely. Yes. Crushing coked-out folktales with my arm
around her waist. "Listen now." I say. "I mean they robbed
her. She won't say it, she loved dad too much, but they robbed

her. They did. I should've done something. I should've slit that mortician's throat and took him up to the mountains near Pikes Peak, thrown him over to the bears. Nobody would've ever known. Nobody. I mean, come on. Fifteen thousand dollars for a casket? Is he out of his mind?" My lover chomped her gum and made a noise like she were coughing. Completely dismissed me. In truth, now that I see her in the right light, she isn't beautiful at all. Her hair is hideous red beaver glare on whitewashed porcelain china. When I returned last night from Colorado, I should not have agreed to see her. It should have been the end. We should have been quite over.

This is an autoportrait of December as best I can give it. See the ghosts of my parents on the beach in Santa Monica and remember that. Picture Mother as a squat woman rather shaped like a radish with kinky grey hair short to her scalp, and see father as always in dumpy clothes, gangly like a rodent with a widow's peak. Picture the sun setting over the Pacific, sky jubilant pastel tropical. Tide sizzling and fizzling on shore. This is not the beginning of the story, it's the end. But soon it will begin again and I will be back with my lover, although even after our huge fight in Las Vegas and my eventual solo trip to Colorado, I will, as always, return unexplainably to her arms. You will see. I'll be walking down Sunset Boulevard with her again, into a restaurant called Toi, living the life I don't really want to be a part of. Why? Certainly this is more than just a long jumbled course of calamities. History whispers angioplasty recovery is painful cyclical. Heart attacks. Goddamn my past begetting me.

Say stones thrown from memory mountains equals Colorado Rockies. Sweeping into Fort Collins from the grey morning sky mountainside crawling through thick atmosphere par infantile. Airplane falls the victim. Down, down, down, towards streets called Mulberry then College then Washington.

But don't get ahead. The airplane comes later. Try to keep globe lit present. Lamp contemporary. Give the x-ray of my heart and steam off frothy recollection nightmares.

See her, spot her, pick her out of a crowd.

My mother, my Tricuspid, comes carrying crocodile skins. Both arms loaded, long-nosed heads hanging to one side, battle ram tails to the other. Great crisp scaly shelter turned textile mod gaudy. Happy Madison Avenue vultures will descend ripe wickedly on handbags stitched with the skins. Mother makes a buck and we eat pleasant food. If we speak linear, this is back in time. Go non-diegetic sound. See picture with silence. Mother through the throng of Farmers Market shoppers, an oversized straw hat hanging against her back on a string around her neck, sunglasses slipping off her nose, crocodile skins stacked up to her chin, it's not easy, see the strain of the weight in her neck muscles tightened. I'm her knee-high or less little boy, but I'm not there. This is what I call pseudo-imaginary. She's alone, but for the strangers, but for the hawkers and suckers hot-potato passing merchandise between themselves. Mother smiles and I know it's honest because no one else is watching. I may be making this all up. I may not remember. But no matter what, she is my right ventricle pumping blood to all my organs except my lungs.

Father is my Pulmonic valve for breathing.

Seeking solace in the idea of gills in outer space; or, some other non-terrestrial example of love; for he did most certainly fail miserably. No, not to be forgotten how he kept my blood moving in the right direction, but were it not so darkly tainted I could see. He is left ventricle for blood to lung communication. I smoke to make him suffocate. Each cigarette makes a difference so I smoke two packs a day. Pause to face his image. Shave your beard, old man. Comb your hair for once. Express yourself in different ways than hunting jackets and overalls.

No need to nullify. Once he took me fishing. Just he and I out on a rented boat with our rented gear, but he didn't speak the entire time. I watched him wrestle with a couple rainbow trout, I never got a bite, and at the end of the day the only thing he said was, "You're very disappointing," and then he shook his head and held my face with his eyes.

My sister is my Mitral, pump, pump.
Once, before I knew what love was, love is, love could ever be, I loved her so bloody unconditionally. But now she's gone ground I won't set foot upon. Ring on the rim of a time we shared footsteps through forest searching caves for dinosaurs. Nobody else to wrestle away her affection. Father gone to hide. Inside, I must of jumped and danced because I still do now when I marinate on it. True she was obstructive, I'm not forgetting everything. Calories not burned. Things such as this. Introduction to cocaine candyland. Little matchboxes full of baggies sporting white by the gram. Free for the first few times. Quick. Quick. Quick. Got way too loud. "Don't go be all debutante," in the mirror she rehearsed, "all faux crunk mythically!" She did-herself-in wickedly. Quite literally. My sister sunk to the sleaziest slums. Did shit you hear about in horror pictures; across the border shit with who-knows-what objects or animals and/or how many. Bottomed out and marked up like a wall of graffiti with tats and scratches and bruises and sores and piercings and scars and stretch marks like tire tracks. Probably lived in a cage. My poor, poor mitral valve.

Out in the backlot at Sony slash Fox Studios, walking around the production bungalows, poking my head into different soundstages to see the construction of other people's movies, smoking, listening to a group of extras dressed in Victorian garb speak Russian. I prepared to face down the studio with my screenplay in my holster, prepared to

264

clear my throat and explode with enthusiasm, bravado, charisma and all that. I'd sell them my fucking idea. Took a final drag on the smoke to kill my father a little more before entering the building. Straightened my tie. Sampled my smile and introduction in the reflection on the glass door. Saw a bit of all four valves in my complexion.

My sister used to treat me like Nosferatu.
At cathedral, she's nine and I'm seven, just after communion, returning to our places in the pew. She sits down next to me smiling which makes me smile. Then she reaches over and takes my hand and holds it with our fingers interweaved. Came out of nowhere. Made me feel so connected. My heart beat perfectly. My feet, too short to reach the ground, are swinging giddy, my dimples brimming. She's wearing her crushed red velvet dress with the white bow in her hair. I'm wearing a blue butterfly collar under a yellow sweater and my dress slacks. Father polished my shoes right before we all got into the car. My sister is diamond beaming. She squeezes my hand. I giggle. And then she leans close to me, puts her mouth right by my ear. I prepare to hear a secret. And then she whispers, "You're God's biggest mistake."

My lover hired a stylist to decorate her apartment,
ricochet heartthrob. Per verse tragedy. Some out-of-work day-time soap star hunk. Real manly man. Buff, ripped, and into car engines, watches football religiously. Had me sweating something serious. Didn't even look to see if she was there, I stormed right past, slammed the front door loudly, no need for turning my head, what goes unseen with her and some dumb fuckface goes unknown historically. What happens when I'm not around is fair game goddamn deplorably. After pitching my new script to those fake ass relaxed Armani suits with Brazilian leather briefcases, after wrangling my tongue, squirming like a prisoner, averting my eyes as much as

possible, hoping to get a smile, a small executive chuckle, something. Instead, I got long faces like the Florida peninsula. "No Sir, no bundle, didn't think I needed it." They ask, I say no. No bundle. No package. No director attached. No actors signed on, it's just the script. My stupid agent said nothing beforehand. Now, hanging cowbell jaws swivel to share a mutual look of trains leaving the station. Fox Studios says they certainly are not interested. I was home, not mine but hers, equipped now with Burberry throw pillows and 19th century inspired Gaultier curtains thanks to the fuckface male model interior designer with a hankering for style and a friendship with the director of The Cook, The Thief, His Wife, and Her Lover, who happens to always be over, helping my lover "think about ways to brighten the bedroom while still keeping the darker tones." I was in no mood for disappointment. Hell bent and serious, I wanted to tie my lover to the bed and say forget it, goodbye, it's over. I can do without my Aortic valve. Wish to paint clear enough a picture. Teakettle fashionably broken. Just absolutely sick of it, bushed from playing the supporting role. Goddamn drained from it. Being in her shadow. A matter of being continually chopped on the block. Quartered. Slice-slice into muddles. Right. Instead, I'm mute. That's how I learned to be. "Has anybody read this? Directors? Actors?" No. I'm afraid not, Mr. Executives. No bundle. No package. Sorry. Thinking worst case scenario, I could pull out my lover's name—drop it—say she's interested in playing the lead. Just scribble out a lie and get them wet for it. Those people love my lover. She's an automatic Green Light. They'd be sick over each other thanking me. But I can't bring myself to do it. "You guys are getting First Look," I say. Yawn. They could give a shit. I want to start crying. I can feel the hairs on my cheeks rise. I want to plead to them, "Please, I came to this city to build a new life. To get away."

266

Unfortunately, those goddamn suits see money signs voraciously. Myopically. Not a one of them honors the human condition. They don't want to hear the story. They don't care what it's about. All they want to know is who's attached. How much box office can they project? Bottom lines. Numbers. Money fucking money. Think money, more money, can't get enough money. Need it greedy need it. Eat it sleep it fuck it, money. It never mattered anyway. They'd made up their minds before we even got into that rotten florescent room. I was out the door wondering why they even took the meeting in the first place if they already knew they didn't want to do my picture? Had my lover, in her sheer disappointment, orchestrated the whole mock meeting behind my back? Had she pitied me so severely that she called in a favor, asked someone nicely, threw her weight around on my behalf? Am I the pathetic tagalong who gets thrown the occasional salvage for being with someone important?

In disgust I leave the crooked metropolis of Loss Angles, its muzzled effluvia, condensed caldron of ambition, to escape The Industry as well as past life regression. To avoid transgression. I could answer the phone when my sister calls and return to Colorado, or I could run away—so I choose to flee and beg my lover to accompany me. Work is just not doable right now, not possibly likely or remotely considerable. And family is worse than work. Lose now my lover? I cannot do without. No amount of coke can help me cope. If I stay in LA, I'll be plagued by gravity, so, no thanks. I'm better in outer space, just like father taught me. Love? For what? I mean, why now be summonsed? Let the lawyers handle what's left of mother and father's estate. Why bother me? Let my sister money grub and choke phony blasphemous. Was she even at mother's funeral? Cry a tropical storm silly melancholy reactionary. Pose and make your face look sympathetic. Daddy had his little girl. I

267

couldn't possibly hate him more. I will not return to see him buried. I object to caring. Fine? Wash my hands with it, scrub up in truck stop restroom and be done with it.

Stupid celestial majesty. Stupid vault of night.

Buy-buy Hollywood. Head out east to Las Vegas proper to forget work and father's death like serum from apothecary. No more history revision or edits needed. Be it Final Cut. Let time endeavor to bless me perpetually inexhaustibly forever. Ruminate on the meaning of Death Valley as I drive past going ninety. Father and mother gone split ridiculous ending. Just me and my cracked-up sister left gawking, left standing around with warm entrails in our arms. Neither of us sure what to do or where to go or how to be. She in Colorado close to father's death, and me in Santa Monica wanting to get even farther away were it not for the ocean and Hollywood blocking. My sister is alive and so is my lover. They are my heart remaining. Right and left atria hold returned blood then release it into the right and left ventricles, my now dead ventricles.

This moment,

with my lover in the car to Vegas, is no different than the last moment regardless and never ending chimera. Such sickening repetition. Does she speak? No, no, of course not. It would be too much to ask. Does she ever give a clue? Any little bits of herself for the sharing? Ever say so of her past? About the twenty-nine years before I knew her? Forget it. I'm not investment worthy. I'm a stop temporary on the side of a desert road. A habit to her. I joke, "Father use to hold me up by my throat against a wall, he had to use both hands to get me a foot or so off the ground, to make his point, to feel real manly and all, and his face would get red like a plum, almost purple. From the third person, he must have looked ridiculous." No smile. She's a hydraulically sealed vault. I'm rabbit pellets bouncing off her Kevlar. Better she knows than to be vulnerable. This is such. So then goddamn the tyranny of my optimism. How sadly it sheer conflates with desperation for a strong aorta. Willing to take the loneliness of her company versus being alone.

Father coming into the house after baseball practice at the cages,
I'm eleven, and he's angry with me for missing so many pitches. Didn't speak to me on the entire drive home. Pulmonic silence. Maybe if he would've had a job he would've been gone to it instead of always being around. Always lurking. If only I could've been so lucky. To halt his endless position on the couch with potato chips and soda pop and television. To end my daily embarrassment. To hide my sister. I wished I could've employed him myself just to make him disappear.

I've learned a clever plastic surgery repair.
How to patch up the damaged implosions. Acting like it's love when it's really over, when it's really, really over. Driving past Barstow with my lover in the shotgun seat silent. A little coke in the nose. Unflinching, I ate the black and white night rushing towards me with my eyes. Tickers ticking hyphens. Bug gut splotches paint the windshield. Absent moonglow, surroundings shrouded in thick steel wool blankets on either side sealing us in a moldy sarcophagus. I catch sight of falling stars as if they were being sprinkled from a salt shaker. Make countless wishes. She's here with me. My lover. Quietly monitoring my handle of the wheel, making comment on my swerving with her eyebrows, checking my speed incessantly. See: Cardiomyopathy. Without use of either ventricle, as mother and father are gone, the heart grows abnormally enlarged, begins to thicken. Stricken. She's a broken isthmus. Missing much important levity. Wait. Look. No marriage in her future, see it lack in her smile fumble when she mumbles the word love. Love. Love.

Mother took me to see Annie
at the theater in old town when I was four or five. We went to a
hobby store first and got supplies to make jewelry boxes even
though I didn't own any jewelry. My sister liked jewelry, not
me. Mother told me there was nothing wrong with a boy
having a jewelry box. I could keep whatever I wanted in it, but
wouldn't it be nice to make something of my very own? My
sister was off with father. I don't recall a single frame of the
movie, I just remember mother at the hobby store smiling,
holding out a jewelry box just for me.

Collapse from block on block walking
when we get to Vegas. Tropicana Boulevard to Desert Inn.
Strip staring, neon fantasy bastion. Slot machines jingle, tick
tick tick—coins clinking expelled from guts of slot into
aluminum trays like medical surgery apparatus. Umbilical
cords stretching from machines to belts on sixty year old ladies.
My lover with auburn hair, tiny nostrils and ears, plays for
broke and comes up short. Think of father with mother's
paycheck. Dice on tables fall. Mother making dinner with
arthritic fingers, father watching television. Roulette spins
black and red rainbow. Father dancing with my sister at
cotillion. Smoke makes casino look dungeon. Astrological
design. Loss in one, loss in another. All in doubt until the
identity of my lover becomes known. Then, miraculously, free
tickets to Cirque de Soleil and room comps come fast and easy
as if Vegas participates in fourth dimension reality. Pluralistic
duality. My famous lover parts such big waves. Everywhere she
goes she ranks currency. Legions in her aftermath, even here
where Los Angeles seems eons away and Colorado gets
bludgeoned by fake Paris façade. After pocketbook depression,
after long line waiting for inadequate buffet, refusal to eat
luxurious, after tonsil searching body exploring four position
tattoo checking, after sheets ripped from bed in melodramatic

fashion, morning comes sassy dancing forward unaware. Back to shower, shave, cocaine and toothpaste. Back to fidgeting through another day. Conference call with execs at Castle Rock and Warner Brothers. Motors bantering, proverbial penises on table for measuring. I get in two words edgewise. "Be back…" I say, before I am reminded that no one cares. I'm just a writer. They say goodbye to each other and I wonder why I was even asked to be in on the conference.

The last time I saw father he played crippled. I wanted to sit him down and teach him method acting. Explain the theory of motivation behind his actions. Seriously, he did miserable. "Could you bring me the remote control?" he goes, couched on the sofa like always in the mold he'd spent thirty-six years creating. With the most obvious deliberation, he eyebrow scrunched to assume pathetic saying, "I don't have the energy to get it." What shit. Mother dead turns man who use to be independent into man who never learned to manage on his own. For him impossibly. Said he didn't know how to cook, didn't even know how to turn on the oven. What, did he forget? Was it not like riding a bike? Washing machine scared him, so he went weeks in the same clothes until he smelled so bad the cats would not come near him. It's a wonder the cats never starved. I imagine my sister took care of them as she took care of him, however secretly. Father was falling apart. He wasn't eating. Even when my sister brought him hot meals he wouldn't touch them. No. He was starving himself because he wanted to waste away. And a large part of me hoped he would. But I got him the remote control, handed it to him, eyed his eyes and said, "I'm sorry you lost your wife." Air got oatmeal thick. Remote removed from my hand, he opened his mouth to speak but nothing came out. Look like vivid recollection. Closed his mouth. I stood my ground. To leave without a response, I couldn't do. But believe me he felt the

271

shoving arms inside my eyes even though he made no effort to pay attention. Heavy handed hearted readily departed. Without looking, he spoke mock quietly, "She was your mother." And that was all. I knew it. And since nothing else could be said, I got in my car and crossed borders till I hit ocean.

So, I haven't said it yet, but my lover lost the glow, lost the age old atom bomb blew up explosion rocking thermo diacritical markings into hieroglyphic arrangements. Las Vegas was such the perfect backdrop. I must explain specifically. See: total cardio hemorrhaging. Born into a valley raining shards of glass. Whirlpool confetti shrapnel. Pink, green, clear. Slicing and puncturing my helpless body. No more indecision buoy. Wish to find a strong umbrella. For behind her eyes plays tempestuous villainy. Shadow pictures flicker when I catch her watching me. Given potency, she should've hit the floor with drink. Should've lost her lunch in the ladies room, but nothing. Absolutely nothing could stop her. Through walls she went walking. Me? I had no season. December or not, famous or not. Because I love her, because she's my aorta, because I told her the secrets about my father. Each vocal measurement chopped the tree. Happened quick like a sprained ankle. My lover upside-down furious at each detail of father's hidden sickness. I'm saying to myself, "No, this isn't happening." Time snaps photo-tornados spinning whirling phonebooks at my head. Out and out screaming. Disgust became molasses in the air. I'd lost everything in one hand and I could barely breathe to finish speaking. One little slip up, call it what you will, and she hates me more than a thousand baby-killing Hitler-loving Christians. Said the day I die the world will bloom great roses. Tick, tick, tick. Heart murmur. Piecing little scraps of history together to reveal a hideous repulsive cretin. "I am not my father," I say. But she fears I will be,

272

someday. "He is a monster," she says. "That means you too will be a monster, too." Her future cannot contain a monster. "You are not my future," she says. "And to be quite honest, you're just barely my right now." Never should I have let myself be vulnerable. Never should I have told the truth. Never should I have confessed my most secret of secrets of all. This is exactly why men should not be vulnerable. Ever. Never ever. Men should be the wiser. Men should know that secrets make their way back round to being daggers. Should've kept my mouth shut. Should've never said.

Father too waxed inappropriate.

Felt obliged to overcompensate. Trying always to be the manliest man with shoulders back and women in the kitchen, women doing laundry, having babies subservient glorification. Oh what wrong he taught me. The way I sat in third grade watching one girl after another thinking sex and domination. Thinking one of them would make a cherry wife. How my sister came to idolize father I will never know. Or maybe I do know, but simply will not say. Perhaps he was more to her than he should have been. Father saying women should speak when spoken to, and no objections. Rules come from bible and church and history and morals and ethics more ancient than words. He with such lack of those things. He with such perversion. "Treat them like they're goddesses, my boy, but treat them like they're women."

Mother must have worried so. She must have felt disastrous.

See her there in the dim-lit washroom wringing out socks and underpants to hang over the rusty shower rod. Basket full of wet clothes and two more piles to get started. Smudge of grease on her forehead from fixing the lawnmower earlier. Me walking in, six years old and smiling, showing her a toy I was fond of, and her leaning down and kissing me on the cheek and me running off plum pleased and confident.

So now if now is now, but it's not.

Now is then and then is what the future hates. I know it's hard to grasp. Attempt to compress the past in present tense or future in the past. Life remembers things not yet done and forgets things we wish for and live up to without forgetting. Heart beats are universal. We all know rhythm from our internal drum. Mine just happens to be sooty muck ruddy and tarnished. Forever in a droning cycle of repetition. Forever diseased for something I had no control over.

Mother getting on a plane at Stapleton Airport with her crocodile skins to sell to vendors in New York City; or, going wherever it was she always disappeared to for months at a time. Gone again till until then. Now it's just me, my father, and my sister. Again. Hushed-up romance and sickening. Tricuspid failure. My sister's birthday. Hiding my report card from father. Absolutely nothing made a difference. Like talking to my lover, mother wouldn't listen when I asked her not to go. She helped me put on my jacket before we left for the airport and I asked her and she said she couldn't stay, not this time, but she'd be back for sure she thought. Perhaps. Most likely. How I cried and cried and cried. I haven't stopped crying.

Can you see me standing out in the cold? I'm only about nine years old. At the bus stop waiting to go to school, dressed warm with extra layers for the winter. I've got my science project with me. It's a three foot robot made out of Plexiglas, coffee cans, and electrical wire. Inside, it has a tape recorder that plays a tape of Supertramp when I use a remote control to work it. There's my sister, ever grumpy and unkind. See her kicking snow at me? She unzips her mauve colored jacket, reaches inside and brings out a picture of me crying in the bathtub when I was two or three. She says she's going to show everybody on the bus and tell them I'm still a big crybaby.

Right before I leave for Colorado, at my lover's place in Burbank,

I cut myself. Just a nick on the thumb, but deep. Blood all over the couch in her living room. She's asleep in her bed. I shouldn't have even been there, to be honest. We hadn't spent the night together. Early I was up and over to her house, stuck my key in the door and slid in quietly so as not to wake her. I was fixing to just leave her a note but somehow I got cut, it doesn't matter how, and instead of running to the bathroom to get a bandage I decided to drip the blood all over her couch. So it wasn't an accident, the blood on the couch. It was planned. I wanted to paint the beige Egyptian cotton sofa with my carnage.

LAX is such a complex mathematical equation.

I get there an hour before my flight and still I barely catch the plane. In the air I gulp a couple tequilas, almost vomit on the landing, get in an argument with some lughead over luggage, rent a Firebird and drive the hour and a half up to Ft. Collins. Slideshow panorama of places past, where winter still wants to keep its hands on the place. I forget the highway, stare out at the vast snow-topped land, the mountains backlit ominous, sky purple and sherbet-orange, the fields abandoned till late spring, houses out beyond the farmland look haunted. Daunting.

I see that dead sonofabitch in his casket.

Quietly Beethoven plays. I stand above father's lifeless body and all I can think is that he looks exactly as he always had. Unmoved. If only we could bury him on that goddamn couch. I don't cry. I don't get choked up. I notice only the hairs in his ears. Realize funerals are uncomfortable. My sister makes a fool of mourning, spilling her water on our uncle, weeping like a widow for our father. Any other actor would've been fired. If

275

it were my show, I'd have pulled the plug, stopped financing, Red Light no more nothing. Both of them looked ridiculous, dead father and weepy sister. Tell the studio to get a new Director. My weepy sister is atrocious and father can't even play dead.

Truncated apologies go round.

Slip. Slip. Sorry. Pedestal descending, open range of emotional gaslight trickery. Succumb to new unusual strategy. My sister in orange Marc Jacobs Mary Janes, a green and purple Proenza Schouler color blocked silk chiffon dress cinched with a white satin belt, still trying to be the life of the party circa 1988, her hair frizzed and sprayed with glue, eyes as always sullen. Mother lurks in her midsection. I try to ask her how she's feeling. She says nothing. I can see father's fingerprints all over her. "How much was the casket?" I ask, "This funeral? How much did all of this cost?" She makes tight with her lips and looks away. I'm in my yellow Ralph Lauren sweater, my hair a mess per usual. "I want to help pay for it," I say, "Just tell me how much." Cross section, quadrangle, typhoid on her face. She shows me that she hates me by tapping her Marc Jacobs Mary Janes loudly, crossing her arms and crooking her jaw in a curious way that makes me know she wishes it were me in the cemetery and not father. Without blinking she says, "The casket alone was fifteen thousand."

Dumb compassion show.

Ft. Collins pangs the tendrils in my chest spread out like cobweb to left arm throbbing. Shortness of breath. Back along the sidewalk in Hollywood walking into that posh restaurant on Sunset Boulevard called Toi. My lover stops for the fan who wants the photo without me. Again I step away and watch her assume that fashionista pose, the come hither. Always the same never-changing disappearing fantasy. All of this has yet to happen. Has already happened. Will never happen. Butcher up the grey when it comes to love. Secrets and words for love. Cast off management of heart disease. Think about the flight back to Santa Monica, walking down to the ocean to see the ghost of my mother and father on the beach just north of the pier, even though neither one of them ever set foot in California. Sun setting sparkle on the glass top of ocean. No one else for miles and miles. Empty all up the coast. Seagulls calling. Smell like the kelp on the shore. It was them. Is them. Always will be them.

My ventricles healed imaginary.

Think about the word abandon.

Responses from Neighbors

[The following responses come from interviews conducted shortly after Mooney disappeared, in the summer of 2007.]

The Doddridge Family

Weldon Doddridge

This probably don't mean nothing, but not once in all the years I lived here did Mooney ever say hello. He never smiled, never even acknowledged my existence. I used to steal his Sunday paper every once in a while; he would walk out and see that I'd taken it, then turn right back around and forget it, without looking up, without any sorta emotion at all: like it was a routine or something.

Jeffery Wentz Doddridge

I knew Mr. Mooney real well. He was like a brother, if by brother you mean boyfriend. I am not alone. There's a whole lot of people in this neighborhood who've been in Mr. Mooney's basement, if you know what I mean. Mr. Mooney liked to have a good time.

Elizabeth Doddridge

My one son, Jeffy, spent a lot of time with that writer guy Mooney. Jeffy idolizes him or something. Now he wants to be some kind of writer or something when he grows up or whatever. He went about lessons with that writer guy Mooney pretty regularly. Guy never charged us nothing for the lessons either. Boy seemed to like it, said he learned a bunch. I never really met the writer guy Mooney. My husband always thought he was queer, like a gay fella or something. I couldn't tell yuh. He always smiled at me at the co-op, always held the door open for me at the pet store or the donut shop or wherever. I seen him help somebody broke down on the side of the road once. I know he had a bunch of cats and that he bought Girl Scout cookies from Penny, so he was a fine enough fella by me.

Gaspar Doddridge

Jeff says he was cool. I never talked to him. I read one of his stories once. The one about the circus, the history of the circus or whatever. I read it in a class and then I watched this Jodorowsky movie called <u>Santa Sangre</u> where a woman with no arms starts a no-arm cult, and in this one scene blood comes out of a dead elephant's trunk and then it cuts away to the protagonist in a bathroom in front of a mirror bent over a sink and all this blood gushes out of his nose in like perfect matching shots, back and forth between the kid and the elephant, both bleeding out of their noses; it was awesome! And the knife thrower in that movie was crazy, plus the tattooed lady, but Mooney's story or essay or whatever it was, it was cool. I liked the part about the glass eye with a fish in it. It would have been cooler if it had armless women or more bleeding animals, for sure.

Penny Doddridge

I hated him.

The Sheffield Family

Ernie Sheffield

I took writing classes with Marvin K. Mooney. Me and like five other guys in the neighborhood. I couldn't have gotten into the MFA program I got into without his help. He would tell us, "Story comes from the dialectic of a character's wants and needs. Do not think story, think sentence." I remember this one time when he showed us a Chuck Close painting where Close used individual fingerprints to construct twelve-foot portraits, then Mooney said, "This is not inconsequential, this is something to marinate on." He loved telling us to marinate on things. "Marinate on that for a moment," he'd say. During that period of my life I did a lot of marinating.

Anna Sheffield

All because of Mr. Mooney, our son is a published writer on his way to a master's degree. Mooney was a godsend. Ernest always tells people he owes his success to Mr. Mooney, and I believe him. That man was very kind to those boys. He would call me and rave about how talented he thought Ernest was; how certain he was that Ernest would be a success. Pretty often. He really believed in Ernest and many times put in good word with certain publishers on Ernie's behalf. I'm thankful for Mr. Mooney, and I'm saddened by his disappearance.

Alvin Sheffield

We used to go to the horse track together, but once we got there he wouldn't ever want to sit with me. He drove us out, paid for my ticket, bought my first beer, but after that he would hand me the program and tip his hat. I wouldn't see him again until the final race, at the front gate, where he would either be belligerent over a loss or ecstatic from win. It was always one or the other. He never came out of a race lukewarm, that's for sure. Wherever he is, I'm betting he's near the ponies.

Cal Pendergrass

He was a great guy, a real nice guy. I liked him, I really did. He was always friendly. Knew a lot about basketball. Me and him would drink together down at the pub. He always drank bourbon with a splash of cherry syrup from the maraschino bin. Called it a John Updike. We'd talk basketball and that guy would cry his eyes out over the Lakers. The year Phil quit and they traded Shaq to Miami, the year after somehow losing the championship to Detroit, with the dream team of Gary Payton, Karl Malone, Kobe Bryant, and Shaquille O'Neal. Marvin wept for days. He started smoking cigarettes again after quitting for like three years. My girlfriend bought him flowers. It was sad. I felt bad for him. He never talked about his writing though. I guess he kept that part of his life a secret. I mean, everybody knew he was a writer of some kind. I never asked if that was what he did for a living, but I've certainly had fun trying to guess what he did in my head. I've imagined him doing some kind of computer work, or else maybe living off a gigantic trust fund. Once, I imagined that he was a secret agent: I think he'd once mentioned something about living abroad, maybe he said he lived in Africa. Thus, I was convinced for a long while that he was an agent of some kind. I liked Mooney, but he was a strange guy.

We live across the street from his house; our house faces his. He had a grip of cats. Sara regularly saw him walk the fat ones around the block on leashes like little furry dachshunds. Elizabeth never saw it because Elizabeth never woke up after dawn. Anyway, we always invited him to Thanksgiving. One year Sara cornered him at the co-op and asked him how many cats he had; he said he couldn't remember. But you would remember something like that, wouldn't you? I mean, how could you <u>not know</u> how many animals you had to feed? To be honest, at that moment I thought he was either totally fucking insane or a pathological liar; either way, I never felt comfortable around him again. It's not that he ever looked at either of us funny or nothing, I mean, he never seemed lecherous or nothing like that, but yet he was still creepy kinda sorta in a weird way. He was weird. Very weird.

The Hurlbert Family

Ted Hurlbert

Mooney taught me how write, sure, but more importantly he taught me how to ignore my inner critic. Some kids go forever enslaved to theirs. Not me. I'm free and clear. Mooney showed me how to confront my fears and overcome them in creative ways. As he would always tell us, "Without a plan there is no attack, without attack there is no victory." I now have a plan and am in attack mode, set for victory. What that means, I do not know. But I'm not beating myself up about anything anymore, thanks to Mooney. I marinate on everything. It works. I'm convinced. The proof is in the output. See where I'm at right now: this house, these cars, a plasma television set, a surround sound theater in my bathroom, all kinds of toys, not to mention the money piling up in my saving account. I'm golden, on account of Mooney's training. I lead a very successful life and aim to be even more so in the very near future.

Zed Hurlbert

Like my brother, I studied with Mr. Mooney. I thought he was pretty mean. He screamed a lot. He was really angry. He made Jeff Doddridge cry a couple of times. He never really liked anything I wrote. As a matter of fact, I don't think he ever said one nice thing to me. At the top of one of my stories he wrote: "After the first paragraph I found absolutely no compelling reason to continue." I would've quit going, but my brother said it would help me to get into college, since Mooney was famous or whatever. He smoked a lot of grass; he always reeked of it. I think he smoked it in the basement. Jeff Doddridge used to go down into the basement with Mr. Mooney all the time and they would come back up with really red eyes all glazed over, each with a grimace. I never ended up asking Mooney for a letter of recommendation because I was afraid he would write some-thing mean or detrimental.

Clyde Hurlbert

Both the boys really liked him; he seemed to treat them with dignity and I think he taught them a great deal. Theodore is doing wonderfully for himself. Zedrick is making good pro- gress. I actually never met Mooney, but I know his work quite well. I teach his story "Hang Up Words For Ardor" (the one about the screenwriter dealing with the death of his father), in a screenwriting course I teach at the community college. I like most the California stories. I haven't read much of the other stuff: the histories or the sci-fi or the surreal stuff, and I haven't read any of the poetry. I guess I just really only know a little about his writing, but I like what I've read. I'd be willing to read more.

Sally Hurlbert

He didn't like to go to the grocery store alone. He said it really depressed him. So, once or twice a week, he and I did our grocery shopping together. I met him in the shopping cart area, just inside the store. He was always there before me. Said he was chronically early to everywhere. We didn't really talk. Once we entered the store we had a pattern that twisted through produce and bakery and then fish stuff on past the red meats and the birthday cards up around the dairy and through the coffee and the frozen foods. He liked to look at the alcohol, but I never saw him buy any. We had that ritual since '96, what, eleven years or so? A long time. He never asked me anything and I never asked him anything: we just walked, pushed our carts, him always behind me, following me as if he needed me to guide him through the motions. One time I had to miss one of our shopping runs, and Marvin wrote me a strongly worded email excoriating my character and what not. It hurt my feelings, but it blew over. In fact, he and I had gone shopping together the morning he disappeared. Actually, I think I might've been one of the last people to see him. He seemed the same as ever; but now that I think back, I think he might have seemed a little more gloomy than normal. He said to me once —that is to say, he did every so often engage in conversation, he was not in fact absolutely silent; in fact, on occasion he would start talking and the things that man would say could break your heart; sure, I cried a few times when we went shopping together: I don't know how you couldn't—"Sally, the secret I've never told anybody is this: I'm not who you think I am." That always haunted me. Still, to this day, I don't know what he meant by it^^^^^^^^^^^^^^^^^^^^^^^^^^^^^^^^^

^^^

^^^^^^^^^^^^^^^^^^^^^

^^^^^^^^^^
^^^^^^^^^^additional material destroyed, will be destroyed, has been destroyed, do not convey additional materail additional material does nto exist

END CHAPTER chapitre de fin

***

Hypothesis #4 Concerning the Disappearance of Marvin K.
Mooney

There are many good reasons to want to disappear from society, just as there are many bad reasons. There are also many good ways to disappear from society and there are many bad ways, too.

So how does Mooney fit?

My theory is not quantum mechanics, not spiritual, not logical, not even economical; my theory is not aesthetic nor is it political; my theory is not dual or binary or even tripartite. My theory is called Disengagement Theory. It is my contention (via my interpretation of Deleuze) that engagement is futile. The house will always win. Mooney was a strong believer in my theory. He and I frequently corresponded. We met often in Los Angeles and discussed our perspectives.

Here is one of his letters to me, which I believe gives a clue as to his whereabouts:

> To answer the major question, "How can you be sure that 'the house' itself did not distribute the idea "The house will always win"?" I would remind you of something Chairman Mao said in his "Talks at the Yenan Forum on Literature and Art" (May 1942):
>
> "We are Marxists, and Marxism teaches that in our approach to a problem we should start from objective

facts, not from abstract definitions, and that we should derive our guiding principles, policies and measures from an analysis of these facts."

The objective fact is: the house always wins. That's the reason why it's the house. If it didn't win, then it wouldn't be the house. (Casino as quintessential example of circular logic.)

This is not to say that individuals cannot experience small victories, on the contrary: there must be small victories or else no one would play. Small victories are a form of incentive. But inherent in them is the problem.

To take this analogy out of the casino and into the "real world" this means that individuals must occasionally see small victories in order that they will continue to participate otherwise they might become apathetic or - gasp! - unwilling to engage. This would be bad for the house, since the house needs individuals to maintain it. So a small victory here and there is actually part of the house's plan: Let them think they're making headway, then they will continue to feed us.

But at the end of the day, the house will stand. This is, as Mao would have it, an objective fact.

So, then, where does that leave us? I agree with you, MLA, Zizek is urging us to develop our critical thinking skills, but I disagree with you when you suggest that he is advocating the "deployment of

288

challenges to hegemony." That idea seems to be missing the point entirely. Action is exactly the opposite of what Zizek's suggesting. "Instigating revolutionary change," as you put it, would mean action, yet Zizek has clearly asserted that "We must withdraw."

In other words, action is participation and participation is not working.

Now is the time to stop participating.

To bring it back to your <u>Sublime Object of Ideology</u> analogy, so long as the people participate in the kingdom the king will have power. But if the people stop participating, the king loses his power.

Remember: any act against the state only legitimizes the state.

Thus, as they say in Vegas, the only way to win is not to play.

This, to me, is one of the liberating concepts D&G invite us to consider. How exactly they make this suggestion could be the topic of a different conversation. For now, I think the important thing to think about is this notion of disengagement, which I don't see as "a mode of defeat or acceptance."—as you put it.

To think of disengagement in those terms means that your perspective is based on a premise constructed by the house. The first thing I would do is question those assumptions: "defeat or acceptance" are exactly the terms the house wants you to use. They certainly wouldn't want you to think kindly of disengagement, would they? Dis-engagement is their worst nightmare! As I stated before, the house needs you to feed it. If you disengage it means you aren't feeding it, thus you are continually taught that disengagement is a bad thing. You are taught that disengagement is irresponsible, defeatist, etc.

This is a lie propagated by the house.

Disengagement is the only truly revolutionary action.

—MKM

That letter is dated July 26, 2008. You're reading that correctly. 2008. Even though the critics and media agreed upon Mooney's disappearance years before. The truth is: he is not gone. He is simply disengaged.

Where is the resolution? What will become of this novel?

[this novel is a search for identity]

I have not found my identity.

[use this quote, it's very apropos: "The three most important concepts in this book are multiplicity, becoming, and affirmation—and indeed the three are intimately related." — from Michal Hardt's foreward to Gilles Deleuze's Nietzsche & Philosophy]

Confession written by Marvin K. Mooney [date omitted] found on the back lid of a shoe box:

This is how I am a stereotype:

I have a beard. I wear glasses. I rock t-shirts under sport coats. I wear black Chuck Taylors—those low-top Converse All-Stars made of canvass. When I was young, I wore checkerboard Vans, Nine Inch Nails shirts and white fingernail polish. I also went through a phase when I wore giant neon orange Cross Colors jeans so big they needed purple suspenders to keep them from bundling around my ankles. Nowadays I wear a robe around the house like Lebowski— The Dude, not the one in the wheel chair. I guess I also keep the same recreational habits, minus the bowling. Plus, I don't have any friends named Donnie.

The squirrel can only work every other day, every other day he needs to rest. I feel the same way. I feel exhausted. But I haven't had a job in almost five years. The stress of it all is enough to make you want to quit...quit...quit it all and buy a spaceship and drag my wife off to the moon and live happily ever after.

That is to say.

What does that say? Towards the opening of the first volume of Musil's The Man Without Qualities, he says something to the effect of, "I have no intention of competing with reality." I agree. I do not want you to think that this is mimicking reality; that I am trying to play the old game where we both agree that I disappear as the writer and you suspend your disbelief and fall spellbound into my story. This is not that. I tremble to consider. These porch swing assassins bleed driblets of misfortune. I can't get no relief. I am half of the stress of the universe combined.

I am sorry every morning I get up.

There are other things to do. There is the library.

What if the library saves my life and that is the story you are waiting to receive from me? I go to the library and research the history of the circus, the history of the Oulipo, the history of the Roanoke colony and the birth of America, and when I am finished I find the true meaning of life is education, and then we all feel warm and fuzzy and content.

Do not listen to Bertolt Brecht. Do not believe in distanciation. It is a myth.

Wait.

Wait.

What is this? This is distanciation. Right here. Right now.

You & me are face to face; I am looking at you and you are looking at me—and what do I see? I see someone who's scared and paranoid and semi-sober. I see the last invitation to a party and the date is something special.

You are not to be forgotten.

When I look at you the rest of the world collapses into pudding on the greasy wooden floor of California. I see blessings in disguise and rare certificates. I see graduation honors and hopes and small amounts of longevity. Perhaps you will outlive your parents.

Or, perhaps you are like me. Do I see a glint of metal in the driveshaft of your responsibilities? I might mistake your smile for a hemorrhage. I am not a doctor. I am a doctor, but not a doctor of medicine. I have a PhD. I am well educated. I have studied Derrida, Foucault, Raymond Chandler.

I grew up watching Sesame Street and G.I. Joe cartoons, just like you. Just like you, I had my first kiss in eleventh grade. Just like you, I nearly lost it. Just like you I missed appointments. I missed many things, just like you.

Flames go analysis and the park plays second fiddle; barrelfuls get knocked down all along your imaginary drive-in Iraqi freedom expedition. You blockhead! You kept me up all night! I could have had candy and all sorts of gifts and all I get is why the long beard. That's ridiculous. Why the crying babies?

Why rain? Why sorrow? Why yellowed beavers?

When we bridge the green gap, can we have our ball back?

Can we play outside?

This Christmas the flood of evergreen saplings threaten to grow half yesterday started sprouting and next week the electronic pianos will need to prepare a eulogy. I am a pin prick or else something grosser. I de-pants strangers. You don't want to know me; or, maybe I don't want to let you get to know me? Maybe I am jet stream? I could hardly tell.

Roll the ankle of promises, yes and yes and yes I said yes and the next thing you know you have to appear in court for copying someone else's material, but you know it is your material, but then even so, you should not let it matter anyway. Writers should write the way DJs make a mix tapes; I don't see any difference. If I want to sample another album, another book, another single, another line, then so it goes.[44]

Listen: good artists borrow, great artists steal.

A trumpet squeals. The addled Miles Davis. I watch the arbor grow. My nephew visits and I take him to the room with the moon. The fridge is a modern convenience. Those in the 1640s never had an image of a glass man, not really, not truly, not without strings attached. The oldest are the ones with the least respect for giving. Think about it. Why not a life for a life and so on? Pick a number, any number. I bet it is either divisible by two or else already part of the family. A pizza we get delivered, or...

---

44   Thanks, Kurt Vonnegut!

see him alone spinning his unpublishable stories

                    to get a flavor of the man
                    one must read lines like these, describing

Kant claims, "We call sublime what is absolutely large."

                         help
                         buy and bye
                         good buy

          what Derrida called

A

                                   an abysmal failure
                         a complete lack of discernable
form
          A failed experiment
          A disorganized consciousness in which anything
     goes!

A madman, Mooney is impossible to explain. You must experience and

Anent
Ameliorate

[What is the Use Value of Use?]

"No, imbeciles, no idiotic and goitrous creatures that you are, a book does not make jellied soup; a novel is not a pair of seamless boots...

...Nothing is really beautiful unless it is useless; everything
useful is ugly, for it expresses a need, and the needs of man are ignoble and disgusting, like his poor weak nature. The most useful place in a house is the lavatory."

—Théophile Gautier
Preface to <u>Mademoiselle de Maupin</u> (1835)

Elocution &
Narrative &
      Opinion-, or
             Textual Construction in free-play

or
      The Deserted Village

OR

a radio station switching to a new station;

how long
should I
let you
listen?

             This is the Club;
      the place.

Ask yourself, how many vanishings make a visit not worth venturing? I object. This is not the object of this sentence.

How many words can you magnet? This is not your party. I have invited you here. That is all.

Son? Is that you? Have you come with flowers? No? Glow away from me! This is not your party to glow. I invited you here. You have been invited by me. By me you have been invited. Have been you invited? Yes, I invited you.

Hang up and walk away.
How can a harp be played?

Only three times, frozen in most cases, I impinge on your protocol.

I don't even know who I'm talking to anymore. Are you there? Hello. My name is Marvin K. Mooney. I am years old. I try not to produce the institution.
Trash truck: the loud noise of the full load of recyclables compacting.

Meteors the entire night, we watched.
            No.
Instead, Consider: We watched meteors the entire night.

You must be proper with your grammar. It must be proper. Or is it properly?

I am allergic to many conjugations. What do I mean when I use infinitives?

Hello. My name is Marvin K. Mooney. I am named after a character in a children's book. My mother changed my name legally, when I was three years old. Before then, my parents called me invisible.

Came right out of a garden, I did. Grown like a cabbage patch kid. Feral mountain goats brought me to fruition under the yoke of soy milk and slaughter.

I am tremble.

I start so many sentences with the word I. I am I and thank you for not being I so I could be, will be, and are I forever, inshallah. Unless a shop opens on the moon where misfits and desperadoes could go to reconfigure their DNA, take one of them pink goo baths; stop breathing; go deep into sleep and wake up an altogether different-looking person; but with the same insides, the same desires. The I would not be I but I would still be. You understand.

Consider death.

"Men are all condemned to death with indefinite reprieves."
–Victor Hugo, 1832, from <u>The Last Day of a Condemned Person</u>

Of Marble Men and Maidens Overwrought

Why Keats? Why now?

> A Poet is a nightingale, who sits
> in darkness and sings
> to cheer its own solitude
> with sweet sounds.
>
> —Percy Bysshe Shelley[45]

"It is among the miseries of the present age that it recognizes no medium between <u>Literal</u> and <u>Metaphorical</u>."
—Samuel Taylor Coleridge[46]

"Human history began with an act of disobedience, and it is not unlikely that it will be terminated by an act of obedience."
—<u>On Disobedience</u>, by Erich Fromm

---

45 "A Defense of Poetry, or Remarks Suggested by an Essay Entitled "The Four Ages of Poetry" (1820) [line breaks are mine, not Percy's]

46 <u>The Statesman's Manual: Or The Bible the Best Guide to Political Skill and Foresight: A Lay Sermon, Addresed to the Higher Classes of Society, with an Appendix, Containing Comments and Essays Connected with the Study of the Inspired Writings</u> (1816)

Be Still, We Will Live Like Thunder

We have luggage because we travel.
We travel because we have money.
We have money because we have jobs.
We have jobs because we need to pay bills.
We need to pay bills because we want to travel.

We are the royal we.

We go on trips because we can.
We can because we save.
We save because we want to go on trips.

Who are we?

We want to test the waters
We want to breach the gate

We want because we want.
We want because we want.
We want because we want.

We three apparitions.

We undeveloped plots.

We future.
We squelch.
We squash.
We make it.
We bake it.
We watch.

At this moment you could be anywhere on the globe and you have no idea where I am, which is how I am invisible. You don't know me. You've never met me. If you are my wife, my mother, or my sister, I am sorry to break it to you like this but you don't know me. You only know a version of me I have given to you over the years, a side of the real me I have decided to show you, not the whole me.

This is me, but I am not Marvin K. Mooney. You understand. I am an American. . I am an American. . I am an American. . I am an American. . I am an American. . I am an American.
I am an American.
    I am an American.
        I am an American.
            I am an American.
              I am an American.
              I am an American.
              I am an American.
              I am an American.
              I am an American.

I am an American!

I am an American!

I am an American!

France: In Three Parts

Part One: "They were hot there, and cold there, and some had
            been born there, and most had died." Marcus, Ben.

I am in bed mirroring Proust. Me, I am in bed mirroring
Proust. The mail, the mail from the city, sounded awful: three
tubas and an elephant victory, a matchbook of ponderosa
pines. I wanted to return, to return and save the daybreak from
escaping. But no use. I had dumbed-up my rickety.

So instead I brush my teeth to have a smoke and make my way
to town. The road is slippery. I am high. The birds are too cold
to chirp. I watch one bird circle a particular patch of prairie
then suddenly swoop down and pluck up a groundhog and
then soar away. I sip a thermos full of coffee and when I arrive
I make the valet whisper my name.

The courtroom is packed. I get a chill. Five men in red rubber
suits come forth to frisk me. I take off my shoes. They wave
huge black wands across my body. I do not beep. The judge
hammers the gavel for order and the prosecuting attorney
sticks his pinky finger in his nostril and sniffs a huge chunk and
smacks his wife and sleeps with his daughter and loses his
entire life's savings while I take my seat and call the ringleader
to the stand.

It is nighttime, so on pop the stadium lights. This is a tennis
court and I am playing for match point against the best player
in the world. It is my serve. I can win this thing. One into the
net, one into the crowd and then my mother has a stroke. I go
to the hospital where the doctors give me two tickets to France.

I go to Paris by myself and learn that it was once known as Lutetia, named by the Iron Age tribe called Parisii, in the third century BCE. Then I drink coffee and eat a croissant. Smoke a Gitanes cigarette like a New Wave femme fatale. Ask a cab driver to take me to Gertrude Stein's house, where I find that she is still alive and living there, grumpy as ever; she lets me in, Alice B. Toklas gives me tea and brownies. We talk about Picasso, and Stein says, "He is dead and he deserves it." Alice B. Toklas says not a word.

My cell phone rings and I am five minutes away from the Eiffel Tower so I go running down the backstreets and over fences to no avail. I am late and I get fired and my secretary tells me she never really loved me anyway. I am heartbroken so I write a country song and sell a million copies and live happily ever after until I am in a library and two elderly Asian men are near fisticuffs over who was a better starship captain: Kirk or Picard? I scream, "What about Janeway and Sisko? What is your problem with women and black men?" The Asian fellows turn to me and I see they are not Asian at all, they are from America and they want to torture me for hours. They say I am an enemy combatant and I ask them to clarify that accusation and they take away all of my teeth, both pinky fingers, the tip of my tongue, both earlobes, one eyeball, and give me a solid purple bruise from one love-handle to the other. Five hours later, minus one kneecap and with a near collapsed esophagus, I pay a visit to the county treasurer in front of the grand jury or whatever was left of it and they find everybody guilty except the one person who wanted me dead. So I flee town and purchase a meeting with a Dali Lama impersonator who asks me a very basic question: "Why?" Since I have no answer for him, he charges me double; I am forced to sell a kidney and take out a loan. The interest rate collapses my savings, crumbles my wallet, and builds my home into the ground. I must devise a new plan.

The new plan works well for the first few years, then it gets sickening and I have to sit in a sauna for three days just to sweat off the humiliation and agitation over the Viking Siege of Paris in 885 AD. Sure, Charles the Fat protected the city and built up the Right Bank, but what was to become of the Left? I am underwater momentarily and I get the brief sensation that I can breathe, but I am too afraid to try.

My best friend from high school shows up and takes me out to dinner where we drink five bottles of burgundy and cry together in the bathroom. I cannot leave Paris because The House of Hugh Capet, ruler of France from 987 AD to 1328, won't let me. He wouldn't have a pot to piss in if it weren't for Clovis he'd still be speaking Gaulish.

Other suggestions suggest various smaller duchies and counties. I am under attack and I have no gun or coverage. This would never happen in America. I try to go home but I am stopped at the airport and asked to take a breathalyzer test, which I fail. My credit card is denied and they ask me to sign a few autographs. I kiss a few babies. They question me in front of the media and I cry for the cameras, which causes the heart of every soccer mom across the country to go out to me until August 24, 1572, when King Charles and the Catholics assassinated Huguenot leader Admiral Gaspard de Coligny, which ignited the St. Bartholomew's Day massacre, which I could not escape. "Kill them! But kill them all! Don't leave a single one alive to reproach me!" said Charles XI.

Forty years pass and René Descartes writes <u>Discourse on the</u>

Method (1637), and Principles of Philosophy (1644). This does nothing for my self-esteem. I am still haunted by the ghost of Marie Antoinette.

King Charles VI was known as both the Beloved (le Bienaimé) and the Mad (le Fol or le Fou), because he was very much loved in his youth but then turned crazy in his twenties. Based on his symptoms, doctors believed he may have suffered from schizo-phrenia, bipolar disorder, or Porphyria: a disease that has been suggested as an explanation for the origin of vampire and werewolf legends, based on a number of similarities between the condition and the folklore first speculated upon by British biochemist David Dolphin. Other famous people who reportedly suffered from Porphyria include: King George III, Mary Queen of Scots, and Vincent van Gough.

Just keep in mind: the Hundred Years' War was actually one hundred and sixteen years long. Charley VI kept the war going. I don't keep wars going. I don't like war. I am not Charley VI. I hate to think about the years between 1337 and 1453. They were awful and they are still awful. Secondly, I am not bipolar. I would know if I was and I don't know that I am so I'm not.

The French Revolution would've been nothing without the signing of the Tennis Court Oath in 1789: "We swear never to separate ourselves from the National Assembly, and to reassemble wherever circumstances require, until the constitution of the realm is drawn up and fixed upon solid foundations." And without the Revolution there would be no Napoleon, which would mean no need for France to try and take Egypt from Great Britain's friends the Ottomans, therefore no discovery of the Rosetta Stone nor Jean-François

Champollion's deciphering of it. We would have never unlocked the mystery of the hieroglyphs. It all had to happen as it did and it did happen and this is why I am here now and have been for quite some time.

Part Two: "The most beautiful fraud in the world." Godard, Jean-Luc.

A bout de souffle (1960) directed by Jean-Luc Godard. Which has been translated as Breathless, but could also be translated as With the end of breath. In the beginning they hotwire a car and then drive away. In jump-cuts Belmondo talks to the camera. Who are we?

I am me and she is just a name I make up. Dark and spicy, these hands are feisty. My wife is my girlfriend is the future mother I cannot see is the woman I have not met is the woman who is French is the woman who is American is the woman is the woman is the woman.

I can see the color red in Une femme est une femme (1961). How could you not? Nothing is more intense. Red is the main character of the film: everything else on the screen seems mortal. When Anna Karina puts on the blue dress, it pops; but not equivalent to the magnification of red: her stockings, the umbrella, the lampshade.

Godard became a militant Maoist. Colin McCabe called him

_____.

Me, split in multiple pieces: one leans forward, one leans back; one watches a waitress, one blows his nose, one gets up to use the restroom, one pulls out a pack of cigarettes and lights up, one pays for his check, one starts a fight with a waiter.

When I sleep I see tin fish in red paint and a small village submerged in hate. I want to burn down the aristocracy, but my lighter is dead. I want to call the police, but my cell phone is broken. I steal an apple from a vendor and throw it at a man in a business suit, which hits him in the face and causes him to stumble, step off the curb, twist his ankle, and fall into the street where a minivan smashes him, one tire rolls over his head, the other tire rolls over his feet. The driver stops and I see her face. She is no one I have ever seen before.

What happened in Godard's 2001 nightmare Éloge de l'amour? Old men? Where is the youth? The youth, it seems, has gone the way of the director. He is old and now his films are a reflection; does it mean the course of Godard's cinematic trajectory mirrors the stages or movements of his own life and/or career? Cinema as mirror, as journal, as diary?

I am paralyzed. This is not me. I am an invention created by an invention, which was created by an author whose name appears at the top of this text. If you have not read Baudrillard, you should stop reading this and go seek him out right now.

If you are still reading, I take it you have made an effort to familiarize yourself with the notion of Simulacra. (What is France but simulacra?)

Alphaville. Directed by Jean-Luc Goddard (1965). "Sensuality is a conquest." "Away, away, says hate." "The heart has but one mouth." "If you smile, it enfolds me all the better." She is reading The Capital of Sorrow by Paul Eluard.

The lesson to learn is: if there is indication of pregnancy, go to the doctor rather than the tarot card reader. Cléo de 5 à 7. Directed by Agnès Varda (1961). This film is Paris. Color for the cards then back to black & white for the main feature. Cleopatra is blonde and ditzy down the streets being commoditized by hungry shoppers. She is famous; she is nobody. The streets are so narrow a bird has trouble opening its wings full sail and I am standing sideways with moneybags waiting for an explosion—in real time.

Curious girl. The way of her fingers on ice cubes cracking orange juice to make for Japan. It is Algeria. I am sick. The flight is wicked. One of me stays home and vomits, one of me gets a first class flight, one of me wakes up in Memphis with Elvis before he walked into Sun Records to make that first album for his mother, pre-pills, pre-three hundred pounds.

Godard puts Anna Karina face down on the bed in a tight shot, implying that she is being penetrated from behind. She washes her hands. I am not those men on the street gawking at her, paying for her, taking her up to that room and damaging her. I am not even French. Vivre sa vie (1962), which has been translated as My Life to Live, but should more accurately be translated as Her Life to Live. The subtle difference isn't very subtle. Then in the end three pimps pull guns and shoot Anna Karina not once but twice. I am not a B movie. I am not the back of people's heads for half an hour. I am not La Passion de Jeanne d'Arc (1928). I am not a silent picture.

I am an American. Not because I chose to be, but because I was born in Los Angeles. Unlike Salvador Dali, I do not recall my time as a fetus, and I certainly do not recall selecting my parents. I made none of those choices for myself. So now I make movies and travel. I am here. I am there. I am in France. I am in England.

Where is England? Potluck? Puppets in the park? Of nose-cones and rummy. By which I am exhausted. One of me is faint, one of me is allergic to nylon. I purchase half a pound of trees and fire up the greenery. This is cause and commotion: a language of sorrow.

With where I am [now] French movies sustain me. Without them I am not.

In the coda of <u>Les Bonnes Femmes</u> (1960), Chabrol has a woman look the audience right in the eye and then cuts away to a disco ball. FIN. This comes after he takes one of the four lead characters—the shy, quiet woman—out into the woods and has a creep strangle her and ride off on his motorcycle. I'm left with half a bag of popcorn and no soda and no money and all of my loneliness intact.

<u>Les quatre cents coups</u> (1959). Here Truffaut is semi-autobiographical, whatever that means. A little boy who catches his mother fucking a man who is not his father, then steals a typewriter to get his parent's attention. Truffaut, who said, "There are no good and bad movies, only good and bad directors."

Part Three: "The definitive differentiation of the fundamental forms." Heidegger, Martin.

I cannot be a father in France. I have no idea what order to begin reading the child great works of literature, let alone music. I am not the right person. Please believe me. A baby would just want to chew up my first editions of Derrida. What good would it do to read the kid Phénoménologie de la perception (Paris: Gallimard, 1945) by Maurice Merleau-Ponty? Even scarier, I fear Sartre's nausea may not properly effect or affect a toddler; but I could be wrong. Perhaps the kid will scratch it's head and lift it's chin and say, "Cogito, ergo sum."

My wife brought a backpack full of unnamable books to our château. I do not believe in war. I have read Giorgio Agamben —even though he is an Italian. I recognize the liminal space between objective and subjective experience is a mere angstrom in size and shape and distance, residing between that false binary is where I'd like to be: that which is neither dead nor alive. Neither up nor down. Neither this way nor that.

Ask yourself: what is grey about rhetoric like With us or against us? Where is Switzerland in all of this? Why must everybody be either guilty or innocent? Why is it either pregnant or not pregnant?

(Don't binaries get crazy-scary when they appear to be immune to deconstruction?)

Now how am I supposed to be a father? Even Lévi-Strauss's raw/cooked binary backfires when poison is consumed; recall his description of that particular merging phenomenon: "a point of isomorphic coincidence between nature and culture." Great excuse, Claude. A baby will not have a hard time understanding that principal. What a bonus; children are helpless at first and thus very shapeable.

I guess I would have to start the baby off with Eric Satie's Gymnopédies & Gnossiennes, then move on to Glenn Gould's performance of Bach's Goldberg Variations—first the 1981 version and then the 1955 version, because a child will first want to understand sadness, and then joy.

I could not be a father in France. The idea is preposterous.

Cannes is 8.8 km in length and 4.5 km in width, with an altitude between sea level and 260 meters above. The name derives from the 10th century Canua word, canna, which means: a reed. This city is a reed. I am from Los Angles. This cannot be the real Notre-Dame cathedral. I can pray in a building from the 17th century? Even though I came to Cannes in search of its reputation: a chic and trendy city teaming with rich and famous holidaymakers. I am not father material. Seriously. I am not cut out to be a father in the reed city.

We should not have gone to those archipelagos, Sainte-Marguerite and Saint-Honorat, nor should we have ventured out to those two micro-islands, Tradelière and St-Féréol.

Cannes is a luxury city & I am pretty much broke.

I should be in America. I should be packing. This misfit outfit itches. I go running for the door but it closes before I get a chance to say, "I'm sorry." I go. It is a long flight. I need Roscoe's Chicken and Waffles on Gower. I need the beach in Santa Monica. Forget the French Rivera; Forget Foucault, remember?

Why Baudrillard? Why now? Why unzip the sleeping bag filled with simulacra cobras?

A better question is this: why does the who of the what when and how could you be? Really? With that intensity, that insensitivity? I am not a robot. I am not Maximilien François Marie Odenthalius Isidore de Robespierre. He was Irish, anyway, not French. And he claimed a middle space: "ni monarchiste ni républicain." (Neither monarchist nor republican.) I would never say something like, "Louis must die, so that the country may live." Or my favorite, his recitation of Rousseau, "This terrible war waged by liberty against tyranny-is it not indivisible? Are the enemies within not the allies of the enemies without?" I would never call June 8th Supreme Being Day like he did. I am not him. I am not Robespierre. I do not adhere to the Law of 22 Prairial, also known as the loi de la Grande Terreur. This is not June 10, 1794. We are not facing south-east. I cannot be a father. Mirabeau is dead. I never joined the Jacobin Club. I do not believe in Terror. I do not believe in anything unless you want me to believe in something. I am an American. I will believe whatever you tell me. I am not France. This is not a pebble in my throat. I will be a tyrant. I will be. I will be a father in France. I will be. There is no way to escape it.

STOP!   *FIN!*

French culture fascinated [Mooney]. At the time of his disappearance, [Mooney] subscribed to three different French Language magazines and two French Language newspapers. He also listened to French Language compact discs frequently on his headset, and always in his car. He was known for carrying a copy of a French Language book wherever he went: to the dentist, the post office, the throat doctor, the barber, the bookie, the grocery. He wrote many stories and essays and poems and other fragments on and about the French culture: the films, the philosophy, the history. He researched Andre Breton—for whom he felt a certain personal affinity— as well as the Surrealist movement as a whole. He also did important imaginary work on the OuLiPo. Like his earlier attempts at historical nonfiction, Mooney embellished the truth handsomely. "Nothing like a little fact mixed with hyperbole," Mooney was like to say. "That's the way we Americans take our news these days. That's the way the media controls us. Culture is a machine without an off switch, a never-ending, self-propelling machine."

What then are you? A machine? A body without organs? Hardly. Probably most people reading this are hardly a body without organs. Hardly. I mean, really. Hardly.

This is a drawing of France:

Dear reader, I'll tell you a fucking story but I'm gonna be pissed off about it the entire time so you have three choices: either quit reading this right now, skip ahead, or accept the fact that telling stories pisses me off and watch how brilliantly I do it despite my irritation.

The setting is Los Angeles. It is not in some bumfuck wheat field in Middle America. The three main characters are interesting: they are not working class, swill drinking, losers. They are well educated, well read people who listen to music that doesn't suck. They watch films based on who directed them, not on the basis of plot or actor or anything else pedest-rian. They are not philistines. There are two women and one man and they are sitting on towels at the beach looking out at the ocean. The man sits between the women. They are all three wearing swimming suits. One of the women is his mother. Her bathing suit is orange. The other woman is his wife. Her bathing suit is green. The man is not very attractive. His bathing suit is a pair of cutoff camouflage trousers and a white sleeveless t-shirt. The mother is attractive for her age and the wife is partially attractive for any age. The mother wants to talk to the man about retirement plans and investment opportunities while the man's wife wants him to play hide the salami. He feels torn. Part of him wants to hear the quickest way to turn his 401k into an empire, while another part wants to hump.

Are you loving this story? It's got sex and family turmoil and all kinds of psychological underpinnings. Lacanians and Freudians are going to drool over the whole mother/wife thing. People are going to write papers about this story right and left. Critical theorists are going to build their careers around it. I'm going to be asked to give reading at Universities

316

around the world. This story has serious tension and a palpable crisis. The main character is being forced to make a decision, to make a choice, to act. People eat that shit up. They love it. You're probably loving it. You're probably saying to yourself: this is a great story, so full of tension. The location should also be pretty satisfactory, since it is on a beach. I assume everyone knows what the beach in Los Angeles looks like; I don't have to explain it—do I? You've been to Santa Monica, right? You've been to Venice Beach, right? Oh my god, if your answer is no you must stop reading this right now. I'm not kidding, stop right now. You have no business reading any further unless you know what I'm talking about. This story was not written for people who do not know what I'm talking about. This story was written for people who are not losers. So until you save up enough scratch to get yourself on a plane to Los Angeles, stop reading this. You must know what I'm talking about when I talk about the beach in Santa Monica just north of the pier. You must know the differences between Venice and Santa Monica or else you may as well give up on life in general, seriously, what are you doing with your pathetic life? Do not read any further—is it further or farther? Anyway, for those of you who are not losers, who have actually been to the beach in Santa Monica, this story should have you desiring more. I understand.

The sun is setting over the ocean; lights twinkle on the Santa Monica pier. Finally the man reaches into his wife's bikini bottom with one hand while taking notes from his mother with the other. He turns his head occasionally to make sure each woman feels like she is getting his full attention. He nods to his mother and scribbles down price indexes. He moans softly in his wife's ear.

317

It is the very dark of midnight and the man's wife is now splayed out on her towel, pink from the sun, spent from having multiple orgasms. The man's mother is standing up, putting on her jacket, folding her blanket, and telling him to consider selling gold. "Now is the time to sell. Gold is through the roof."

This is nothing like my real life. I did not base this story on myself or anyone I know. I used something children call imagination. Past the age of eleven, most people don't have one, so I understand if you're one of them. But unlike you, I still use mine. Instead of recapping tidbits of my boring real life, like most fuckwads who call themselves writers, I sit and imagine stuff and that's where the "story" comes from. There is never any truth in anything I type. My name is not Marvin K. Mooney. In real life, my wife is nothing like the man's wife in this story. My wife & I never visit the cave anymore. To be honest, I haven't even seen my wife in months.

Goodbye Cavelight

You see... the cave is a metaphor, a tool, an illustration. I use it. The cave is symptomatic. The formula for its accurate representation is something like $S2=(2^2)+1$. As I just pasted that formula into this document I realized I do not speak math and therefore could not read that formula aloud were I ever in a situation like a reading where I would need to say the formula out loud. I don't know what S means or what S2 equals, nor do I know how to pronounce that little upside-down V between the pair of 2s. If you speak math, then you know what it means. The facts are these:

A broken whistle. A photograph and a dog-eared copy of Palace Holidays #46, the one where the guy finds out his mother is actually his older sister who was technically adopted so therefore not blood related, and concludes with their passionate lovemaking. I had only read the text four or five times and marked the pages in color code:

Orange = Moments of narrative contention, i.e. modes of sublimating combinatory algorithms.

Yellow = Theme, or what's lovingly referred to as Doom; which is what happens when attempting to evoke mood instead of sticking with the wants and needs of the characters.

[Also, mood is doom spelled backwards.]

Red = N/A

Blue = Setting, or topographical delineation material relevant to or pertaining to the ethereal underpinnings.

Brown = Sex sequences. Also both top and bottom corner of

page is dog-eared.

But why did I start the second chunk of this text with the image of a broken whistle? Especially if my authorial intent was to go off on something else entirely. Why make up the name of a magazine and make up a story and then try to pawn it off as what actually happened? Why did I write that particular title: Palace Holidays? Does it have significance in my life, or did I just like the sound of it? Was it the name of my grandmother's imaginary wonderland? Was it the name of a television show? And why number the magazine 46? What is the relevancy? Do you feel like you should be paying close attention to everything, as if I am trying to trick you, that I'm dropping little subtle clues here and there and then being smug when you beg for answers?

The woman steps into the cave and blank happens. Blank makes blank for blank and puts the largest amount of blank in blank's blank.

A team of bumblebees rob an azalea, spread their seed. I am watching from the basement. This is not a metaphor. I was actually, literally, honestly, truly, downstairs changing the laundry and without any hyperbole, I cracked the frame on my glasses when I slammed my face into the window trying to get a good look at those bees.

I was born in Kansas, but I grew up in Wyoming. That may not be particularly integral to this text, but it is verifiably true, and therefore firmly establishes this piece as nonfiction. I like to think it is also creative, and therefore this text can be described to others as a work of creative nonfiction. If someone asks you:

"Hey, what's that you're reading?"

You could answer a number of things, one of them being: "It is a new work of creative nonfiction by Marvin K. Mooney."

In follow-up, you may be asked:

"What's it about?"

To which you can safely reply: "It is a text about itself. It is pretentious, egomaniacal, megalomaniacal, and hardly worth my time; but for some reason I continue to read it - perhaps I am being forced to at gunpoint, perhaps I am slightly enjoying it."

Wouldn't it be nice to come out from behind the curtain? Just step out and smile, admit to the reader when you think you've written a fantastic sentence and say, hey, I created that, thank you for your recognition. Street performers get cheers and hollers from their crowds. Why not a writer? Or on the flip side, if you write a shabby sentence like, "The moonlight caressed her glorious curvature." You know the line is bad, bad, bad. Why not admit it? Put in a parenthesis and tell the reader why you wrote it and what you were thinking and then you can explain to the reader why you chose to leave it in and what that means about the advancement of the novel (you see, in that sentence I was trying to do this very thing and talk about the sentence I just wrote, which came to me not because of something I heard but from something nudging me in the side: this idea of stepping out from behind the curtain and admitting my role as creator of this text).

There is nothing new about talking to the reader. I cite The

321

Life and Opinions of Tristram Shandy, Gentleman, which appeared in nine volumes, the first two appearing in 1759. That's a long time ago. And since metafiction is rhizomatic and eternally occurring, the meat I feast on now is probably from even longer ago. I know it. I do not pretend to be doing otherwise. All I ask is that the reader remembers Robbe-Grillet's brilliant observation:

> "Flaubert wrote the new novel of 1860, Proust the new novel of 1910. The writer must proudly consent to bear his own date, knowing that there are no masterpieces in eternity, but only works in history; and they survive only to the degree that they have left the past behind them and heralded the future."
> ("The Use of Theory,"
> For A New Novel: essays on Fiction, 1965)

Why did I choose to take that particular rhetorical tone a moment before dropping that block quote? Why did I feign being humble, when we both know I'm the opposite of that? Why the pun? (Writing a novel kind of novel, are you?) What underlying impulse drove me to try and explain myself, and situate myself within the discourse? Why don't I feel confident enough to make a move and stick with it?

I wonder if this work of creative nonfiction began with an introductory paragraph, which outlined the road map of this text? You can check back if you want to, or you can take my word for it, in which case I did not. The beginning of this text opens with a snappy sentence that begins with a contextual discussion of metaphor followed by an example of a simile. The substantive I used was cave.

The cave is on the other side of the house. I am trapped in the gossip of the living room. Outside a car passes by and I metaphysically jump into the passenger seat and ride with the driver to Omaha, but it is not Omaha because it is only down the street a little ways and I live in Ohio, which is about 800 miles away. I invoke the cave to symbolize something. Can you guess what it is?

In the fifth grade I was not allowed to go trick-or- treating because I stabbed my brother with a Boy Scout blade.

The cliché of the cave is one with funny enemies. Think about Plato and his shadows, his theory of forms. I do not wish to conjure up thoughts of Plato. I also don't want you to think about Al-Qaeda hideouts in Afghanistan, or the kinds of caves you've seen in adventure movies. Read the following description slowly, maybe more than one time, and let the words come out of your mouth, let your breath translate the words you are reading, feel the breath that brings the words into being. Say this next sentence out loud, as loud or as soft as you like, don't just read these words and continue past without doing it, and remember to concentrate on the words as they are birthed through lips:

There Has Never Been A Time

In Which I Have Been Convinced From Within Myself

That I Am Alive

Franz Kafka wrote those words in a longish short story called "Conversations with a Supplicant." I wrote a short story and gave it that sentence as the title. You didn't write that, I wrote that. Wrote what? Who are you? I am Marvin K. Mooney! Someone said good writers borrow and great writers steal. Makes me think about plagiarism, pros and cons. Walter Benjamin envisioned a novel made entirely of quotes. Other people's words mixed together, as if the writer were a DJ mixing music. I grew up in the eighties. I didn't have a computer until I was in middle school. The invention of the internet happened when I was a sophomore in high school. When I was a senior in high school, my room had black carpeting. Could that be what the cave signifies? Am I returning to that long black room to drink vodka and type horribly sappy love poems on my typewriter? I am nearing thirty. Closing in, I suppose. I am on my final descent. I should explain the broken whistle.

I made a contract with the reader. Even if I didn't began this piece by promising an explanation, I still owe you one, since the rulebook says so. In fact, the rulebook says I should concisely describe the significance of the cave, explain why I moved dramatically to a fancy math equation, and then bring the piece into some kind of focus. I need to try and salvage this work of creative nonfiction by giving it proper shape, proper dimensions, proper flow, proper usage of proper.

It is easy to write a story. All you have to do is invent a person who wants something and then make it hard for that person to get whatever it is they want. Put obstacles in the way of the protagonist. Give the protagonist an ally, which could but doesn't have to lead to a crisis of the heart. For subtext, all you have to do is introduce some kind of need for the protagonist, which must in some way be opposed to the character's want. That is it. That is all it takes to write a story. So for example, if you invent a character who wants desperately to win the pie eating contest, you contrast that desire with his need to lose weight. Along with introducing a ticking clock element, which serves to manifest the tension; which is half the battle, the other half is everything else.

I am not interested in that type of story. I am interested in lines of flight. At the moment, I have an inclination to rewrite this work of creative nonfiction, structuring it around the character of myself and make my want be validation, but make my need be to gain confidence. I want desperately for you to think that I am a good writer. I want you to be impressed and inspired by me, the way I have been inspired by other writers. (If you want my list of favorite/most influential writers, email me at themarvinkmooneysociety [at] gmail [dot] com.) Did I mention my awareness regarding the outlandishness of my ego? It is interesting that you have continued to read this work of creative nonfiction for so long. Does the cave still interest you?

I received four rejection letters last week, three the week before. I keep them. Most people I know who send stuff out keep them. Chances are, this will never be published. If you are reading this work of creative nonfiction, it is truly an example of a miracle. I am at this moment not feeling particularly confident. Now maybe you can see how the metaphor of the cave is easy to use.

And by typing words on paper and presenting them as factual, as nonfiction, I am placing on public record the contents of my

325

personal warehouse. The time is nearly midnight. I am afraid to go driving, but I must. There are emails to send. I am tired. This is the cave, or it is the opposite of the cave or it has absolutely nothing to do with the cave. The cave is blank and I blank what blank makes blank. Literally.

[This is how it's going to end.]

Three people creep to the cave's mouth and peer out and see us, you and me, and we in turn can see Plato's forms in their eyes.

We shake the hand of Adam. We see the doom and gloom of their horizon.

Suddenly a bunch of angry people surround my front yard. I light a torch. These rookies. These Saturday cartoon watching Joe Piscopo looking Dracula-type characters. I need garlic. I need holy water. I need a SAG card to throw at one of them.

Give me a hand, will you? Help me out of this scene, I'm begging you. Turn the page and help me escape this situation, reader; these fucks are closing in! Think fast. They're getting closer; I can see a couple of them brandishing weaponry. Make the right decision. Hurry, turn the page. Turn it. Please. Turn it.

THE END

Do you want to read an encore?

If you want to read an encore you must clap your hands no matter your location, be it the library, the living room, or the brothel–clap your hands and whistle and shout as loud as you would at a musical concert...

ENCORE!

ENCORE!!!

ENCORE!!!

Thank you.

Thank you very much.

The Invention of America

I.   Prologue

The second son of Otho and Katherine Gilbert of Compton Greenway Estate, Devonshire, came barreling out of poor Katherine's vagina like a cannonball. The nursemaid at hand caught the lad and spanked his bum. He choked. His cord was cut and he was handed to his mother who in turn smiled greatly. The child scrunched his nose and, having breathed the air of life for only mere moments, shouted, "Mutare vel timere sperno!"

Katherine, unfamiliar with Latin, knew not what to make of such an outburst. She looked to her husband for an answer. Lord Otho's jowls jiggled. "I scorn to change or fear," he said, his face alight with pride. "A true Gilbert through and through."

The year was 1537.

Thus began the life of Sir Humphrey Gilbert, English adventurer, explorer, culinary genius, and swashbuckling murderer who faithfully served the crown and enforced the Protestant tyranny of Queen Elizabeth I.

By 1569, Gilbert had invented shepherd's pie and single-handedly slaughtered thousands of Irish women and children. He was the first British military commander to practice decapitation, and by the looks of his letters, he truly enjoyed it. Once, to his mother, he wrote, "The only thing that pleases me more than standing knee-deep in gallowglass blood is preparing a perfect pudding." One can imagine, owing to how he took himself for such a witty sentimentalist, the gleeful twitch of his curlicue mustache as he brushed the quill pen across the paper, proudly trumpeting his triumphs to his mommy.

The Queen was impressed with his butchery, not to mention his delectable chocolate chip cookies. With milk, they made her

336

orgasmic. All combined, the Queen found him to be the perfect candidate to lead the expansion of the Protestant empire in the New World.

To those in Great Britain, it was no secret that Gilbert endeavored to get his bloodstained hands on that unmapped land so he could stab an English flag into her soil, dance around in a megalomaniacal frenzy, and plunder her shrubs for their berries. Plus, he was getting bored killing the Irish. On August 5, 1583, under Royal Charter to discover and colonize "remote heathen and barbarous lands," he got his wish. St. John's, Newfoundland became England's first overseas acquisition. To celebrate his conquest, he ordered his men to round up three attractive adolescent natives and dress them in Persian attire. He prepared a delicious three course meal, which he shared with them before slicing each of their ears off and fashioning a memorial necklace to wear proudly around his neck. For dessert they ate angel food cake.

Unfortunately, his colonial celebration was short-lived. On the return voyage an enormous sea-monster was sighted, one said to resemble a lion with glaring eyes and dagger teeth. Gilbert's tiny ship was no match. The ravenous creature swallowed the vessel whole, just south of the Azores. The rest of the fleet watched through telescopes, while eating buttered corn on the cob. They were closer to shore and therefore safe from the grumbling appetite of the beast.

Gilbert's last will and testament, dated July 8, 1582, made clear that his ultimate purpose had been to establish an English empire beyond the seas, and to be forever remembered for his prowess in the kitchen.

Back in Britain, Queen Elizabeth was more peeved than pleased. Although Gilbert had indeed laid claim to a chunk of North America for the crown, he had not established a permanent settlement nor had he left anyone behind to secure and defend their new property. In short, he made a fool of the endeavor and wasted a great deal of cash.

Spain, on the other hand, now sworn enemy of England, settled down nicely in the New World. They had established a successful settlement in St. Augustine, Florida where they held the first Christian worship service on the North American continent: a Catholic Mass celebrating the feast day of Augustine of Hippo.

When Queen Elizabeth's excommunicated ears heard news that the Papacy had one-upped her abroad, she screamed "No!" so loudly every stained-glass window in the Tower of London shattered, every child on the island cringed, and half the cattle in the kingdom spontaneously combusted. Her shout echoed into the atmosphere where it hung like a rain cloud until it reached Italy, where it fell on the Roman court and struck Pope Gregory XIII. He instantly recognized Elizabeth's voice and snickered.

To expunge the sour thought, she ordered her guards to go to the dungeon and retrieve the five priests being held as prisoners, so she could molest them with her poetry. After reciting her newly composed "The Doubt of Future Foes" to them repeatedly for three hours, she ate a hearty meal and plotted her next move.

For results she looked first to Sir Francis Drake, an extremely popular officially sanctioned pirate who flew St. George's Cross and plundered the sea in the name of the crown. But he couldn't be bothered. He and his cousin Sir John Hawkins were too busy kidnapping West Africans and starting up the first English slave trade expeditions.

The job then fell to Sir Walter Raleigh: part time French Huguenot, inventor of the French kiss, squelcher of the Desmond Rebellion, co-conspirator in The Main Plot against King James, Author of The History of the World, and assassin of Christopher Marlowe. His father had married Sir Humphrey Gilbert's mother once Lord Otho passed away, and in yet a further twist of nepotism, Raleigh's great-grandparents, John Drake and Margaret Cole, were the grandparents of Sir Francis Drake. However, evidence of their having family reunions wherein all three men attended is scant and circumstantial. Chances are, Gilbert, Drake, and Raleigh never played cricket together as children, never sat side-by-side at church or borrowed each other's knickers.But they were family nonetheless.

And so it was that Sir Raleigh took charge of the plot to conquer the unknown world.

II. The Scouting Expedition

On April 27, 1584, Captains Philip Amadas and Arthur Barlowe, who were not at first lovers but would soon become, left the west of England in two barks well furnished with hunky men and premium victuals, to explore the North American coast for Sir Walter Raleigh. On board, un-beknownst to them, was the headless body of Anne Boleyn, Queen Elizabeth's mother, who carried her head under her arm like a bushel of firewood. The headless body of Anne Boleyn, who was of course unseen by virtue of being a ghost, did not interfere in this initial expedition. She merely went along to observe.

When they found Roanoke Island tucked away from the Atlantic by the Outer Banks, Barlowe wrote in his diary, "This place is resplendent, majestic, and so full of scuppernongs that the shore seems to overflow with them."

Also onboard was a brilliant scientist named Thomas Hariot who set up the New World's first science laboratory. He and his men gathered different types of plants to take back to England

for further study. One of which was an unknown root vegetable called a potato. Another was a strange short leaf plant,
which was burned and inhaled purposely in what would come
to be known as the practice of smoking.

On the fourth day of the exploration, the chief of the
Roanoke Island Indians paid them a visit, wearing nothing but
a feathered headdress. Although Amadas and Barlowe were
still sore from their rough lovemaking the night before, neither
could help but stare longingly at the Chief's enormous penis,
which dangled freely about his knees. Fantasies involving its
usage filled both of their minds. The headless body of Anne
Boleyn took a step backwards and raised her severed head.
With her eyes also fixed on the chief's giant member, she
mouthed the word "ouch."

After a short period of trading, Barlowe remained with the
chief. Amadas, somewhat jealous, took seven others to the
north end of the island, to the Indian's palisaded village. Here
the Englishmen were entertained with a primitive but hospitable ceremony. All the while, Amadas brooded. What if
Barlowe ruined their newfound monogamy and took the chief
to bed? As the Indians danced about and shook their feathers,
Amadas vowed that if Barlowe had in fact cheated on him with
the well-endowed chief, he would throw himself from a cliff
and end his life in the most dramatic fashion imaginable.

When the ceremony was over, Amadas and his team returned to their camp. Most of the crew were by this time
sleeping, but Barlowe was nowhere to be found. Amadas
searched every tent, wandered up and down the shore looking
for his lover. By midnight he had searched every possible
location to no avail. The headless body of Anne Boleyn
considered helping Amadas find Barlowe, since she knew
exactly where he was, but at the last moment she decided
against it.

Amadas was exhausted. He crumpled to the sand and started snoring almost immediately. For better or worse, it was a dreamless sleep. When he awoke, the sun beat down on him and the water's edge tickled his feet. In the distance he saw the naked chief and a now naked Barlowe walking towards him, hand-in-hand. Instead of jumping up and running away to hurl himself from the nearest cliff, he clenched his teeth and softly started to cry.

In his official report to Sir Walter Raleigh, a heartbroken Amadas wrote, "The Indians appeared gentle, loving, and faithful - unlike some Englishmen aboard the expedition. The earth bore a most pleasant and fertile ground, replenished with goodly Cedars and other sweet woods, full of grapes, flax, and many other notable commodities, game and fish in abundance - all of which mean nothing, of course, if you have no one with which to share your life."

The expedition party sailed back to England minus Barlowe, who remained on the island as the chief's concubine. The headless body of Anne Boleyn also remained.

Amadas was so full of grief that he gave up exploring forever. When he arrived in Europe he moved to Paris and changed his name to Balthasar de Beaujoyeulx and dedicated his remaining years to the invention of a new form of dance, inspired by his brief but passionate love affair with Barlowe. He called it <u>Ballet</u> - a dance for sad people.

III. A Colony of Men

Besides hearing of the love affair gone awry, Raleigh was pleased. He decided to send a startup colony of 108 men, which included fellows expert in the art of fortification, tree hugging, horse wrangling, spade and shovel making, as well as shipwrights, millwrights, playwrights, carpenters, brick makers, tile makers, bricklayers, tile layers, rough masons, and property lawyers.

The fleet would be commanded by Raleigh's cousin, Sir Richard Grenville, former sheriff of Cork, who once had to stand by and watch as James Fitzmaurice Fitzgerald and those pickaxe wielding Geraldine fanatics massacred his entire garrison. His lifelong dream was to circumnavigate the globe, which he was promised in the late 1570s, but then Queen Elizabeth gave the honor to Sir Francis Drake instead, because, of course, he made her an infinite amount of money from his slave trading. Poor Richard Grenville was relegated to suicide duty: the chances of making it to the New World and successfully setting up a functional colony, then making it back to England to tell about it, were slimmer than a rapier's blade.

Regardless of certain failure, illustrator John White, a self-professed hater of verisimilitude, who would meet death after late stage syphilis twenty-one years later, packed up his water colors and his government issued parchment and joined the convoy to the unknown continent. His assignment, directly from the Queen's lips, was to capture the "raging savagery" of the New World in startling hand drawn detail. She wanted to see what it was she was conquering.

They sailed from Plymouth, England, on April 9, 1585, in seven ships. When they arrived, Captain Barlowe met them on the beach with his husband, the chief, and many of the natives, who greeted the Englishmen with open arms. The headless body of Anne Boleyn stood on a cliff and rued the ship's arrival.

The Englishmen quickly set up their colony on the north end of the island. Seaman third class Ralph Lane was elected Governor. This infuriated Grenville beyond measure. Of all the lowdown, backstabbing, double crossing bullshit, this slap in the face was just too much to bear.

But instead of assassinating Lane, which was his initial idea, he devised a plan. First, he took thirteen of his men into the nearest Indian village. Then he ordered them to burn it to the ground. His justification was simple: there was reason to believe the Indians were plotting a similar attack. "It's a preemptive strike," he told them. "For the safety and security of our new colony."

The men reluctantly followed their orders, sacked the village and burned it to the ground, killing its inhabitants while they slept. Grenville delighted in the spectacle of those Indians who awoke and ran around aflame, women running out of their tents trying desperately to extinguish their babies. "We have done what the Queen would like us to do," he told the men. "We have done good for the future of England."

At seeing such cruelty, the headless body of Anne Boleyn considered intervening. All along she'd been standing beside Grenville, watching him unravel his plot, without allowing her presence to be known. Because she didn't want to give herself away just yet, because she was saving her appearance for the most opportune moment, she decided to remain silent. Her time would come, but this was not it.

Torching the Indian village caused exactly the response Grenville was hoping for: all out war with the natives. The chief of the Roanoke tribe, who at first received the Englishmen hospitably, changed his attitude abruptly. Even though Captain Barlowe was intimately involved with the chief, his influence was miniscule. The chief had four other wives, and two of them bore him children. Barlowe was by any measure lowest man on the chief's totem pole.

As his next move, Grenville convinced Governor Lane and the others he should return to England for supplies and reinforcements. "We've come too far to be torn asunder by savages," he told them. "We must stay the course. We need more troops." The consensus was iffy, but he won their support unequivocally when he stood erect, touched his left shoulder with his right fist, and broke out singing, "O Lord, our God, arise, Scatter her enemies, And make them fall. Confound their politics, Frustrate their knavish tricks, On Thee our hopes we fix, God save us all!"

Upon hearing the lines from "God Save the Queen," Governor Lane became teary.

Patriotism triumphed. Grenville took the ships back to England and left the colonists to die in a war he started, which gave him cause to smile the entire trip home. The taste of retribution was sweeter than sugared milk in his mouth.

By June 1, 1586, the colonists were losing the war. They were in a desperate predicament. Less than half of the group remained. Every night they would huddle together as a group and pray for Grenville's return.

Such were the affairs on Roanoke Island, June 9, 1586, when they heard news of Sir Francis Drake anchored off the coast with a mighty fleet of 23 ships. By order of the Queen, he had just burned St. Augustine, Florida to the ground. The Catholics would have to start over.

The colonists began to clamor for escape.

John White, the illustrator who made inimitable watercolor drawings of the Indians and articulately documented the flora and fauna of Roanoke, loathed the idea of giving up the colony. So did Governor Lane. But the majority of the men wanted to go home.

Drake sailed for England on June 26. Every living colonist went with him, but the headless body of Anne Boleyn remained on the island.

Shortly after Drake and the colonists sailed, a supply ship sent by Sir Walter Raleigh arrived. After searching in vain for the colonists, they returned to England shrugging their shoulders. A fortnight after Raleigh's ship sailed, Grenville returned with three ships. After finding no trace of the colonists, he retired to his cabin where he opened a bottle of wine and drank himself into a celebratory stupor. In the morning he made the last move in his plan.

To finally be a hero, to get his name back in the good graces of the Queen and hopefully into the history books, he left 15 men on Roanoke Island, fully provisioned for 2 years, to hold the property while he returned to England and made a case for why he should be the governor of the New World.

The Indians had had enough. With fervor, they attacked. The only thing the outnumbered Englishmen could do was scramble to their dinghy and flee. The treacherous waters offshore capsized their vessel. None of them were seen again.

IV. The Second Attempt

Back in England, the prospect of continued conflict with the natives did nothing to deter the Queen's plan. The English were quite accustomed to enforcing exceptional brutality while managing their affairs abroad, take Ireland for example, so staging a little massacre or even a complete genocide across the Atlantic would be no problem. Anyway, they could always just poison the unruly beasts, if more conventional means of domination proved unsatisfactory. What mattered most was that England win the race to colonize North America, at whatever cost.

In private, the Queen asked Sir Walter Raleigh to instruct the return party to try and eradicate as many natives as possible. More than anything, the Queen was offended at the audacity of the natives to stand up for themselves. "They are infected with ignorance. Unknowing of their position in this life. With disrespect they assume their posture, in defiance of our bountiful grace in allowing them to exist. Heathens such as they deserve no such graces, Sir Raleigh. Disgust is all I am to muster for those vile creatures. Even death is too handsome for them. They have not the sense nor humility to realize, if I wanted to render them extinct, they would be so."

Raleigh agreed. "Indeed, we best to dispose of them, your Highness. A disgusting blight on our beautiful new land they are."

The sun set and the decision was made to send another, more prepared, group of settlers.

Grenville appeared before the Queen to beg for the governorship. She referred him to Raleigh, who loved his cousin, but not enough to recommend him for governor of the colony. Besides, he knew even before it happened that the honor would go to John White, the illustrator who presented the first pictures of the New World to the eager Queen. Indeed, his work impressed her so much that she knighted him and personally appointed him leader of what would come to be known as the land of the Virgin Queen or "Virginia," named not for the fact that Queen Elizabeth abstained from sex, quite the contrary: she pathologically engaged in raunchy poly-amorous orgies, but because she refused to marry and become merely a consort. White's assignment was to return to Roanoke, patch up the troubles with the natives by slaying as many of them as need be, and find a way to forge a sustainable community.

As she had done before, the Queen stripped Grenville of the one thing he wanted most and instead appointed him admiral of a fleet sent to the Azores to stop the advancement of the Spanish galleons. He took command of the HMS Revenge, a ship considered to be a masterpiece of naval construction, and led a heroic fight against the enemy. After sustaining massive casualties, taking shrapnel in his face and hands, and nearly defeating the entire Spanish fleet, a cyclone hit the harbor and sunk his ship. Grenville died never having accomplished anything worthy of historical record.

On May 8, 1587, the second colonial expedition sailed for Roanoke. This time the group consisted of 150 persons, twenty-three of which were women, eleven children.

When they landed, Captain Barlowe and the Roanoke Island Indians were nowhere to be found. The headless body of Anne Boleyn was present, but she remained hidden.

Governor White led a small group to the colonial site, to confer with the fifteen men left by Grenville the preceding year. When they reached the spot, they found only the bones of one who had not escaped the last ransacking. There was no sign of the others. The houses built by the previous expedition stood unhurt, except that each was overgrown with melons and filled with deer feeding on those melons.

Arrows flew from the surrounding trees. Before the men could react, the ambush killed everyone but White, who stood very still, waiting for his arrow to come. It never came. The aggressors vanished.

White returned to the docked ships and warily began to explain what had just happened when suddenly a group of Indians emerged from the trees. White braced himself for the impending attack, but hostility was not their aim. One of the natives stepped forward proclaiming "Fear Not! Fear Not!" calling himself Manteo, speaking perfect Queen's English. He said he was not a Roanoke Indian. "I am Croatoan." He explained how he had fallen in love with Captain Barlowe and stolen him away from the chief of the Roanoke Indians, which led to a war between the two tribes. Barlowe had in turn taught the Croatoan English before dying of a strange illness that turned his body into stone. It was Manteo and his men who had just saved White. It was a vestige of those pesky, bitter, angry Roanoke Indians who slaughtered his men. "You are all safe now," Manteo told them. "Please, join us for a feast."

Although the headless body of Anne Boleyn knew Manteo was lying, she chose not to give him away.

Time passed and the wide-eyed colonists settled into their new existence. Since things seemed only to be prosperous, and since the Roanoke Indians seemed to be long gone, now replaced with these friendly Croatoans, everyone decided to forget the Queen's command to exterminate the natives. Governor White's daughter, Eleanor, wife of Ananias Dare, gave birth to the first child of English parentage to be born in the New World. In honor, they named her Virginia. Relations with the natives had never been better. All seemed tranquil and promising.

So, on November 27, 1587 White sailed in good faith homeward to obtain supplies for the upcoming winter. He stood at the stern of the flagship and happily waved to his wife, his daughter, and granddaughter for the last time. His intention had been to collect the goods and return in less than two months. He had no way of knowing that he would never see any of them again.

V. The Disappearance

Once the English fleet merged with the horizon, the color of the sky in the New World changed from powder blue to sangria. The salt in the ocean rose to the surface and crystal-lized. All the trees wilted and the fruit soured and the animals dropped dead in unison. The sand on the beach turned to ash. The headless body of Anne Boleyn placed her severed head back where it belonged, then crimped it together by pinching the skin on her neck with the skin around her collar like the crust of an apple pie. In a matter of moments she was whole again. Manteo and his tribesmen appeared from the graying forest and surrounded the colonists, who stood dumb-founded in their farewell assembly on the shore. "Come," Manteo shouted. "We have something very special to show you."

When Governor White reached England, the war with Spain was swelling. Thus the Queen forbade him to return to Virginia straight away. Instead, she ordered him to the front line, where he spent three years fighting Philip II's rabid Catholic soldiers.

The Spanish Armada was crushed. England shook their victorious flags. But unfortunately, by the end of it, White was penniless, completely without means to return to his family in the New World. As well, the crown suffered such setbacks from the struggle that funds were too tight to allocate a sufficient sum necessary for his return expedition. Grief-stricken, White took heavily to the drink. He also began to frequent less expensive whores, who in turn introduced syphilis into his bloodstream. Day after day he guzzled spirits and slept with streetwalkers to combat the sorrow of knowing his tiny granddaughter was growing into a pigtailed toddler without him. The pain ratcheted, mounted, threatened to strangle him from within. But just when it seemed of utmost hopelessness, by the grace of slave trading the money finally appeared. He asked no questions, looked no gift horse in the mouth, and hurried to organize a return party.

They set sail on March 19, 1590.

When they finally anchored at Roanoke three months later, White spotted black smoke rising from inland. He blew the trumpet to alert the colonists of their arrival, but no one rushed to greet them nor returned their call. The eerie silence haunted the sailors as they fitted the dinghy to go ashore and make contact.

As they climbed the sandy escarpment toward the settle-ment area, White spotted the letters "CRO" noticeably carved in a cedar at the brow of the hill. Going from there to the dwelling site, they found all the houses destroyed and the site enclosed with tree posts like a jail. One of the main posts had its bark peeled off and the word "CROATOAN" carved in it. At first White took this to be a signal that the colonists had gone, for whatever reason, to live amongst the kindly Croatoan Indians, but what troubled him was the absence of the Maltese cross, which served always as an identifying code to fellow Englishmen. Without that symbol, White had no reason to be-lieve the colonists were responsible for the markings. But, White considered, if it were not done by the colonists, then by whom?

Things refused to add up. The site was completely overgrown with grass. Not a single colonial remnant remained: no bodies, no artifacts, no signs of destruction, no indication of battle. It was as if the previous group had never existed there. "Surely this is but a dream," White said to his men. "We must scour this island for our countrymen. They are here, by my honor, I am certain." But just as the words escaped his lips, stormy weather brewed above. Rain began to sizzle on the tree limbs. The ground began to soften into mud. Fog appeared as if a cloud had suddenly fallen. In seconds White could hardly see his hand in front of his face. "Men," he shouted. But there was no response. He turned to shout in the opposite direction and slipped down a small embankment. When he regained his feet he noticed a patch of bright light cutting through the fog in front of him. He took a few steps towards it and stopped. Before him stood the now whole body of Anne Boleyn, backlit by the radiant light.

"Who are you?" he asked.

She smiled. "Do you wish to know what has become of

your family and friends?"

"Yes, of course," he said.

She stepped toward him. "I will show you, but first you must swear to never speak a word of what you are about to see."

"I swear," he said.

Without another word, she reached out, took his hand, and led him into the light.

The Marvin K. Mooney Society
dot com